THE
HIGHLY
EFFECTIVE
DETECTIVE

ALSO BY RICHARD YANCEY

Confessions of a Tax Collector

A Burning in Homeland

The Extraordinary Adventures of Alfred Kropp

THE HIGHLY EFFECTIVE DETECTIVE

A Teddy Ruzak Novel

RICHARD YANCEY

Thomas Dunne Books
St. Martin's Minotaur
New York

THOMAS DUNNE BOOKS.
An imprint of St. Martin's Press.

www.minotaurbooks.com

Library of Congress Cataloging-in-Publication Data
Yancey, Richard.
    The highly effective detective / Richard Yancey.—1st ed.
        p. cm
    ISBN-13: 978-0-312-34752-9
    ISBN-10: 0-312-34752-9
    1. Private investigators—Tennessee—Knoxville—Fiction. 2. Knoxville (Tenn.)—
Fiction. I. Title.

PS3625.A675H54 2006
813'.6—dc22

                                                                                    2006042521

10   9   8   7   6   5   4   3   2

TO SANDY

Yet in these thoughts myself almost despising,
Haply I think on thee—and then my state,
Like to the lark at break of day arising
From sullen earth, sings hymns at heaven's gate
        —William Shakespeare, Sonnet XXIX

Take note, take note, O World.
To be direct and honest is not safe.
　　　　—*William Shakespeare*, Othello

THE
HIGHLY
EFFECTIVE
DETECTIVE

CHAPTER ONE

I'D HAD THIS DOPEY IDEA TO BE A DETECTIVE EVER SINCE my mother gave me an illustrated Sherlock Holmes book for my tenth birthday. For months, I walked around the house with a bubble pipe and two baseball caps on my head, one turned backward so I would have that double-billed look. I outgrew the ball caps and the pipe, but never my dream of being a detective.

Then when I was twelve, somebody gave me one of those *Encyclopedia Brown* books, about a boy detective who was smarter than his own father, the chief of police no less, and solved all the crimes for him. The answer to each mystery was in the back of the book for those people like me who wanted to play detective but could never figure out what the solution was. I liked that kid detective so much, I started calling myself "Dictionary Ruzak," because "Encyclopedia" was already taken.

After high school, I went to the Police Academy, but they kicked me out. I couldn't run fast enough, and I never could pass the driving and the marksmanship tests. Then they put me in what they called "scenario training" and the bad guy always killed me. I must have died a hundred times, and would have died a hundred more, but the Academy concluded I wasn't cut out for police work.

After I flunked out of the Academy, I took a job as a guard

with a company that provided security for a local bank. I wore a black uniform with a gold badge embroidered on the shoulder. I had the midnight shift, which I liked. It was quiet, I had a chance to read or listen to the radio, and nothing ever happened. I worked there for fourteen years. For ten of those years I lived with my parents, until Dad died of a heart attack and Mom told me if I didn't move out, I never would, because with him gone, the temptation would be too great to live with and take care of her as an excuse not to strike out on my own. She kept on me to go to college. I worked nights, so my days were free, but somehow, like a lot of things people plan for, I never got around to it. I also could never figure out how I was going to work a full-time job, go to college, and sleep.

So the day came when I was thirty-three years old and was still doing the same thing I'd been doing when I was nineteen. I was hunkered down. Flunking out of the Police Academy had taken something out of me, a pretty big chunk of my resolve or spirit or whatever you want to call it, and I was waiting for something. I couldn't put my finger on what I was waiting for. Maybe it was some kind of mystical call to action, but I was never the type who believed we all have a destiny to fulfill, like a cosmic apple hanging from a tree that we wait till it's ripe to pluck. My outlook on life tended toward the prosaic. I wasn't much of a dreamer or go-getter, since the two usually go hand in hand. But sometimes, usually midway through my shift, about 3:00 A.M., when things were their most quiet and I was tired of reading and all the late-night radio talk shows had signed off, I would feel an aching somewhere in the vicinity of my heart, not in the heart itself, but about two or three inches below it, which I interpreted as some soft groaning of my unfulfilled soul, only I didn't know what to do about it except wait for it to go away.

CHAPTER TWO

THEN ONE NIGHT IN THE WINTER OF MY THIRTY-THIRD year, my mother called me to tell me she was calling from her deathbed. So I drove to her house in Fountain City. It was the fourth house she had lived in since I'd been born. Dad was a salesman and moved around a lot. He wasn't a traveling salesman; he just wasn't a very good salesman and he moved to follow what he called the "consumer trends." I spent the first twelve years of my life in Brooklyn, where Dad sold furniture. Then we moved to St. Louis, where Dad sold cars. Then to Raleigh, where he sold life insurance. Finally, when I was sixteen, he moved us to Knoxville, where he sold more cars, more life insurance, and more furniture. The house in Fountain City was about fifty years old, renovated several times, big and drafty, with a pee smell in the hallways that Mom could never get out, so she burned a lot of candles, though Dad stomped around and said one day she was going to burn the whole place down.

Mom had cancer. When it was diagnosed, I told her she should find a smaller place. She said she felt closer to Dad there. She had had cancer for three years, and this was about the sixth call from her deathbed, so I didn't rush over. I even stopped first at the DQ drive-thru for a chocolate sundae. It was for her. Mom loved chocolate sundaes.

"Mom, I brought you a chocolate sundae," I said. She was lying propped up in the bed, with about a dozen pillows behind her back. She didn't look good, and I felt guilty for not going straight over there.

"I don't want a chocolate sundae. You eat it."

I sat on the edge of the bed and ate the sundae.

"Tell me how I look," she said.

"You look great, Mom."

"No, I don't. I look terrible. Don't lie to me, Theodore."

"I never lie to you, Mom."

"You lied about breaking my kitchen window."

"Mom, that was twenty years ago. I was a kid."

Her eyes narrowed at me. I looked away.

"How old are you now?"

"I'm thirty-three, Mom. Mom, you know how old I am."

"You've gained weight."

"I've always been big, Mom."

"Now you're bigger. You shouldn't have eaten that sundae."

"You told me to."

I set the empty plastic cup on her nightstand.

"Teddy," she said. "I'm dying."

"Mom, you say that every time I come over."

"This time, I am."

"Okay, Mom."

"I doubt I'll make it through the night."

"You want me to stay?"

"No, I'm sure you have to work tonight."

"They'll let me have the night off, if you're dying."

"Really? How kind of them." She coughed. She motioned to the box of Kleenex by her bed and I gave one to her. She pressed it against her mouth as she coughed, then examined it carefully for any sign of blood.

"Teddy," she said after she caught her breath. "I have a confession to make."

"Okay."

"When your father died, there was quite a bit of life insurance. I was working at the time, as you know, and we really didn't need the money, so I set it aside—the life-insurance money, I mean."

I didn't say anything. I was remembering all the times she'd complained about us not having any money.

"I knew if we started to spend it, it would just be gone. Woosh! Right out the window. So I invested it. There's quite a nest egg there, though the medical bills have taken their bite, and now that I'm dying and you're thirty-three years old, with half your life gone already, I thought it was time to give it to you."

I thought about it. It was a lot to think about.

"It's quite a bit of money, Teddy," she whispered. "And you shouldn't spend it. Invest it. Like I did. You make a good living. You don't really need it."

"How much is it, Mom?"

"One hundred and twenty-five thousand dollars, give or take a few pennies."

CHAPTER THREE

I FELT BAD WHEN SHE DIED THE NEXT WEEK. BAD FOR NOT believing she was really dying and bad for being angry with her for hoarding that money, which we really could have used. Most of all, though, I felt bad because she was my mother and she was dead. She was the only family I had.

I put the house up for sale and gave most of her things to charity. A couple of items, knickknacks she treasured or things I remembered from childhood, I kept, but I put them away in one of my closets.

They gave me the night off the day of her funeral, so I decided to eat out, though having a steak that night made me feel a little guilty. I drove to the Old City Diner on the corner of Western and Summit Hill. Felicia was working that night. That made me feel a little less bad. She was my favorite waitress. I liked her nose. It was a small nose and crinkled in the middle when she laughed.

"Teddy, how are ya?" she asked when she came to take my order.

"Okay," I said. "Except my mom died."

"Oh God! I'm sorry. Wasn't she real sick, though?"

"Cancer."

"My uncle died two years ago of throat cancer."

She took my order. I said, "She left me sixty-five thousand dollars."

"Get outta here!"

"No, she did. Plus a little insurance money to boot, and I've sold the old homestead. She told me not to spend any of it. Didn't make me promise, though."

"So what're you going to do with it?"

"Well, it's always been my dream to have my own detective agency."

She put her hands on her hips and laughed. Her nose crinkled. Felicia had goldish blond hair that she pulled up into a bun for work. I only saw her at work, so I didn't know how long her hair was or what it looked like when she took it down. She saw I was serious, and stopped laughing.

I pulled a piece of paper from my pocket as she slid into the seat across from me.

"See, I'm working on some names for it. So far, I've got Ruzak's Detective Agency, Detection by Teddy, AAA Detectives—you know, that way, you get the first listing in the Yellow Pages—Just Like Sherlock Detective Agency, and Dick Ruzak Agency. See, *dick* is another word for detective."

"I don't think you should call yourself 'dick,' Teddy," Felicia said.

"I'm not crazy about any of them."

"Well, I'm sure you'll think of something."

She left to put in my order. I studied my to-do list, things like renting an office and buying furniture and getting some phone and electrical service. Felicia came back with my steak.

"You know what I would do with sixty-five thousand dollars?"

"What would you do?"

"I don't know. But I'd quit this stinkin' job."

"I'm quitting mine tomorrow. It isn't the greatest job in the world, either, but it's the only job I've ever had, so it's been like contemplating the void, working myself up to quitting."

She didn't seem too interested in my contemplation of the void.

"How about the Ultimate Detective Agency?" she asked.

"Maybe something that's an acronym," I said. "You know, a title that spells something out, like CIA."

"CIA isn't an acronym, Ruzak. An acronym is a pronounceable word, like NATO. TUDA."

"TUDA?"

"For The Ultimate Detective Agency."

"That seems too close to *tuna*. If I'm going with an acronym, I should go with something that's related, not something that's going to make people think of fish."

"Related to what?"

"The thing itself."

"The thing itself?"

"Detection."

"How about Private Investigator & Gumshoe Ruzak?"

I thought about this. "Doesn't that spell out PIG Ruzak?"

Her nose was crinkling at me.

"Anyway," I said. "I'll think of something."

CHAPTER FOUR

THE NEXT WEEK, I RENTED SOME SPACE ON CHURCH Street, in the old Ely Building, about two blocks from the Tennessee Theater, where fading singing stars came for concerts and where old movies that hardly anybody came to see played on the weekends. My new office was one floor above the only dry cleaner's downtown. It was in a drafty old building, and you had to walk up this narrow stairwell to get to my door. The ventilation wasn't very good and I never could figure out a way to keep the stench from all those dry-cleaning chemicals from seeping up through the creaky boards. The other place I looked at was bigger, but it was above a Chinese take-out joint in Market Square and the rent was twice as much. I realized after a week that I should have taken the bigger place. I didn't take it because I didn't like Chinese food and the rent was higher, but smelling Chinese food all day would have been better than smelling chemicals.

I finally settled on a name and hired a man to stencil it on the door. I bought a desk, a filing cabinet, an electric fan for the top of the cabinet, an executive office chair, a typewriter, and a telephone. Everything was secondhand except the telephone. There was a little space near the door that could be a secretary's office, but I was trying to economize. I figured I would hire a secretary once I got my first client.

But I didn't get a client. I went to my office every day and sat by the phone, but the phone never rang. A couple of letters came addressed to "Current Occupant" and some bills, but no one called and no one came to the door.

I put an ad in the paper and printed some handbills. I hired this little Latino boy to walk around the block and hand them out, but I didn't monitor his work, so I don't know how many he handed out or if he handed out any at all. I drank too much coffee and ate too many Krispy Kreme doughnuts. I thought about my mother. I thought about my old job. I missed my mother. I missed my old job. I started leaving the office earlier and earlier. I'd go to the diner in the Old City and sit in my booth and Felicia would ask me how it was going and I would say fine and she would laugh and wrinkle her nose at me.

Then one day, there was a knock on my door. I thought it was another salesman, so I didn't answer it at first. About twice a week, the salesmen dropped by. I bought some stationery from one, and when it came in, it had my name spelled wrong at the top: Theodore Rusak. This really ticked me off, because people were always spelling my name wrong or saying it wrong. It was Ruzak with a *z* and pronounced "*Rue*-zack," not "Russ-ick" or "Ruh-zick." I called the salesman, but he refused to give me a refund or redo the job unless I paid him full price again.

The person kept knocking, so I got up and answered the door.

"Theodore Ruzak?"

"That's me."

"I saw your ad in the paper. May I come in? I know I don't have an appointment. . . ."

"That makes it tough," I said. "But I'll squeeze you in."

He was a small guy, maybe five four, no more than five five, balding, with little white wisps of the remaining hair dancing in the air like the tops of dandelion heads. Dandelions reminded me of summer and my father's irrational, visceral hatred of the weed, yanking me out of bed at six o'clock on Saturday mornings to pull them from the yard and flower beds, fussing at me for breaking them off at ground level, leaving the root intact to generate a new plant. Dandelions have very stubborn roots and are ingeniously designed to snap off at the top if you pull too hard. I've got one of those free association–type brains, where my thoughts bump around like pinballs, and I often come off stupid in conversations because I've bounced about ten thousand miles from the spot where I should be.

He was wearing Levi's, brown work boots, and a flannel shirt that was really too warm for the weather, like he was trying to come across as a farmer or a day laborer, but I wasn't buying it. He was too old for day labor, for one, and the shirt was pressed; I mean, what sort of farmer irons his flannel? I waved him to a chair. He was a spry little guy; he reminded me of Fred Astaire in that movie musical about the Irish leprechauns. He had the same thin, sharply chiseled features and the rather triangular-shaped head. I figured he was in his late sixties and kept himself fit, maybe with tennis or golf, despite the fact he wore flannel and people who wear flannel generally don't go in for the effete sports.

I sat down behind my desk, pulled out my legal pad and my mechanical pencil, and wrote the date across the top.

"My name is Parker Hudson," the old guy said. He didn't have an East Tennessee accent—definitely not a local, then—and his voice was strangely youthful, not cracked and quavering like you'd expect an old man to sound. He was no farmer all right. No self-respecting farm couple would name their son Parker. That was inviting trouble.

"All right, that's great," I said, and wrote his name beneath the date.

"Have you been a detective long, Mr. Ruzak?"

"Only about a month. But my background's in security."

"I tried going to the police," Parker Hudson said. "First they thought I was a crank; then they practically laughed me out the door."

I wrote beneath his name the words *crank* and *laughed*.

"What are you doing?"

"Making notes."

"I don't like the fact that you wrote 'crank' beneath my name."

"Sorry."

I erased the word. Now all I had was "laughed" beneath his name. I wondered how much sense that was going to make to me later, so I erased that word, too. *Police* made more sense. I wrote "police" while he watched me write "police."

"Do you have a license, Mr. Ruzak?"

"A driver's license?"

"A PI license."

"Do I need one?"

"You're the one billing yourself as a private investigator. Don't you know whether the state requires a license before you can privately investigate?"

"You know what, Mr. Hudson, I bet they do. I mean, you can't even fish in this state without a license, and PI work is at least as taxing."

I wrote "license (?)" beside the word *police*.

"So the answer to my question is, you don't have a license."

"Don't turn me in," I said. "I'll get one. Meanwhile, Mr. Hudson, maybe you oughta check out another agency. If I'm gonna make a go of this, I might as well do it legally. I know what right and wrong are. That's one of the reasons I became a detective, though maybe I shouldn't say that, because technically I'm not one till I get a license."

All of a sudden, he laughed. I wasn't sure why he laughed.

"Will you give me a discount?"

"Well," I said. I didn't really know what to say, since I hadn't thought out my rates. I tapped the eraser end of my mechanical pencil on the notepad and gave him what I hoped was a calculating look, like I was figuring what discount he might be entitled to, first for hiring an unlicensed detective and second for not turning me in for being an unlicensed detective.

"I'll pay you fifty dollars an hour, plus expenses, of course."

"Of course," I said. My mouth was dry. Fifty dollars an hour! My top pay at the security company had been twenty-two dollars an hour. Why had I waited this long to go into the detective business? That was the way my mind worked: On the heels of euphoria came depression, thinking about all the wasted years. "Expenses?"

"Gas and supplies and the like."

"Yes, and the like . . . that."

"Good."

"What is it you want me to do?"

"I want you to find a murderer."

I stared at him for a second.

"Did you say a murderer?"

"And once you find him, I want you to bring justice to his miserable soul."

CHAPTER FIVE

PARKER HUDSON PAID ME A RETAINER OF TWO HUNDRED dollars. I promised I'd be on the case the very next morning and we parted very up on each other. I honestly thought he thought he had found the right man for the job. I didn't have the heart and felt it didn't make good business sense to tell him I had no idea what to do next.

I drove to the diner in the Old City to celebrate. Felicia came over right away to take my order. She was wearing bright red lipstick and matching red nail polish. Her hair was up, as usual, and she wore the same white uniform with the name tag, and it occurred to me I had never seen her wearing anything but that white polyester waitress uniform.

"So, how's it taste?" she asked.

"How's what taste?" She had totally thrown me, since I hadn't even ordered yet.

"The canary. You look like the cat who swallowed it."

"I'm celebrating."

"You got a client."

"I got a client. How much do you make, Felicia?"

"What's that?"

"What's Freddy pay you to wait tables?"

"Two-fifty an hour, plus tips. Why?"

"I'll pay you twelve bucks an hour, with a two-week paid vacation every year."

"Huh?"

"I need a secretary," I said. "I'm getting clients now and I need somebody to answer the phone and do the mail and get the door . . . you know, a secretary."

Her nose crinkled. "You want to hire me to be your secretary?"

"Sure."

She thought about it.

"Okay," she said. She called over her shoulder, "Hey, Freddy! I quit!" She took off her apron and slid into the seat across from me.

"Okay, tell me about him."

"Who?"

"Your client, Ruzak."

"His name is Parker Hudson."

She took a sharp breath.

"You know him?" I asked.

"No. I just thought that I was supposed to do stuff like that. You know, like in the movies. Like, 'Oooh! Not *the* Parker Hudson!'"

"He dresses like a farmer, but he's a retired banker."

"He's loaded."

"I don't think he's hurting for cash."

"Ka-ching," she said. "But why would some big-shot retired banker with loads of cash hire someone like you?"

"The police won't help." It kind of bothered me, the way she said that, "hire someone like you," with the emphasis on the word *you*.

"Why won't the police help?"

"Well, technically I guess it's a crime, but it's not the sort of crime they take seriously."

"What is it, jaywalking?"

"Hit-and-run. Murder. Well, it was closer to manslaughter, but the 'man' part's misleading."

Her nose crinkled. "What is this, Teddy, some kind of joke? What really happened, his wife lose an earring?"

One of the other waitresses came over. Her name tag said LACEY. Lacey was an enormous woman with steel gray hair and very small hands for such a large woman. She told Felicia that Freddy was pissed that she had quit like that and doubly pissed because we weren't ordering anything. Only paying customers got booths. I started to order something, but Felicia stopped me.

"Let's get out of here, Teddy."

"It's my favorite place."

"We've been shut down three times by the Health Department."

"I'm hungry," I said.

"We'll pick something up. The food here sucks." She said this real loud. She wanted to make sure Freddy heard.

CHAPTER SIX

FELICIA KNEW THIS CHINESE PLACE CALLED #1 CHINA
Buffet down on the Strip, the main drag through the campus of
the university. A light rain was falling, the kind of rain that's between real rain and fog, kind of a foggy rain. It was never easy
finding a parking place on the Strip; I had to park three blocks
away, and we walked together in the rain. Felicia was wearing a
green overcoat. I didn't have an overcoat or an umbrella.

"Since when do the cops not take murder seriously?" she asked.

"I guess it's got something to do with the victims."

"Victims? Like more than one?"

"Yeah, like that."

The rain made her face look softer somehow. Maybe it was all
the moisture in the air.

We picked up our food and sat on bar stools at the long counter
against the window and watched the people go by on the street,
students mostly, since the Strip ran right down the middle of
campus. She was having a bowl of noodles and I had some pork.
The pork was soggy and the pieces seemed to take too long to
chew. I didn't really care for Chinese food, which is how I ended
up over a dry cleaner's in the first place, but Felicia had been
pretty excited about the food here. I should have chosen the noodles, I guess. I wondered why only Chinese and American foods

were done buffet-style. You never saw an Italian buffet or a Mexican buffet.

"So who were the victims?" she asked around a mouthful of noodles.

"Geese."

"Did you say *geese?*"

"Parker Hudson was taking a walk one morning a few weeks ago, and there's this nice big lake he walks around, and as he's walking, he sees these two geese with their babies, six of them, crossing the road."

"Okay, okay. I see where this is going."

"And while he's watching, all of sudden this big SUV comes roaring up behind him and—"

"Don't say it."

"Runs right over the baby geese. The goslings." That's what Parker Hudson had called them, *goslings.* I wasn't completely sure what that meant, so after he left my office, I looked it up. My name didn't used to be Dictionary Ruzak for nothing.

"Didn't slow down, didn't try to swerve. Parker's sure whoever was driving saw them. And if they didn't see them, they sure as heck *felt* them. So I asked him why they were crossing the road. . . ."

She laughed. "You didn't."

"Why not?"

"Never mind."

"Okay. Anyway, the two adults didn't get hit—Dad was leading and Mom was taking up the rear—and they went berserk, flapping their wings and honking to beat the band, refusing to leave their dead babies even when other cars came up, so Parker's running up and down the road trying to scare them back to the lake. . . ."

"Oh God. That's awful."

"Anyway, he didn't get the guy's tag number. Just says it's a big SUV with white-rimmed tires, something like a Ford Expedition or maybe a GMC. Might even be a Jeep. He's just not sure."

"So he wants you to find who killed the geese."

"Goslings."

"And when you find them?"

"First I have to find them."

"Okay, say you find them. Then what?"

I shrugged. "I guess Parker files charges, I don't know, reckless driving or something like that."

"He's a big animal lover, huh?"

I thought about it. "I don't know about that. I don't think it was the dead baby birds that got to him so much as the person who hit them, like life was nothing to him."

"It was probably just an accident."

"That's what I said," I said. "And he said, 'If it was an accident, why didn't he stop to see if the birds needed help? He must have known he hit them, so why did he keep going?' "

"He didn't care."

I nodded. "That's what got to him—Parker, I mean. That somebody killed something and just kept driving."

"The world's full of assholes, Ruzak."

"Yeah, but that doesn't mean you don't take them to account."

She pushed her empty bowl away. One of the dishes on the steam table had been Peking duck. There were Peking duck and General Tao chicken and sweet-and-sour pork and beef and vegetables. It wasn't disrespectful to eat the animals in those dishes, though. The whole reason they were on the earth was to be killed and eaten by people. The geese murdered that morning were wild geese that nested by Parker's lake every spring.

"Okay, detective, how're you going to solve this murder most foul? Sorry."

"I'm working on that."

"Witnesses?"

"Just Parker. It was pretty early in the morning."

"He lives around there?"

"House right on the lake. There're two or three subdivisions on the other side of the road, but he didn't see which one the car came out of. It might not have come out of any of them. The road connects to Kingston Pike."

"Busiest road in Knoxville."

"Right."

"Could be anyone."

"Right."

"Any one of about five hundred thousand people."

"Right."

"In a black SUV, the most popular kind and color of car in East Tennessee."

"Right."

"Or it might be someone from out of town, out of state, even."

"Right."

"Well, this should be easy."

"I'm not so sure."

"How much is Mr. Hudson paying you to hunt down this bird killer?"

"Fifty dollars an hour, plus expenses."

I was looking out the rain-streaked window, but I could feel her eyes on the side of my face.

"You're kidding, right?"

"He gave me a two-hundred-dollar retainer."

She whistled. "And I was making two-fifty, plus tips."

"Blood money," I said.

"Huh?"

"People like me. And cops. Even doctors, I guess. Somebody has to suffer so we can earn a living."

"Teddy, these are geese we're talking about."

"Tell that to the goslings."

"I never knew you had a sensitive side."

"Money never could motivate me that much, Felicia. Why else would I stay a security guard for fourteen years?"

CHAPTER SEVEN

I DROVE FELICIA BACK TO THE DINER TO PICK UP HER CAR. The foggy rain had turned to just fog.

"I still don't understand why he decided to hire a detective," she said.

"He told me for three weeks he's been staking out that same spot and the car hasn't been back. He drove through all the neighborhoods around there, but he didn't see any car that looked familiar."

"So what does he think you can do that he can't?"

Again, she emphasized the word *you*.

"Well, he did say that when he wants his house painted, he doesn't do it himself. He calls in the experts. That reminds me. I gotta get a license."

"What kind of license?"

"A detective's license."

"Oh Ruzak. That bird killer's as good as in the cage."

"You're ribbing me. That's okay."

I pulled into the empty space beside her car. Before she got out, she asked, "Where's your office?"

"How come you want to know?"

"Don't I have to show up for work tomorrow?"

I waited until she was in her car and the doors were locked, so no crazed dope fiend or bum could get her. The Old City could be kind of rough. When she slid into the driver's seat, her white skirt pulled up and I saw a lot of thigh. Her stockings were the same shade of white as her uniform and she was wearing those thick-soled white shoes waitresses and hospital workers wear because they're on their feet all the time. A few strands of goldish blond hair had slipped from the back of her bun and hung down her neck, swaying as she got in the car. I watched her pull out and waved to her as she drove away, but she didn't wave back. Maybe she didn't see me.

Nothing can make you feel lonelier than hanging out with a pretty girl. All at once, I felt like crying. I knew I was luckier than most people. I had fulfilled my childhood dream. And so what if this wasn't the coolest or sexiest case any detective'd ever worked? At least now I was a detective and making more money than I ever had as a security guard. I guess if my mom hadn't died and left me that money, I'd still be a security guard making twenty-two dollars an hour, but at least my mother would be alive.

I drove back to my apartment, but I didn't feel like going inside. I decided to take a walk.

I walked up and down Gay Street, all the way to the Tennessee Bank Building and back. Not many people live in downtown Knoxville. Most of the people I knew by sight, though I didn't know their names. I passed three dedicated joggers damning the rain and some couples arm in arm, and the people walking past seemed more real to me than I did to myself. I'd always heard that the reality is never the same as your dreams when they finally come true. That it doesn't feel like you thought it would. Then I thought maybe it wasn't my dreams coming true that was making me feel so empty and ghostlike. Maybe it was something else.

By the time I got back to the apartment, I was hungry again, so I cooked some pasta, and right in the middle of washing my plate,

I burst into tears and cried for about an hour. A lot of people say you feel better after a good cry, but I didn't feel better. I felt pretty crummy for the rest of the night. I took a shower and tried to watch some TV, but there was nothing good on. Maybe it's just me, but there's never anything good on TV unless you have something else you have to do and can't watch TV. I thought about walking to the video store and renting a good detective movie, but just thinking the word *detective* made me feel crummier. I told myself I was crying over my mom, but deep down I was wondering if I was crying because she died or because I felt bad I hadn't cried enough over her dying. Maybe it wasn't about her at all. Maybe I was crying because I didn't want to be a detective but had become one after a lot of hassle, just to find out that after all the dreaming about it, the reality sucked.

The next morning, I was still feeling lousy, so I stopped by the Krispy Kreme and picked up a dozen doughnuts and two large coffees. Felicia was waiting for me on the sidewalk outside the Ely Building. She followed me up the narrow stairs, pausing at the door.

"What the hell is this?" she asked.

"What? Oh, it's the name I picked for the company."

" 'The Highly Effective Detection & Investigation Company,' " she read.

"You like it?"

"What does that— Teddy, that spells out 'THE DIC.' "

"Yeah, that's another name for a PI. Only I couldn't think of a word that started with a *K*, so I left it off."

"What?"

"The word I couldn't think of that started with a *K*."

"So that's where I work now? I work at a place called 'THE DIC'?"

"I figured it'd be a catchy way for people to remember. Don't you think it's catchy? The copy in my ad says, 'Got a mystery? Come see THE DIC.' What's the matter? Too wordy?"

"No, it's just . . . well, it makes you wonder why it took you so long to get a client."

We stepped inside and she cried, "Dear God, what is that smell?"

"The dry cleaner's."

"We're gonna have to do something about that."

I showed her the fan and said it wasn't too bad with the fan on and the windows open.

Felicia ate two doughnuts and I ate the rest.

"You feelin' okay?" she asked.

"I feel pretty crummy."

"It's this place. It's a dump, Teddy."

I gave her the card of the furniture salesman and told her to go ahead and order a desk for herself and a chair and maybe a filing cabinet if she thought she needed one. Felicia was wearing a nice powder blue business-type suit and high heels. Her hair was down and reached just past her shoulders. It was the first time I ever saw her with her hair down and wearing heels, and I told her she looked nice.

"You want to go to the movies with me sometime?" I asked.

"I have a boyfriend."

"I didn't know you had a boyfriend."

"You never asked me."

"Some detective," I said. I went into the john and washed my hands. She was standing by my desk when I came out. She looked just like Lauren Bacall. I told her she looked just like Lauren Bacall and she asked who the hell Lauren Bacall was.

"Never mind."

The glaze from the doughnuts had given her red lips a luster, and for some reason I thought of a bowling alley, those lanes waxed and polished till they shone.

"What's your boyfriend's name?"

"Why do you want to know his name?" she asked.

"Just curious."

"His name is Bob."

"Bob?"

"Why, what's wrong with Bob?"

"Nothing."

"We've been dating for three years."

"That's a long time."

"He's a fireman."

"That's a very important job. I wanted to be a cop once."

"Why don't you have a girlfriend?" Felicia asked.

"I used to."

"What happened?"

"I had just flunked out of the Police Academy. She told me she wanted somebody with a future."

Her name was Tiffany, like the lamp, but everybody called her "Tiffy." We started dating my senior year. I made the football team that year, after four years of trying. I was big and hard to knock down, but I got confused in the huddle because studying the playbook gave me a headache, so I didn't play much. But if we got ahead in the game, the coach put me in at left guard and I would hunker down and just let them hammer me. "You've got a soft head and a softer body, Ruzak," he told me. "But we're leading fifty-two to ten, so go hit some people." Usually, the opposite happened. Tiffy played in the band, and one Friday night she noticed this guy standing out there like a big dumb post for two quarters, and something about this lummox standing in there play after play while he had the living crap beat out of him impressed her, so she asked the tuba player about me. The tuba player, who was actually bigger than I was, introduced us after the game and we dated the rest of my senior year. We were even talking about marriage once I graduated from the Academy, but of course I flunked out and she dumped me for a guy named Bill Hill, which is the kind of name you never forget, so I was stuck with always knowing the name of the guy my girl dumped me for.

I picked up the phone.

"What are you doing?" Felicia asked.

"I'm using the phone."

"How long are you going to be using it?"

"I don't know. Why?"

"I need it."

"What?"

"The phone, Teddy."

"Why do you need the phone?"

"I'm calling an interior decorator."

"Why are you calling an interior decorator?"

"For the office, Teddy."

"But I just gave you a furniture guy's card."

"This place doesn't need a furniture guy, Ruzak. It's gonna take a whole lot more than a couple secondhand chairs and tacky prints on the walls."

She disappeared around the corner. I wondered how much an interior decorator cost while I got the number for the Tennessee Private Investigation and Polygraph Commission.

"You can't be a PI unless you meet state requirements," the lady at the commission told me after I was on hold for twenty minutes. She had the same sharp, impatient tone as most people who staff telephone lines.

"What are the requirements?"

"They're on our Web site."

"I don't have a computer. That isn't one of the requirements, is it?"

"Are you saying you don't have access to the Web?"

"I'm saying I don't have a computer. That's what I said."

"But that isn't what I asked."

"But you can't have one without the other. That's like making a phone call without a phone."

"Do you want that address?"

"I might want it, if I had a computer, but I don't have a computer. Could you just tell me what the requirements are over the phone? I own a phone."

"Obviously you own a phone, sir."

"Well, what if I was calling from a pay phone?"

"Are you calling from a pay phone?"

"No."

"Then why did you say you were?"

"I didn't. I was posing a hypothetical. The bottom line is, I happen to own a phone but not a computer. Would it be possible—to save you some time and the state some money—to tell me what the requirements of becoming a PI are, right now, while we're talking?"

"Your local library should have Internet access. . . ."

"What, so I have to apply online?"

"Did I say you had to apply online? I said if you wanted to look up the requirements online, you could access the Web from your local library."

"Ma'am, in the time we've taken to exhaust the Internet-access option, you could have told me what the requirements are."

"That's an assumption on your part, sir."

"That may be, but you assumed I was talking from a pay phone, like I didn't have the wherewithal to own my own phone."

"Sir, you're the one who brought up the pay phone."

"I really don't want to quibble," I said. "I feel like we've started off on the wrong foot, and I'd like to step back onto the path and reach my goal of knowing what the requirements of being a PI are."

"Hold on," she said snippily, and music started to play in my ear. I was on hold for quite a while and began to wonder if she had cut me off or was taking a break, or if the list was so lengthy that it took this long just to assemble it.

Then she came back on and said, "Okay. There're eight."

"Now we're getting somewhere," I said. I waited with my mechanical pencil. "Now we're cooking."

"First, you have to be at least twenty-one years of age."

"I'm thirty-three." One down, seven to go.

"Then you can check that one off, I guess. Are you a citizen of the United States or a resident alien?"

"What's a resident alien?"

"I—I'm not sure. Do you think you might be an alien?"

"No, I'm a citizen. I was born in New York, though. Are you a resident alien if you were born in another state?"

"You can't be a citizen and an alien, sir, resident or nonresident."

"How can a nonresident be an alien in the United States? I mean, if you're not living here . . ."

"Sir, I have six other people on hold. . . ."

I told her I was sorry, but I reminded her we would be much further along if she hadn't bogged us down with the Internet option. I gripped my pencil hard to try to keep my thoughts from pinballing.

"Have you been declared mentally defective?"

"Not for years. But you know kids can be pretty cruel."

"By a court of competent jurisdiction, sir."

"Oh, no, nothing like that."

"Do you own your own company?"

"Yeah. It's my own company."

"Are you of good moral character?"

That one brought me up short. I'd always thought of myself as having good moral character, but who was I to say? What did the state want as proof? What did that mean, "good moral character"? I hadn't been to church since I was a teenager, so I'd be hard-pressed to find a preacher or other moral authority to vouch for me. It was one of those tricky questions where the answer flipped back and forth in your head. If I said yes, that I had good moral character, I might be lying, in which case, I didn't. But if I said no, that I didn't, that would be telling the truth when a lie would be better, and didn't that prove I did?

"Sure," I said. "You bet."

"Do you suffer from habitual drunkenness or narcotics addiction or dependence?"

"I have a beer every now and then."

Felicia appeared from around the corner and leaned against the jamb, crossing one ankle over the other and her arms over her chest.

"Beer? Who are you talking to?" she asked.

"Sir, you know that's not what I'm asking."

"The state of Tennessee," I said to Felicia.

"I beg your pardon, sir?"

"Nothing," I said to the phone lady. "No, no drunkenness or narcotic, um, ness."

"You also must submit your fingerprints for processing. All PIs must have a clean criminal background."

That sounded funny to me, "a clean criminal background." Did that mean I could have a criminal background, as long as it was clean?

"Okay."

Felicia rolled her eyes and disappeared again.

"And you have to pass the exam."

My heart gave a little roll. "There's an exam?"

"Tennessee also requires a minimum of six hours of continuing education per year, acceptable to the commission."

"What, like at a college or something? Do I need a college degree, by the way?"

"No, you do not."

"That's good, because I don't have one."

"Really? Is there anything else I can help you with today, sir?"

"Sure. How much does a license cost?"

"There's a two-hundred-and-fifty-dollar application fee."

I whistled. Her voice warmed because she was enjoying this part.

"And a one-hundred-and-twenty-five-dollar licensing fee, renewable every two years."

I didn't say anything, and she said, "Are you there?"

"Yeah."

"Would you like me to send you an application?"

"Sure. Yeah. That would be great. These fees, are they tax-deductible?"

"Sir, I'm not qualified to answer that question. Talk to your accountant."

"I don't have an accountant."

"Maybe you should get one, sir. Seeing that you're running a business."

"That's not a bad idea. Thanks."

I gave her my address so she could mail the application, then hung up. I was sweating hard and my fingers were shaking a little. Felicia came back into the room.

"Can I use the phone now?"

"Felicia, do you think I have good moral character?"

"I hardly know you, Ruzak. You're a good tipper."

She disappeared again. When Felicia was in the room, I felt bigger somehow. My mental weight expanded about twenty to twenty-five pounds. I wondered if I should call Parker Hudson and tell him it really wasn't moral for me to work as a private investigator on his bird case when I didn't even have a license, no matter that it didn't bother him. If I had good moral character, I wouldn't practice detecting without a license. But then I would give up the fifty bucks an hour, plus expenses, default on my lease, and fire Felicia. She would have to go back to waitressing, and she hated waitressing. I told myself not to worry so much about this PI exam. There must be study guides, and maybe it was even an open-book test. In general, people panic before they have all the facts.

I yelled into the vestibule to ask Felicia if she knew any good accountants, but she was already on the phone to some interior designer, setting up an appointment to "appraise the space." Maybe she would back off the interior designer thing if I hinted that only people with no taste hire interior designers. But then she might get sore at me. I'd have to balance the cost of her getting sore against the cost of hiring some fancy-pants interior designer. When I was younger, they were called interior decorators. *Designer* sounds more artsy, I guess, and somehow more technical, like an engineer, someone who designs rockets for NASA or something.

Felicia came back into the room and said, "They're coming this Thursday."

"To give an estimate, right?"

"What are you worried about?"

"I have to take an exam."

"You want me to help you study?"

"You'd help me study?"

"It's purely selfish, Teddy. You don't get that license and I go back to being a waitress."

"Why were you a waitress, Felicia?"

"What's that supposed to mean?"

"I mean, somebody as smart and pretty as you—"

She sat down across from me and said, "Maybe we should get something straight right from the beginning, Ruzak. My personal life is off-limits. Our relationship is going to be strictly professional. I won't stick my nose in your business and you won't stick your nose in mine."

"Don't get sore."

"I'm not. Look, I've got lots of single friends who'd love to—"

"Oh, I'm not looking for a girlfriend."

She narrowed her eyes at me. "How come?"

I shrugged and looked away.

"Are you still carrying a torch for her?" she asked, meaning Tiffy.

"She's married, Felicia. A guy named Bill Hill. Anyway, I thought you just said we weren't going to stick our noses in each other's business."

"Now you're sore," she said. "Don't get a crush on me, Ruzak."

I promised I wouldn't, though it probably wasn't worth the breath it took to say it. It goes back to moral character: You make a promise like that and there's no way you can know at the time if you can keep it.

CHAPTER EIGHT

A COUPLE OF WEEKS LATER, I WAS SITTING IN MY OFFICE, which didn't even look like my office anymore. There were potted plants, some huge thing in the front that Felicia called a receptionist desk, a computer on that desk (with high-speed Internet access), colored prints on the walls, a throw rug, new towels and a fancy toilet paper holder in the john. My old secondhand desk was gone, replaced with a huge mahogany number and a leather executive chair. Two matching visitor's chairs were in front of the desk. There was a big globe of the world on a stand in one corner.

Felicia brought in the designer, and I guess they had a high old time. Felicia said I had to project a certain image or people wouldn't trust me to be their detective. "You have to look successful to be successful," she said. She was wearing a new designer outfit, though she said she'd gotten it on discount. She'd charged everything to the business account, even her outfit and the three others she had bought, also on discount. "It's like an advance. I'll pay you back, Teddy." The total for everything, including the shiny gold pens and stationery with the right name on it, was $26,546.74. This could have bought a nice car, even a convertible. I already had a car, but I'd always wanted a convertible.

Felicia had also bought me a tape recorder to make dictation on. All I had to do was tape my letters and reports and she would type them for me on the computer, to make everything very professional, she said. I was fooling with the taping machine when Felicia buzzed me on the new intercom system to tell me Parker Hudson was there to see me. She was sitting about ten feet away, so I heard her voice over the intercom and from across the room, as if there was an echo.

He was wearing a white sweater over a polo shirt, Docker slacks, and Birkinstock sandals. Except for the sandals, again he was dressed too warmly for the weather, which was eighty-three and sunny. Maybe he had poor circulation, like my mother, who had been dead now over two months, and still I hadn't been to her grave. That meant nobody had been to her grave, since I was the only somebody she had left. I clicked on my new tape recorder and said, "Flowers for her grave."

"Whose grave?" Parker Hudson asked. He sat down in one of the fat leather visiting chairs and looked appreciatively around the room.

"You've redecorated," he said.

"My mother."

"Your mother redecorated?"

"My mother's dead."

"I'm terribly sorry. I didn't know."

"I did."

"I'm sure you did."

"No, about the redecorating."

"Flowers would add a little color."

"No, the flowers are for her grave. I was just making a little reminder for myself, but I never remember to check the tape for reminders, so I'm wasting double the energy."

He nodded. He seemed confused. "I hope this isn't an inopportune time."

"No, pretty much any time is opportune." I pulled my pad in front of me and picked up my mechanical pencil, clicking out some fresh lead.

"I was in the neighborhood, visiting an old colleague at the bank, so I thought I'd drop by and check on the status of my case."

He stared at me and waited for me to say something.

"Is there a status on my case?"

"I'm working on some theories."

"Theories?"

"Scenarios. Hypotheticals. Possibilities."

"What are you talking about, Mr. Ruzak? It's been three weeks since you took my case and I haven't heard a word from you. Do you have any leads?"

"No, not really."

"Have you been to the lake?"

"I've been meaning to get out there. . . ."

"Canvassed the neighborhoods for any potential witnesses?"

"That's on my list."

He crossed his arms over his chest and said, "You haven't done a blessed thing, have you, Mr. Ruzak?"

"Legwork isn't all there is to detection, Mr. Hudson. Have you ever heard of Mycroft?"

"No."

"He was Sherlock Holmes's older brother. Smarter than Sherlock, if you can believe that, but he hated the legwork. He cracked cases completely in his head."

"And that's your strategy? To crack my case completely inside your head?"

"Like I said, I'm working on some theories. Without theories, you're just thrashing around in the dark and billing a lot of unnecessary expenses. I'm trying to save you some money here, Mr. Hudson."

"You're not charging me for all the time you spend concocting theories, then?"

"No, concoction is free."

"Because, after all, how could one call it work?"

"You couldn't in good conscience. Though most work these days is with your head, when you think about it. There're not many manual laborers left. . . ."

"Mr. Ruzak, I get the impression you're not taking my case very seriously."

"Oh, no, Mr. Hudson, I am taking your case very seriously. I think it's terrible what happened to those birds. It's a damned shame and whoever did it was damned shameless and you're to be commended for spending your money to track down who did it. And anyway, I'm grateful as hell for the work, but most of all for the confidence in hiring an unlicensed detective, though I'm in the process right now of getting one, a license, and letting him feel his way through his first case. To be honest with you, it's also my only case, so I've got a pretty strong interest in solving it. Maybe not as strong as you, but pretty strong."

He laughed suddenly, like he did the first time we met. One minute he was still and stoic as a Buddha, the next his face crinkled and cracked open and he was all teeth and tongue and guffaws.

"Well," he said after he got control of himself. "I suppose I can't complain too much. I haven't paid a penny and I've managed to find the equal of Mycroft Holmes."

"Oh, I never said I was his equal. Mycroft was very big in the smarts department. It's a matter of technique, not ability."

"That certainly seems true."

"But I'll get an answer for you, Mr. Hudson. I'll nab this bird killer. You've got my word on that."

He left after that and I was more than relieved. I was ready to throw his painting metaphor back at him, something like, When you hire somebody to paint your house, do you trail behind them, questioning every little stroke? Lucky for me, I didn't have to.

Felicia stuck her head in the little opening and said, "Two things."

"Yeah?"

"You wanna put a door here. I heard every word."

"I don't mind."

"Your clients might. One day, you'll get a case that requires delicacy, you know? Maybe something a little more serious than a dead bird."

"It was more than one."

"You know what I mean."

"I'll talk to the landlord. Have you ever heard of Mycroft Holmes?"

"Not till three minutes ago."

"Ever heard of Moriarty?"

"Sherlock Holmes's little brother?"

"No. His archnemesis. Maybe that's why I'm having trouble getting into this case. There's no, um, worthy adversary."

She just stared at me.

I sighed. "What was the second thing?"

"Paul Killibrew is holding for you."

"Oh. Who's Paul Killibrew?"

"He's a reporter for the *Sentinel*. He thinks this case will make a great human-interest story for the paper."

"Really?"

"Sure. It's got it all, Ruzak. Pathos, humor, a man chasing his dream. He said it might make the front page of the 'Lifestyle' section."

"That's terrific."

"And maybe the killer will read about it and come clean."

"That would solve the case," I said. I never considered myself a lucky person, but this was luck with a capital *L*.

"I wonder how he heard about it," I said, picking up the phone.

"I called him, Ruzak."

So it wasn't luck, unless you considered my hiring Felicia lucky. If it was, it was of the dumb variety. I thought I had hired her to answer phones and do the mail, not to be the brains of the operation.

CHAPTER NINE

PAUL KILLIBREW WAS A REAL NICE GUY AND SEEMED GEN-
uinely moved by the story of the dead goslings. He came by with
a photographer after we talked and took a picture of me behind
my desk, grimly gripping my mechanical pencil, the little point
poised above the legal pad, as if he and the photographer had
walked into the middle of some important detecting. The story
ran on Sunday, a half-page spread with a big color picture of me
behind the desk, holding the poised pencil. The first thing I
thought when I saw it that morning was that I had no idea how fat
I'd gotten. My weight had always been a problem and one of the
big reasons I'd struggled so much at the Police Academy. The police take it very seriously, the ability to chase down criminals
without suffering a coronary. The second thing I thought was
how proud my mother would have been. I'd never been in the paper before, except when the *Sentinel* ran my senior picture, but
they run everyone's senior picture, so that didn't really count. The
third thing I thought when I saw it was that I still hadn't visited
my mother's grave and what kind of son was I anyway?

So I cut out the article, threw on some sweats and my Nikes,
and jogged down to the Central Baptist Cemetery on Central Avenue, where my mother was buried. The church's parking lot was
packed when I got there; it was only a little after noon. After

I caught my breath, I told her, "Ma, I didn't bring you any flowers, but I brought this." I laid the clipping at the foot of the headstone and weighed it down with a stick.

"I look pretty fat in that picture," I said. "So I'm starting an exercise regimen today. I ran all the way here—well, most of the way, anyway—and I'm going to run back. I'm taking up karate, and there's this new thing I saw an ad for in the paper today, this hand-to-hand battle technique perfected by the Israelis, called Krav Maga. It's kind of like street fighting, only more deadly, because it's their secret police who invented it, and those guys are some tough sons a bitches. Sorry, Ma. And I'm cutting back on the doughnuts and the Three Musketeers. And no more swinging by the DQ after work for those damned sundaes. Anyway, I wanted to show you that clipping because maybe you'll think I'll make something of myself one of these days. I'm getting some free publicity out of the deal, which is great for business, or at least that's what I hope. I guess I should tell you it wasn't my idea. It was Felicia's. I don't think you ever met Felicia, but she's this girl I know from the Old City Diner—you know, in the Old City—and she's really smart and nice, too, when her mood's okay. I think I've got this kind of crush on her, but she has this boyfriend named Bob, who's a firefighter. That's a pretty heroic profession, though being a successful PI is nothing to sneeze at in the courageous department."

I was still slightly out of breath from my run, and talking so much wasn't helping. I was tired of standing at the foot of her grave, so I sat down.

"So that's what I've been up to, setting up the office, hiring Felicia, working on this case. . . . That's why I haven't been by sooner."

I could hear voices behind me. I looked over my shoulder and saw people in the parking lot; church was letting out. I ducked my head. I had grown up going to this church, but I hadn't been back since I graduated from high school. My father had been a lapsed Catholic and never went, but Mom had been a dyed-in-the-wool churchgoer and dragged me in every Sunday when I was a kid. The old minister I knew back then had long since retired and the new guy was young and very energetic and kept getting Mom's name wrong at the service. Mom had been too sick to go to church much in her later years; this guy barely knew her. When Dad had his heart attack, he begged for a priest, until finally Mom relented, and then Dad got in an argument with the father during the Last Rites; the first priest he'd spoken to in thirty years and he gets in a fight with him, but that was Dad—very cocksure and querulous. I had trouble understanding why he'd summoned a priest to ready him for the afterlife, only to badger him about Church dogma. What especially set him off was the priest performing the sacrament in the vernacular. Dad wanted Latin, and when the priest said his Latin was rusty, Dad said, "What kind of goddamned priest are you?" I was worried he'd have a second heart attack, fighting with a priest, of all people, and that if there was anything to the Church's teachings, the priest would never get out of there, because Dad kept sinning up to and past receiving absolution.

I hunkered there until the last car left the lot, told Mom goodbye and that I'd be back soon, then started my run back to the apartment, thinking about a hot shower and maybe a package of those little white-powdered doughnuts ninety-nine cents for six at the Walgreens right on my way home. I told myself my problem was willpower, in that I didn't have any. I had just made a promise to Mom about sweets, and already I was planning to break it.

I stopped by the Walgreens on Gay Street, about five blocks from my apartment in the Sterchi Building, and bought three more newspapers for two dollars each, a bottled water, and a bag of unsalted peanuts. Peanuts are excellent protein and good for you, according to the Atkins book. I had never read the Atkins book, but I'd seen a lot of stories about it on television. I went through a phase in my twenties when I read every diet book on the market and bought exercise tapes and even joined a gym, which I never went to. I was into diet culture the way some homely guys get into porno. Maybe later I'd rent a movie (not porno) or call one of my old buddies from the security company, Glen or Farrell, to see if they wanted to come over and read the paper. Thinking of my old friends from work made me lonely all of a sudden, and I thought about getting a dog, even though it was prohibited in the lease. Then I thought how pitiful that was, so lonely that I was willing to pay for companionship. Growing up, I had just one dog, a collie named Lady, who died one summer while we were down in Florida for a family vacation. I begged for another dog, but my dad told me I wasn't going to get another dog until I learned how to handle my emotions better. I guess I never learned to handle them to his satisfaction, because we never got a replacement for Lady.

I jogged down the sidewalk, the green plastic Walgreens bag bumping against my thigh. You don't think a newspaper is heavy until you stuff three Sunday editions in a bag and jog with them. Traffic was very light on Gay Street. It was Sunday and the downtown pretty much died on the weekends, despite millions of dollars spent on revitalization and all the tax breaks and rent subsidies they handed out, trying to get people to move downtown. I barely glanced both ways before crossing at Jackson, and I was hopping onto the curb on the east side of Gay Street when it hit me—not the car itself, but the fact that it was a big vehicle and that it was black, and the fact that it was going very slowly, like it was following me.

CHAPTER TEN

SINCE I DIDN'T KNOW WHAT TO DO AT THAT POINT, I DID what most people do when they don't know what to do: I just kept doing what I was doing. In this case, running. I slowed up, expecting the car to pass me. The speed limit downtown was twenty-five, but there was no way I was running faster than twenty-five miles per hour, so why was this guy driving so slowly if he wasn't following me? Maybe he had blown his chance to run me down like those poor damn goslings and he was waiting for another. I thought about stopping, just stopping and turning around to get a good look at him. It occurred to me I didn't have a gun and that, being in PI work, I might find a gun useful, but I hated guns—even when I was in the Police Academy I hated guns—and besides, I was a terrible shot—probably because I hated guns. I'd have to get a permit for one, and you have to pass a marksmanship class to do that, and I sucked at marksmanship. It had been my worst subject at the Academy.

I could see the Sterchi Building up ahead. Less than three blocks to go, and now I could hear the rumble of its big eight-cylinder engine and I tried to remember if the windows were tinted or not. It might not even be worth it to stop and look, if the windows were dark.

Then all choice was taken from me. The engine roared and the big SUV swept past, and I saw the windows *were* tinted. I also saw it was a black Ford Expedition with Tennessee plates. I was so overwhelmed with information at that point, I didn't catch all the numbers, but the first three letters were *HRT.*

I sprinted the last two blocks and up the three flights of stairs to my apartment, then collapsed against the wall beside my door, clutching my keys in my hand, saying over and over to myself, "HRT. HRT. HRT. History's really tough. Her rotten tomatoes. Harry rips tissue. . . ." I kept muttering things like that to help me remember.

When I had my breath back, I went inside, threw the dead bolt, dropped the Walgreens bag on the counter, and looked up Felicia's number in the phone book. A guy answered on the fifth ring. It sounded like I woke him up. I asked if Felicia was there. There was some mumbling, then a loud *clunk,* like somebody'd dropped the phone.

"Hello?"

"Felicia, this is Teddy. Did I wake you up?"

"No. No. It's my boss. . . ." She must have been talking to Bob. It made me feel funny, hearing her call me her boss.

"Did the article run today?" she asked.

"Yeah, but that's not why I'm calling. I think I spotted the killer."

"What killer? Oh. The geese. What do you mean, you spotted him?"

"He's stalking me." I told her what had happened.

"Teddy, the odds that—"

"The only thing I can't figure is how he knew where I lived. . . ." I looked down at the counter. "The phone book! I'm listed! He read the article this morning and looked me up!"

"Ruzak, think about it. Even if this was the person who hit the geese, why would he come looking for you?"

"I don't know . . . maybe because he's mad. I'm sorry. I shouldn't have called. I'm a little shaken up." My face was hot, and it wasn't from sprinting two blocks and three flights of stairs. "I visited my mother's grave this morning and I guess I'm a little spooked. I'm sorry I bothered you, Felicia."

I hung up. Bob must live with her, I thought, although last night was Saturday and it wouldn't be unusual for a guy to sleep over after a date.

Felicia was right: There were hundreds of black SUVs. It was crazy to think this was the one. Crazy, too, that the guy would be so incensed that he'd jump in his car on a Sunday morning to track me down and . . . and what? Stop me from fingering him for killing some baby birds? But if it wasn't him, why did he slow down like that, pacing me as I jogged? Or was he pacing me at all? Maybe he was talking on the cell phone, which people do, and they say that's as dangerous as driving while drunk. Maybe he was having a fight with his wife. One of the things you have to be careful about when you live alone is the tendency to put yourself too much in the center of the world, like everything that goes on around you is related to your existence, when in reality, your existence doesn't amount to a hill of beans. That's tough for a lot of people to swallow. For centuries, people believed the sun revolved around the Earth, because we thought we were so damned important. What's my life going to matter in a hundred years? Or fifty? Or even twenty? I wondered how long a goose's memory was, if that mamma and poppa goose still remembered their babies and mourned. Parker Hudson had told me they went berserk when that car flattened their children, honking and flapping their wings and refusing to move off the road. That tore him up almost as much as seeing those goslings murdered. That, and the way the SUV sped up right before impact, like he'd *meant* to hit them.

"It was him," I said aloud in my empty apartment, which seemed emptier than usual. I figured maybe I should get a more low-maintenance kind of pet, like a parrot, something you could not only talk to but that would also talk back. That way, I would have an excuse for talking to myself. But I had heard a parrot can live a hundred years, and that made me feel funny, having a pet that would outlive me. I went to the living room window, pulled up the blinds, and looked for his car parked on the street, but there was no black SUV.

I couldn't be sure it was him, of course, not like I was sure about the Earth moving around the sun. I couldn't *know*, but I *knew*. Black Ford Expedition with Tennessee tags beginning with the letters *HRT.*

It was a start.

CHAPTER ELEVEN

I took a shower, changed into some shorts and my NYPD T-shirt, made myself a roast beef sandwich on rye with some Lay's baked potato chips and a Clausen pickle, the spear-cut kind. Then I grabbed my keys and took the stairs into the garage below the building, thinking again about maybe investing in a gun. I could write it off my taxes, and being motivated might help me pass the marksmanship test, though in the Academy I'd been motivated—I'd really, really wanted to be a cop—but I couldn't get it down.

Checking my rearview mirror the whole time, I took Kingston Pike west into Farragut. After driving around for about forty minutes, I finally found the road Parker Hudson lived off of, with the lake sparkling beside it in the afternoon sun and the pontoon boats, waterjets, motorboats, and bass boats, and shrieking skiers and two little groups of fishermen angling off one of the neighborhood piers. A sidewalk followed the lazy curves on the opposite side of the road, broken here and there with entrances to subdivisions with names like Water Sound and Lakeview and Rocky Creek. Families were everywhere, kids on bikes and trikes and scooters and older ones on skateboards. It was a warm Sunday afternoon in late spring, the kind of day that makes your heart ache, although you're not sure what for.

I pulled into the lakeside park and shut off the engine. More families here, tossing a baseball or a Frisbee, and lots of dogs sniffing the bushes. I looked for Parker Hudson. Part of me wanted to see him and another part wanted him to see me. I'd tell him of my encounter with the evildoer on Gay Street and see if the make, model, and tag number jogged his memory. I checked out the cars in the parking lot, but although there were lots of SUVs and even some black ones, there weren't any with the tag HRT.

There was a paved walking trail that snaked through the park about fifty feet from the water, past picnic pavilions and under mature oaks and maples; then it wrapped around a softball and soccer field before looping back to the parking lot. I walked the trail, practicing my powers of observation, wishing I had worn a hat, because the sun was high and hot. Looking to my right as I neared the softball field, I saw them cruising the little inlet about a hundred yards away, two geese with dark heads and white bands around their necks, and I wondered if these were the parents of the babies who had been slaughtered. It occurred to me that, in a way, these geese were my real clients and Parker Hudson was just an agent acting on their behalf.

I left the trail and walked down to the water's edge and the geese checked me out in the way wild birds do when they're used to the occasional handout of stale bread. You would think after several centuries of humans giving them the bum's rush, wildlife would be more wary of us, but maybe there hasn't been enough time for the information to be encoded in their genetic memory. I was a little fuzzy on evolution; it taxed my imagination, getting from some slimy vertebrate dragging itself onto a primordial shore to Teddy Ruzak standing on another, man-made shore in an NYPD T-shirt and Nike running shoes.

A couple of shirtless boys, neither one older than ten, I guessed, appeared beside me and immediately found a couple of rocks and hurled them toward the geese. Before I even stopped and thought about it, I told them to cut it out. They gave me that shocked look of kids called down by a total stranger and took off toward the trail. "It isn't trivial!" I yelled after them. Life is not trivial, no matter whose life you're talking about, although some people might ask what mosquitoes or those tsetse flies in Africa contribute. That was Parker Hunter's whole point, why he got out his wallet, and the reason this case was important: You have to battle total disregard wherever you find it, in whatever form it takes.

The geese turned their backs on me and glided toward deeper water. To tell the truth, I have always been a little afraid of geese. They are the most aggressive of the freshwater North American fowl. I was charged by one more than once in my childhood, and I shrieked with terror and dashed behind my mother's legs.

It was a time for a silent pledge to the bereft parents, if these two really were them, but I didn't because I couldn't promise I'd find the killer, only that I'd try, and that would be more poignant than reassuring, and besides, to promise more would not reflect well on my moral character.

I walked slowly back to my car. A couple of lovers were reclining under the shade of a willow tree by the shore. He was reading something to her from a book and she was staring at the water with a bored expression, but it was like something out of a movie or a painting, and for a second I was pretty lonely and feeling self-conscious and sorry for myself because I was the only person in the crowded park who was alone.

I figured it was a good time to cruise the neighborhoods around the lake, since it was Sunday and the odds were better the SUV would be at the perp's house. If the perp lived in one of the neighborhoods around the lake, that is. If the perp had gone home after stalking me. If the car I saw even belonged to the perp. I drove slowly through Rocky Creek, Lakeview, and Water

Sound, all newer developments with two-story brick or stucco houses, clean white driveways, and perfectly manicured lawns. I was thinking the whole time, This is it. This is the American dream, with bare-assed kids splashing in the plastic wading pools, big yellow fish painted on the sides, with the pretty teenage girls and shaggy-haired boys lounging on the patios beside blaring boom boxes, and the sometimes strained, disembodied laughter floating from unseen backyard cookouts, and the young trees, dogwoods and Bradford pears and oaks, their leaves still blushing the bright green of spring. Here there was no room for my sorrow over the goslings or my self-pity; here was bursting secondhand happiness and the riches of suburbia. No wonder people moved out here, a good twenty-five miles from the city. Twenty years ago, Farragut had been a sleepy little hamlet, a farming town named after the famous admiral who was born somewhere near here. The farms had been sold to developers, cut up into tracks, and the humans rushed in, pushing out the native deer and raccoon, rabbit and opossum. And the geese. I might have told Parker Hudson those babies were as much victims of urban sprawl as human viciousness and indifference, but we would both have known the truth.

I didn't see the Expedition, so I drove home.

CHAPTER TWELVE

I WAS LATE GETTING TO THE OFFICE THE NEXT MORNING. I hadn't been able to go to sleep Sunday night and kept getting up to stare out my window at the street outside until about 3:00 A.M., when it dawned on me that the goose killer was probably indifferent about my life, too. Then about three hours later, the sun itself dawned on me because I'd forgotten to close the blinds, so I crawled out of bed and closed them, then fell back asleep, not waking up until half past eight. For fourteen years, I was a night watchman, and that screws up your body's inner clock; it was still hard for me to stay awake during the day and go to sleep at night, though human beings are programmed to be diurnal.

Felicia was already at her desk when I came through the door at a little after ten o'clock. She was wearing a red short-sleeve sweater-type top and a short red skirt, but I thought it lacked something, maybe a red carnation behind her ear or a rose, although maybe that was too far on the flamenco dancer side. A stack of Sunday *Sentinels* lay on the desk, along with a large frame with the backing removed. She was wielding a razor knife.

"I was about to call your apartment," she said.

"Sorry," I said, even as I wondered why I was apologizing to my secretary. "I overslept. You know, human beings are diurnal creatures and—"

She cut me off. I was disappointed. I wanted her to be impressed by the fact that I knew the word *diurnal*.

"Thought maybe you had a wild night."

"I was reconnoitering the scene of the crime yesterday." Again, a word worthy of any college professor, but she remained stubbornly unimpressed.

"Did you see it again?" she asked, meaning the SUV.

"No, but I saw the geese. At least I think it was them."

"Hard to tell. They all look alike."

"Unless you're a goose."

"Duck, duck."

"What?"

"Didn't you ever play that game when you were a kid? Duck Duck Goose?"

"Oh, sure."

"Well." The tip of her tongue came out of her mouth as she cut the newspaper with the razor knife. For some reason, this reminded me that I hadn't eaten breakfast, and I had a vivid image of a Krispy Kreme doughnut, then an even more vivid image of Felicia biting into one, the glaze glistening on her bottom lip, which was the same color as her sweater. Her tongue chewing also reminded me of my father, who'd had the same habit when he was concentrating on something. Thinking about my dad with one part of my brain and Felicia's lips with the other made me feel weird.

"What are you doing?" I asked, to change both subjects, the outward subject of childhood games and the inward subject of the odd pairing of my old man fixing a lawn mower with my longing to watch Felicia eat a doughnut.

"I'm framing your article. I'm gonna hang it on that wall right there so when people come in, they'll see it. They'll think you're a celebrity. People love celebrities, Ruzak."

"About the only thing I watch on TV is old movies, so most of the celebrities I love are dead."

"That's kind of morbid. Anyway, you are one now and you've got to make the most of it."

"Felicia, Ben Affleck is a celebrity. I'm an unlicensed detective with one case, which I can't even solve."

"That doesn't matter. What has someone like Sarah Ferguson ever really accomplished, except marry into a famous family and use that to sell diet plans? You put too much stock in personal achievement. Most of the time, it's just luck, being in the right place at the right time, or luck like Ben Affleck's looks."

"Well," I said. "I was never too lucky with that."

Though I kind of opened the door for her to argue with me, she didn't.

"We've had six calls already this morning."

"You're kidding."

"Three well-wishers, two potential clients, and a kid who wants you to find his lost hamster. He suspects his big brother's taken it, maybe killed it, even, and buried the evidence in the backyard. He's found a fresh hole."

"That's three potential clients."

"No pro bono work, Ruzak, until your bank balance is triple your IQ."

I was trying to figure out if she'd just insulted me as she went on. "Parker Hudson called, too; he wants you to call him back. I didn't tell him about your sighting or whatever it was yesterday. He's very excited, calling it a stroke of genius—the article, I mean."

"Did you tell him it wasn't my stroke?"

"Why would I tell him that? Anyway, nobody's called yet to fess up, so the jury's still out on whether it was marketing genius or detecting genius. Dear God, Ruzak, what are you wearing?"

I looked down at myself. My most comfortable pair of jeans, a white oxford that maybe was a little old and maybe one of the little collar buttons had popped off, but I thought I looked pretty good, in a casual kind of way.

"What's the matter with it?" I asked.

"Your shirt's so threadbare, I can see the moles on your stomach. Your jeans are about a half inch too short and your socks don't match."

"My jeans aren't too short."

"Then how else could I see your socks?" She proceeded to lecture me for about five minutes on the importance of image and how I had to project a certain kind. You're judged by the way you look, and people in the public eye especially are judged, and not kindly. Dress like a bum and be treated like one. Dress like a million bucks and one day you'll be worth it. The longer she lectured, the more maternal she became, and this didn't sit well with me, mostly because of the sweater and short skirt.

"It's like redecorating this dump. It's the same principle. People walk in expecting a professional's office to look a certain way. First impressions, Ruzak. Bad first impressions will kill you. Good ones will make you rich."

I told her I didn't have anything against getting rich, then went to my desk to call Parker Hudson.

"Hey, Teddy," he said. It was the first time he'd called me by my first name. "Terrific article."

I got right to business. I figured he'd appreciate it, because he was being billed for the call.

"Do the initials HRT mean anything to you?"

"HRT?"

"HRT." I told him about the black Ford Expedition and the slow, spooky "chase" down Gay Street.

"Well, the car I saw was definitely black and it might have been a Ford—those Expeditions are quite large, aren't they?"

"Huge."

"But HRT . . . I wish I could remember. I was focused on the geese. . . ."

"Sure. I saw them yesterday, by the way."

"You were at the lake?"

"Drove through those developments out there, too, but I didn't spot anything. Maybe I'm being overly optimistic, Mr. Hudson, but I'm thinking we might just have this thing cracked wide open by week's end. I've already gotten six calls."

"Tips?"

"Actually, no tips yet, but I'm thinking if our guy doesn't turn himself in outright, somebody else will. Might call or write a letter to the paper, or even to me. Meanwhile, I'm gonna figure some way to turn up the heat a little."

"How?"

"I'm working on that."

"Well, I thought the newspaper article was a stroke of genius."

Now was my opportunity to tell him it had been Felicia's stroke. I had assured the state of Tennessee I was of good moral character, and this was an issue of moral character if ever there was one. Felicia had acted like telling him the truth was counterproductive to earning a buck. And anyway, she didn't seem to mind giving me the credit, since she didn't tell him when she had the chance. I was quiet while I wrestled with these pros and cons.

"Teddy?"

"Yeah?"

"I thought we were disconnected."

"I am, usually. Mr. Hudson, you ought to know that article was my secretary's idea."

"It really doesn't matter to me whose idea it was. I should have thought of it, saved myself some money."

"Are you firing me?"

"Are you kidding, Teddy? You're doing a bang-up job. Keep me informed on your progress."

Felicia stepped into the room and said, "Why did you tell him?"

"Because the next one would be easier."

"The next what?"

"My mother always said that once you've told the first lie, the next one comes easier and the one after that even easier and so on."

She looked at me for a second. Her shoes, which I hadn't noticed till now, were the same color as her skirt, had three-inch heels, and were very glossy.

"You miss your mom, don't you?" she asked.

I nodded. "Is that a new outfit?"

"What's it matter?"

"The shoes are very shiny." I added quickly, "I've been practicing my powers of observation."

"Observe this," she said, and stuck her tongue out at me. She turned on her three-inch heel and disappeared behind the little wall.

"How about some Krispy Kremes?" I called after her.

CHAPTER THIRTEEN

A COUPLE MORE CALLS CAME IN BEFORE NOON. ONE WAS from an old lady who wanted to tell me about all the skunks on the west side of town and how motorists kept smashing them in their haste to get to the mall or Wal-Mart or wherever their lives took them, then asked me if I thought anything could be done about it. The smell was awful, she said. I told her no, probably nothing could be done. The other call was from a potential witness.

"I know who hit those geese," the caller said.

I picked up my mechanical pencil and readied myself to crack the case wide open.

"What's your name?" I asked.

"I'd rather not give you my name."

"Sure, I understand. That's perfectly reasonable. It's a friend of yours?"

"A neighbor."

"Man or woman?"

"Woman. She's a nasty little woman, too, and I wouldn't put something like that past her. I see her all the time on that road in the mornings, and do you know what she's doing, Mr. Ruzak?"

"No. What?"

"Putting on her makeup! Can you believe it?"

"Once I was on Kingston Pike and I saw a woman strip off her work clothes and change into her aerobics gear."

"While she was driving?"

"No, it was at a stoplight."

"What in the world did you think?"

"I thought that life had gotten too hectic." I also felt guilt—guilt that I watched her and guilt that I had completely abandoned any pretense of keeping an exercise regimen.

"So you didn't actually see her hit the goslings," I said.

"Oh, no, nothing like that. But she drives a big black SUV all right."

"Ford?"

"No, it's a GMC, I think."

"You sure it's not a Ford?"

"No. I'm pretty sure it's a GMC."

"What's her tag number?"

"I have no idea."

"Could you get one and call me back?"

"I'm not walking over there and writing down her tag number, Mr. Ruzak."

"What's her name?"

"You want her name?"

"Isn't that why you called, to give me her name?"

"Why do you want her name?"

"Because the whole point of this case is finding out who killed those geese."

"If I give you her name, she'll know it was me."

"How could she know that?"

"Oh, she'll know. She'll know. You don't know her. She's a nasty, nasty person."

"Well, there's not much I can do about that. Not much of anything I can do, really, if you won't give me her name."

We went around and around like this for another five minutes. It was like playing Twenty Questions. "Does she live in Knoxville? Does she live on the west side? Does she live right off the road by the lake?" I continued asking questions, with her getting more and more cagey, until finally I gave up.

"Well, thanks for your call," I told her.

"No problem," she said. "People should stand up for what's right."

After I hung up, Felicia came into the room, holding her purse.

"I'm going to lunch."

"I didn't even have breakfast."

"I'm meeting Bob. Wanna join us?"

I thanked her but said I'd probably work through lunch. The thought of being their third wheel was mortifying. "How did you and Bob meet?"

"At his brother's wedding. His brother is married to my cousin."

"Doesn't that make you sort of related?"

"How do you figure?"

"I don't. Sorry. Is he nice to you?"

"You got a crush on me or something, Ruzak?"

"No, I just wanted to know if he's nice to you."

"He's very nice. Don't get a crush on me, Ruzak."

"Okay." I had never seen Bob, but I pictured him as tanned and buffed, like those models in the Calvin Klein fragrance ads, maybe mustachioed, possibly a black belt, and certainly possessing more than his fair share of machismo. In other words, the complete opposite of me.

"You ought to buy one of those little refrigerators and a microwave," she said on her way out the door. "That way, you wouldn't have to go out for lunch. Save yourself some money." Then she was gone, out to lunch. First, a complete makeover for her, then one for the office, and now a company break room. One of the reasons I'll never be rich is the financial concept of spending money to make or save money is something I've never been able to wrap my imagination around.

She hadn't been gone ten minutes when there was a knock on the door and an old lady stepped into the room. And I mean, as old ladies go, she was quintessential, from the shapeless flower-print dress to the blue-gray hair and the large purse clutched in both hands and pressed against her chest.

"Are you Theodore Ruzak?" she asked.

"That's me," I said. I went around the desk and led her to one of the visitor's chairs. She had those thick knee-high stockings old ladies wear and she smelled faintly of lavender talcum and cheap hair spray.

"Thank you," she said. "My name is Eunice Shriver."

I wrote down her name with my mechanical pencil on a fresh sheet of my yellow legal pad. When I finished, I stared at the name for a second.

"No, I am not *that* Eunice Shriver. No relation at all, though I've been asked all my life."

"Sure."

"My maiden name is Sparks, and in 1943, I married a young sailor on a three-week furlough. His name was Nathaniel Shriver—of the Kentucky Shrivers, no relation to the Yankee Shrivers."

"You bet," I said.

"I made quite certain of that."

"Who wouldn't?"

"His family owned several thoroughbred racehorses, though none ever raced in the Derby."

"Is that so? I'm not much into the ponies myself."

"The vice of vices!" she exclaimed. "It nearly destroyed my marriage, and it certainly destroyed my husband."

"He gambled?"

"Of course he gambled; he was from Kentucky and his family owned horses. When I say it destroyed him, I mean it literally: He died in a stable accident when a horse kicked him in the chest. Killed him instantly. I was thirty-four years of age, with four children, and he was gone. Not that he was a wonderful provider to begin with, God rest his soul."

"Insurance?"

"A little, but that's hardly any of your business, Mr. Ruzak."

"That's right. My business has to do with detective work."

"As I should well know! I saw the article in the paper yesterday and that is why I am here now talking to you, though you seem almost too interested in my private affairs."

"I'll back off."

"I never married again after the horse killed him, if you must know. I'd had my fill. Are you married, Mr. Ruzak?"

"Oh, no."

"Why not?"

"I guess I haven't found the right person."

"What hogwash! There is no such thing."

"Maybe you're right—you've lived a lot longer than I have and been around the track a few more times, if you'll forgive the pun, so I can't really argue with you except to say you gotta let the young be idealistic, because it's so darn hard when you get old."

"What's hard?"

"Idealism."

"You don't say!"

"Is there something I can help you with, Mrs. Shriver?" I had trouble understanding why she was sitting in my office giving me a hard time, as if I were the one who had arrived unannounced and without an appointment.

"I am here regarding the matter of those poor little goslings."

"Terrible thing, wasn't it?"

"You're to be commended, Mr. Ruzak. Most people could care less about the fate of six baby geese, particularly since the adults are such unpleasant and noisome creatures."

"Oh, I really couldn't agree with you there, Mrs. Shriver. I think a lot of people actually do care about it, or the *Sentinel* wouldn't have run the story in the first place. But now we're back to idealism."

"That's very insightful," she said. "Like several things quoted in the newspaper. You strike me as particularly sober and level-headed for one so overweight, bless your heart. I mean to say, it's rare to find someone of your bulk so given to philosophizing."

"Really, you don't think so? Again I'll have to bow to your experience, Mrs. Shriver, and the truth is, I can't think of a single fat philosopher. But my weight really is offset by my height; I'm nearly six six."

"Really! Did you play football in college?"

"I didn't go to college."

"I find that extraordinarily difficult to believe."

"Most people don't."

"And modest, too. I must say I find even more to admire in person, Mr. Ruzak. I believe I've made the right decision by coming here today."

"Gee, I hope so," I said. I looked at my watch, and she caught me looking at it and frowned.

"You won't think I'm wasting your time when I've spoken my piece, Mr. Ruzak."

"You're not wasting my time, Mrs. Shriver. Really, I'm what

you might call a people person, and this is pure bread and butter to me."

She leaned forward and whispered, "I know who killed those goslings."

"I figured maybe you did."

"I was there. I saw it all. It was grotesque, terrifying, an absolute and utter tragedy, the likes of which I pray I never witness again. And I probably won't, because guess how old I am."

"You want me to guess your age?"

"Go ahead."

"Seventy-five."

"I'll be eighty-six years old next month."

"I'm not good with ages or names."

"And I still drive my own car."

"That's terrific. Now, you say you saw the car that hit these geese? What kind of car was it?" I was poised to write "black Ford Expedition" on my yellow legal pad.

"Why, it was my car."

"Your car?"

"Yes." She opened her purse and pulled out a white hankie and dabbed her eyes with it. "That's the worst of it. Now that's done. I had no idea how I would say it, but there, I've said it. The baby killer sits before you, Mr. Ruzak, in all her shame and sorrow."

"Oh, that's rough. I'm really sorry about the shame and sorrow, but . . . you hit those geese?"

"I just said so; must I repeat it?"

"What kind of car do you drive, Mrs. Shriver?"

"What does that have to do with anything?"

"Is it a black SUV?" It was hard for me to picture it.

"I don't even know what an SUV is. I drive a white Buick Monte Carlo."

"That's funny," I said. "Because my witness says it was a big black sport-utility vehicle."

"Well, your witness is mistaken."

"He seemed pretty sure of it."

"Then he is a liar."

"Why would he lie about that?"

"I have no idea why he would lie about that. Perhaps you should ask him, since you are the detective."

"Okay." I tapped the eraser end of my mechanical pencil on the pad. "Tell me what happened."

"Well," she said, scooching forward in her chair, bag clutched in her mottled grip and resting on her wide knees. "I was on my way to the market and running late, as usual, and I simply didn't see them until it was too late. Smack! Smack, smack, smack! Oh, it was horrible! Terrible!"

"Why didn't you stop?"

"I did stop! I am not a monster, Mr. Ruzak, no matter what that newspaper article implies."

"My witness says the driver didn't stop."

"Again, your witness must be lying."

"But if you'd stopped, he wouldn't be my client, there wouldn't be a newspaper story, and you wouldn't be sitting here." I laid my pencil on the desktop and said gently, "Mrs. Shriver, you didn't hit those geese."

"I beg your pardon, but I most certainly did!"

I thought about it. You have to pick your battles in life, and what was the point of arguing with the old lady? She wanted to confess; it made her feel better, for reasons I really didn't want to get into, so I dropped the whole thing, took a statement from her, which she signed with a dramatic flourish, and eased her out the door, promising I'd fax her confession over to the police

ASAP. I warned her to be careful driving home, saying there were other animals and even pedestrians out there, though she'd probably already filled her quota. She got offended when I offered to help her down the stairs, and she huffed down to the street alone. I went to the window and watched her climb inside a sky blue Lincoln Town Car and pull with painful slowness into traffic.

I went back to my desk, tore the page off the legal pad, wadded it up, and threw it in the garbage.

About twenty minutes later, there was another knock on the door. Most businesses' doors you don't knock on first; what was it about PIs? I yelled that the door was open.

A Knox County sheriff's deputy walked into the room.

"Teddy Ruzak?"

"Hi, yes, that's me. How're you doing?"

We shook hands. He introduced himself as Gary Paul and pointed to the framed clipping now hanging on the wall directly behind Felicia's desk.

"Saw the article yesterday and thought I'd drop by."

"You're not the only one. I just took a confession."

His eyebrows went up. "Really?"

"From a professional. Not a professional goose killer. A professional confessor. Or maybe that would be confesstrix."

He laughed. "We get those types all the time."

"Have a seat." I waved him toward the chair Eunice Shriver, no relation to the Yankee Shrivers, had just vacated. "You want anything? The coffee's pretty old, but I could make a fresh pot." My heart was high up in my chest and I was slightly out of breath, a common reaction around cops, even back when I was at the Academy. That probably should have been a sign to me I wasn't cut out for police work. I was also thinking Felicia had a good point about the refrigerator. You want to make your clientele feel at home, and there wasn't so much as a bottled water in the place. I wondered how much those minifridges cost. Deputy Paul sat in one of the visitor's chairs and I plopped down in my big leather number behind my oversized desk and tried to look professional despite my threadbare oxford shirt that you could see my moles through and my too-short blue jeans. Deputy Paul's uniform was immaculate. He was probably around my age but about twenty pounds lighter and three or four inches shorter, with very small dark eyes and slightly oversized lips. His skin had this reddish tint to it, pocked and deeply scarred, most likely from severe acne in his adolescence. He was losing his hair but hid the fact by clipping it very short, like that guy on the *Today* show.

"What a creep," he said, referring to the gosling killer.

"Yeah. Either very cruel or very thoughtless."

"Either way, a creep."

"It's one of those things that can make you question the basic goodness of human beings. But again, all the calls this morning have had one thing in common, and that's a sense of outrage. Some people might say all that means is that people are basically silly and sentimental, but it gives me hope."

"Hope for what?"

"Oh, you know, for humanity. That everything's going to come out all right in the end. I'm basically an optimist; that's why I took the case in the first place, despite the fact there were no leads and no witnesses, besides my client." I didn't add the chief reason I'd taken the case—that I didn't have one and Felicia was draining the bank account for designer dresses.

"Well, that's kind of why I dropped by," Deputy Paul said. "I wanted to let you know not everybody on the force thinks it's funny what happened—couldn't believe it when I read that they laughed your client out the door—and also I wanted to help."

"Oh man, that's terrific, Deputy."

"Call me Gary."

"I couldn't appreciate it more, Gary. I'm kind of in a reactive mode, waiting for a tip or some kind of break, like the perp coming clean." This felt great to me, talking shop with law enforcement. It was almost like being part of the fraternity. Maybe your dreams do come true, but never in the way you imagine they will.

"Strictly on my own time," Gary said. "You know, informally. I've got resources you probably don't."

"That's true. You know, I went through the Academy a few years back."

"You were a cop?"

"No, I didn't finish. Another opportunity came up." This wasn't precisely a lie, but it wasn't precisely the truth, either. I never gave much thought to my moral character. Not many people do, I guess, because it's something most people take for granted, assuming theirs is pretty good for the most part. I didn't think most people sat down and considered whether their moral character was up to snuff. Maybe religious types do, like priests and certain fundamentalists. Although fundamentalists probably start with the assumption that everybody's moral character falls more than a little short of the mark: If everybody is so damned good, why do we need God in the first place?

"So tell me what you got," Deputy Paul said crisply. Down to business. He was probably on his lunch break, since he said he was going to help on his own time.

"Well, I've got a description of the vehicle from my client. . . ."

"What's his name?"

"Parker Hudson." I hadn't told the paper his name, but I didn't think Parker would mind if I told a cop. Gary wasn't taking notes. That meant either he had a good memory or I hadn't told him anything yet worth writing down. "Big black SUV with

Tennessee plates. But I think I've got a little more on that." I told him what had happened on Gay Street with me jogging down the sidewalk with my Walgreens bag.

"What was that partial tag?" he asked.

"HRT."

"And it was a Ford Expedition?"

"That's right, fairly new, maybe a 2001 or an '02, with tinted windows. That's why I couldn't make the driver."

"Did you check with DMV?"

"Check with them how?"

"Motor Vehicles can run those letters through their database and match them up with registered vehicles throughout the state."

"Gee, I didn't know that."

"I'll have it run for you, if you want."

"That'd be terrific. That'd be great. This is an incredible stroke of luck," I told him. "I've been having this unbelievable run of luck lately, and to be honest, it makes me a little nervous. I forget who now, but somebody once said that luck is the residue of design, but I've always been a little deficient in the design department."

He laughed. He had needed some dental work as a kid and didn't get it. That and his pockmarked face got to me. Pity is the swiftest way to my heart. When I see a stray dog, I immediately look the other way, because if I didn't, I'd have half the strays in the county living in my little apartment.

He told me he'd give me a call in a couple of days with the list from the Department of Motor Vehicles, we shook hands, and he left. I was starving; it was nearly one o'clock and I hadn't eaten anything since Sunday night. I put up the sign Felicia had made on the new computer—GONE TO LUNCH. BACK IN ONE HOUR— and walked down to Market Square. I was feeling pretty ebullient.

It was another warm, sunny day and the square was filled with the late-lunch crowd, and even though I didn't have a license, I was about to solve my first case. For the first time since Mom died, I didn't feel so crummy, and I had a salad for lunch with low-fat dressing and a glass of ice water.

CHAPTER FOURTEEN

FELICIA WAS STILL AT LUNCH WHEN I GOT BACK TO THE ELY Building. On my walk back from Market Square, I got an idea to capitalize on my terror on Sunday. I was excited because, one, I actually had an idea and, two, it was a pretty good idea and, three, you should always find some way to exploit your fear, because otherwise it's just a destructive waste of time.

I called Paul Killibrew at the *Sentinel* and told him I might have a lead in the case and asked if he was interested in running a follow-up article based on my encounter with HRT. He sounded interested and said he'd run it by his editor.

About twenty minutes later, Felicia showed up, and there was something I'd call fuzzy about her: one side of her red skirt higher than the other, her blond hair windblown-looking, though there was no breeze, a fresh coat of lipstick. The Hilton was two blocks west of the office and she had been gone over two hours. She hadn't asked to take a long lunch, and I knew I had certain responsibilities as an employer, but would I be reprimanding her for the long lunch or the fact that she was fuzzy and the Hilton was only two blocks away?

"What's wrong?" she asked.

"Why do you think something's wrong?"

"You were smiling when I came in and now you're not smiling."

"I guess no smile lasts forever."

"Bob took me to the Bistro—you know, where all the bankers and lawyers and other big shots go—and the service is always slow there. And to top it all off, the waitress brought us the wrong check." Felicia, as a former waitress herself, could be righteously indignant when a fellow professional did substandard work.

"What'd you have?"

"The special."

"What was the special?"

"This some kind of test?"

"No, just curious."

"Why? Ruzak, did you skip lunch, too?"

"No, I ate at Market Square. A cop came to see me after you left."

I told her about Deputy Gary Paul and my idea to get another article in the paper about the latest development in "The Gosling Affair," as the *Sentinel* called my case.

"Only you don't know that Mr. HRT was our killer," Felicia said.

"Funny coincidence if he wasn't. Anyway, you've got to go where the leads take you."

"You know, one day after you're world-famous, I'm going to publish a book of your sayings. Like 'Go where the leads take you.' "

"Are you sore at me or something?"

"Why would I be sore at you?" she asked crossly. She went to her desk, out of sight, and now I was sure she hadn't lunched at the Bistro; she'd been at the Hilton, or maybe not the Hilton, but some other private place for a quickie (though technically, two hours couldn't be called a quickie), and her being sore had to do with guilt.

There were a few more calls in the afternoon. Felicia set up a couple of appointments for prospective clients and then around four o'clock, she said she had to take off early because she had a hair appointment. This made me wonder if she was a natural blonde. A lot of women in East Tennessee aren't but want you to think they are. My mother had called it "the Dolly Parton effect." After Felicia left, like some cosmic switch had been tripped, the phone stopped ringing. And I was out of ideas, since I'd used up my allotment for the day. I hung around till five o'clock, making notes, like "Check on minifridge" and "F/u on PI app." Then I cleaned off my desk and trooped around the office, watering all the plants Felicia and the decorator had placed around because they were convinced the oxygen produced by all the foliage would help cleanse the air of dry-cleaner fumes. By the time I finished, I was a little sore at Felicia. Watering plants was definitely a secretary's job, but then I realized the idea to call the newspaper with the story that might break the case was the detective's job.

There was a young woman standing on the sidewalk outside the Ely Building when I left. She was a good-looking girl of about twenty, with shoulder-length dark hair and very large brown eyes. She didn't have much shape, but she was tall and held herself well, like a girl who's had some breeding. She was holding a section of the newspaper—the "Lifestyle" section of the Sunday *Sentinel.* I could see the top of my shaggy brown head above the fold. What a sheepdog! I decided right then to get a haircut first thing in the morning.

"Guess what? I'm Teddy Ruzak," I told her.

"Oh, good," she said. "I didn't know if this was the right address. You saw me standing out here?"

"Actually, I was on my way home."

"I'm sorry. Mr. Ruzak, I need to talk to you. . . ."

"Okay. It's nice out. You want to walk?"

She hesitated, but only for a second, before nodding, and we set off east, toward Gay Street. The air had begun to cool and there was a springtime moistness to it that reminded me of flower gardens and the way wet grass feels beneath your bare feet. The gentle atmosphere played counterpoint to this girl's agitation. She was definitely distracted and nervous about something. HRT, I thought. She's going to tell me she's HRT, the goose killer. I cautioned myself not to get my hopes up. She might be a chronic confessor, like Eunice Shriver.

"Where are you parked?" I asked. "Because if you didn't feed the meter, they'll still ticket you after five. They're very aggressive about it downtown. It's a cash cow for the city." I thought I was being pretty clever. I wanted to see her car. If it was a black Ford Expedition with the partial tag HRT, I had her.

"I parked in the Hilton's garage," she said.

Well, there went that lever to pry the truth out of her. If she didn't confess, I could tail her back to the garage to check out the car.

"Did you want to see me about the article?" I asked.

"Yes." She dropped the newspaper into a trash can mounted on a light pole on the corner of Gay and Church. Her putting my picture in the garbage kind of hurt my feelings.

"My name is Susan Marks. I saw the article yesterday and . . . I don't know what good it's going to do, but . . . I wanted to ask you something, Mr. Ruzak."

"Go ahead. But call me Teddy."

"Okay," she said. "The article didn't mention the name of your client."

"I protect the identity of all my clients," I told Susan Marks. Of course, I had only one client, but she didn't know that. The trap of the human ego is the desire to impress other people, even total strangers. It's led to more misery than half the wars in history. I wondered if I should tell Felicia that one so she could put it in *The Wit and Wisdom of Theodore Ruzak, Master of Detection.*

"I understand that, Mr. Ruzak, but I hope that after you hear my story, you'll change your mind. You see, I'm a little desperate."

We turned left on Gay Street and walked north. A guy passed us walking a big German shepherd that was wearing one of those thick black leather collars with the rows of glittering silver spikes. German shepherds are very smart but too aggressive and big for my little apartment. I wouldn't want one of those little yippy-type dogs, though, the kind you dress in sweaters in winter, and the males especially annoy me, the way they daintily lift their hind leg to pee.

"Have you ever heard the name Lydia Marks?"

"No."

"Maybe you've seen her picture before."

She pulled a piece of paper from her purse, unfolded it, and handed it to me. It was a flyer with MISSING printed in bold black letters at the top. Beneath the word was a picture of a pretty woman with auburn hair, maybe around my age or a little older.

"They ran it in the newspaper a few days ago. She's my step-mother and she's been missing now for over four weeks."

"You want me to find your stepmom for you?"

"I want *anybody* to find her. The police sure haven't had much luck." Susan Marks had a small, slightly upturned, freckly nose and a full bottom lip that was out of proportion to her top one, which gave her a kind of puckish look. She went light on the makeup and could have passed for a boy if her hair had been shorter or maybe hidden in a ball cap. She had the fine features of a pixie.

"What's this have to do with my client, Susan?"

"When those baby geese were killed—that was around the time she disappeared. She always took a jog that time in the morning—always."

"She lived near the lake?"

Susan nodded. "We aren't sure she was abducted that morning. See, my dad travels a lot for business and my little brother and

I live on campus. Dad flew to Brussels on Wednesday and didn't get back home till late Saturday night."

"You don't call or go see her on a regular basis?"

"We aren't that close. Don't get me wrong, Mr. Ruzak. I like Lydia, I really do, but she was Dad's thing, you know? He met her in Ireland about four years after my mom died. I was a senior in high school. She was a lot younger than he was, but they were in love. And it *was* love. She wasn't like some kind of gold digger or anything."

We had doubled back toward Market Square. She sat on a bench beneath an oak tree and I sat beside her. I was still holding the poster and I looked at her stepmother's picture as she talked.

"What have the cops found out?" I asked.

"Not a hell of a lot. There were no signs of a break-in. Nothing is missing in the house, the Mercedes is in the garage, and Lydia's purse is on the kitchen counter with her driver's license, all her cash and credit cards. The only thing we can't find are the house keys."

"And none of the neighbors saw anything suspicious?"

She shook her head. "Dad talked to her on Wednesday night. He tried calling again the next night, Thursday, but there was no answer. He wasn't too worried, because Lydia often goes to the movies at night when he's out of town."

"By herself?"

"She was—she's a very shy person. America was overwhelming to her. She hated America, I think, but Dad tried to help out the best he could. He even gave her a job managing some of his properties while he was away, Mr. Ruzak."

"Please, call me Teddy."

She nodded. "She didn't know anybody in America when Dad moved her here after the wedding and she didn't meet people easily. I don't think she has any close friends here."

"So what makes you think somebody abducted her? Maybe she hopped a cab and flew back to Ireland."

"That's the first thing the police thought, so they checked all the manifests. And anyway, you can't get on any plane these days without a driver's license."

"Maybe she ran away."

"She had nothing to run from."

"I mean with somebody else."

"Lydia's crazy about my dad. If you ever saw them together, you'd know that's impossible."

"Okay. No friends. No lovers. Enemies?"

She shook her head. "Not that I'm aware of."

"And your father was in Brussels."

She gave me a cold stare.

"The police must have brought that up, too," I added quickly. "Family members are the first people they look at in a case like this."

"My father loves Lydia. He adores her. I'm talking to you because he can't. Or won't. He's in some major denial right now. He can't bring himself to deal with this, so I have to. We're desperate, Mr. Ruzak. The police have no leads, no evidence, and no witnesses and I don't know where to turn. Maybe it's grasping at straws, but your client might have seen something. Even if he didn't see what happened to her, at least if he did see her jogging on that trail that day, we could narrow down when she disappeared."

I nodded. "Sure. That makes sense. I'll ask him."

She looked down at her hands. They were small and her fingers were very thin. I remembered a line from a poem I had read once, or maybe it was from a movie: "Nobody, not even the rain, has such small hands."

"Hey," I said. "Are you hungry, Susan? I didn't have breakfast this morning and all I had for lunch was a salad with low-fat dressing and a glass of ice water. You want to get something to eat?"

She looked up at me with a startled expression. The last thing she probably expected from me was a dinner invitation. I wasn't sure why I had extended one. It probably goes back to my weakness for the bereft of this world, those holding the short end of the stick, from stray dogs to poor people with bad teeth. She was obviously pretty broken up by her stepmom's disappearance and knew deep in her heart what all cops know: that the longer someone's missing, the greater the likelihood they'll never be found.

CHAPTER FIFTEEN

WE WERE A BLOCK FROM MARKET SQUARE AND THE TOMATO Head was still open, but I have this constitutional aversion to eating at the same place twice in one day. There're not a lot of restaurants or any kind of place that stays open past 7:00 P.M. in downtown Knoxville, because there're not a lot of people living downtown to patronize them. I thought about getting my car from the garage and driving somewhere, but we were about seven or eight blocks from my apartment and I was afraid if we walked all that way, it would give her too much time to change her mind. About the only other decent place was the Bistro on the corner of Jackson. It was attached to the Bijou Theater and frequented by the city's theater crowd at night, actors and other artsy types who constituted Knoxville's version of counterculture. The servers were all either actors or students studying to be actors and therefore could be counted on to be temperamental. I thought the place was overpriced for the quality, but it was kind of cool, with brick walls and wide-paneled wooden floors and a bar that ran the length of the room. A large painting of a naked fat lady hung over the bar; she was reclining on a bed with about fifty pillows and a small white dog, maybe a Pomeranian—I didn't know, as I wasn't up on the small breeds.

So we walked back to Gay Street and turned right onto Jackson.

A breeze had picked up, the first real one in a couple of days, and some clouds were moving in. Susan Marks walked with her thin arms folded over her small chest. Maybe it's just my impression, but androgyny seems to be more prevalent in the upper classes. Look at all those royals and superstar celebrities, especially the singers, only they don't call them singers, but "recording artists." I guess you couldn't call people like Jack Kennedy or Paris Hilton androgynous, but those are the exceptions that prove the rule. It's like money breeds the sex right out of you, though you hear that money is the ultimate aphrodisiac—or maybe it's power, which in this world is the same thing. If I had a lot of money, I'd hook up with the most voluptuous woman I could find, just to safeguard against the asexual factor.

"Where do you go to school?" I asked. It was the first time I'd spoken since she said she'd have dinner with me. "The university?"

She nodded. She had this habit—probably born of self-consciousness, because her bottom lip was so much larger than her top—of sucking in her bottom lip and chewing on it with her teeth.

"What's your major?"

"I'm studying to be a vet."

"Hey, that's terrific. I love animals. I've been thinking about getting a dog, although technically it's not allowed. I haven't had a dog since I was a kid and my collie died."

"We always had a dog, usually two or three. And a cat. And a cockatiel, fish, turtles, a couple of hamsters—you name it."

"Since you're in the field, maybe you can tell me what the deal is with these ferrets that are so popular now and maybe what kind of dog I should get and your thoughts about somebody my age getting back into school. . . ."

She stopped walking all of sudden.

"What's the matter?" I asked. We were a block from the restaurant.

"This feels weird to me," she said. "Having dinner with you."

"Well," I said. "Why are you?"

She shrugged. "Why did you ask me?" She had folded those thin arms over her chest again and her dark eyebrows had moved close together. She wasn't exactly frowning at me, but she wasn't smiling, either. I guess she was wondering if this was some kind of seedy quid pro quo, like I wouldn't help her if she didn't have dinner with me. It wasn't that at all; she just seemed so lost and I felt bad for her. And, like a lot of guys, I equate eating with comfort—that's really what it was all about, comfort. But would she believe me if I told her that? I wondered. One of the saddest developments of the modern age is the cynicism of the youth. There was another quote for Felicia's book.

"I'm pretty hungry, to tell you the truth, and probably the last eighteen or nineteen meals I've eaten, I've eaten alone. It's pretty crappy to eat alone. There's nothing chic about it, and besides, it's dangerous to your health. I read somewhere you tend to eat more when you eat alone, but I might have that wrong, because sometimes you read things and you remember them wrong because you're justifying something—in my case, the fact that I need to lose about twenty pounds."

She laughed and her eyebrows sprang apart.

"It may have said that you eat faster," I said.

"You're funny," she said. "You're not what I expected at all."

We started walking again.

"What did you expect?" I asked.

"I don't know."

"Probably someone like Philip Marlowe or Columbo. You don't run into too many PIs in day-to-day life, so it's one of those professions where stereotypes flourish. I never liked Columbo, chiefly because there's something mean and snide about pretending to be stupid when you're not."

"Who's Columbo?"

It was a dark night for the theater, so we didn't have any trouble getting a table. Susan Marks folded her arms on the table and looked around the room; she had never been to the Bistro before, she told me. There was a tiny potted plastic flower arrangement on the table and an unlighted candle. I ordered a beer and Susan ordered a raspberry tea. I asked our waitress when her shift had begun and she told me four o'clock that afternoon, so she wouldn't have known if Felicia and Bob had actually eaten there. I wondered why I was trying to catch Felicia in a lie, then decided it was because detective work is a vocation, not a job; you can't leave it at the office at five o'clock.

I asked what she thought had happened to her stepmother.

"I think she was jogging and somebody took her. I don't think she ran off with the yardman or joined a commune or is playing some sick game on my father to get him to notice her or anything like that."

"But we're talking broad daylight on a well-traveled road with lots of moms around walking babies and retirees strolling the trail. Not exactly the ideal spot to be abducting someone."

"There's no other explanation."

The waitress came back with our drinks. I ordered the filet mignon and Susan ordered the North Atlantic scrod, which was one of the specials on the chalkboard at the front of the restaurant. I thought about telling her you should never order fish on a Monday because restaurants serve the leftovers from the Friday deliveries, but we weren't that intimate, and anyway, it was sort of a big brotherly or, worse, fatherly thing to say, so I kept my mouth shut.

"I guess the cops told you that's one of the hardest cases to solve."

She nodded. "Unless we can turn up a witness, there's not much hope."

Tears welled up in her eyes and I looked away. An older couple, maybe in their seventies, were eating at the next table, not saying anything to each other. You see that a lot when you eat out, old couples who've been married for a million years eating and not saying a word, but it never looks uncomfortable. After all that time together, they've probably said all that's worth saying. The best way to take someone's mind off their problems is to get them to talk about themselves, because most of us think our problems come from someone or something else, so I asked her about school—if she was going to specialize in any particular type of vet work, if she was going to work in the research field or be a practicing vet, if she was going to stay in the area when she graduated, and if vets had to do internships like people doctors. This kept the conversation going through the bread and salad and halfway into the entrée. When she relaxed, she had this habit of talking out of the right side of her mouth; she reminded me of those kids in that old movie *Bugsy Malone* trying to act like gangsters. She should let her hair grow some and wear more makeup, I thought, but vet work is kind of a butch science for a girl, a tomboy occupation. She had an athlete's body, inclined more toward swimming or basketball than softball or soccer. To test my theory, I asked if she played any sports, and she told me she was on the tennis team. Well, tennis would fit, too.

"I played football in high school," I told her. "Left guard. I wasn't very good, but I was big and could take a lot of hits. People just bounced off me like little moths off a naked lightbulb. I haven't been very active since then, but I'm gonna get into this Krav Maga deal. Don't know if you've ever heard of Krav Maga, but a lot of girls do it; it's a great workout, plus you learn self-defense. You really find out how to beat the living crap out of someone. I'm thinking I can write off the entire cost of the class, since knowing martial arts would come in handy in my line of work."

She asked how I got interested in my line of work, so I told her about reading Sherlock Holmes and the Dictionary Ruzak moniker. She laughed about me calling myself Dictionary Ruzak. She had very good teeth and didn't show too much of them when she laughed, like a lot of thin-faced girls, which reinforced my notion that she had some breeding, that here was a girl who had wanted for nothing in her life, that her stepmom disappearing was the first real trouble she had had.

The check came and she insisted we go dutch, but I told her I needed the write-off, because technically I was entertaining a client.

"But I'm not a client," she said.

"Well, it's sort of like you are, though one client removed, like a second cousin."

She laughed. "You say things that don't make sense and make sense at the same time."

I blushed, as if she had paid me a compliment. It was dark when we stepped outside, and I told her I was walking her to her car. Downtown Knoxville can be pretty rough at night, after the library closes and all the vagrants hit the streets. Knoxville is known as a good place to come if you're homeless: The cops don't hassle you too much and people are generous. The air was heavy with a storm coming in from the west. The leading winds of the front had died and there was that before-the-rain stillness in the air. We didn't say much on the ten-minute walk to the Hilton, and I was feeling a little like we were television reenactors on one of those true-crime programs, tracing Felicia and Bob's route from the Bistro to the Hilton, if they even went to either the Bistro or the Hilton.

Her car was parked on the third level, a brand-new cherry red Mitsubishi convertible. My car was a 1992 two-door Nissan Sentra. I stood a couple steps back while she opened the door. She thought of something, pulled a pen from her purse, and scribbled her number on an old bank receipt.

"Will you call me right away after you talk to your client?"

"You bet."

"An English sheepdog or maybe even a Great Pyrenees."

"Huh?"

"The kind of dog you should get."

"Oh. Okay. Thanks. I'll look into that."

A lopsided smile. A hand on my shoulder. A little bounce on the balls of her feet and a kiss on my right cheek. She got in her car and I waited until her top was up and she was pulling out to turn, then walked back to the stairs. The rain had started and I had left the umbrella at the office. I was going to get soaked to my Skivvies, and I'm not such a romantic that I like walking in the rain.

CHAPTER SIXTEEN

I CALLED PARKER HUDSON FIRST THING THE NEXT MORN-
ing. A lady answered the phone—his wife, I guessed—and told
me he was playing golf. The rain that had moved in the night before was still hanging around, having turned misty overnight and
now promising to stay all day. Sometimes the clouds swoop down
upon us from the Cumberland Plateau and settle in the valley for
days. I left a message for him to call. He must be a dedicated
golfer to hit the links in this kind of weather, I thought, or else he
is lying to his wife. Although Parker Hudson didn't strike me as
the lying type.

It was Felicia's turn to show up late. She didn't get in till almost ten o'clock. She was wearing black knee-high boots, a suede
skirt, and a white peasant-looking blouse that showed a lot of
cleavage. As always, when she first walked in the room, I felt myself expanding like that fat kid in the Willy Wonka movie.

"Don't tell me I'm late," she said.

"How come?"

"Because I already know I'm late."

"Car trouble?"

"Yeah, something like that."

I wondered what could be like car trouble but not car trouble.

"You'll never guess what's happened."

"You've caught the killer."

"No, but the plot's thickened." I told her about meeting Susan Marks and about her missing stepmother. For some reason, I left out the fact that I'd had dinner with Susan.

"That's a weird coincidence," Felicia said.

"It would explain why the driver didn't slow down or stop."

"Because he was in the midst of an abduction?"

I nodded.

"On the other hand, maybe she's wrong and the stepmom took off on her old man."

"She's sure that didn't happen."

"Stepmom was a lot younger, right?"

"Uh-huh."

"Dad's out of the country a lot, right?"

"Uh-huh."

"Stepmom's a looker, right?"

"She's kind of pretty, yeah."

"A foreigner in a strange country, no friends, no family around except the stepkids off to college . . ."

"Maybe I should look into this deeper."

"Why?"

She was leaning in the entryway, one ankle crossed over the other, and as she talked, her thigh muscles clenched and unclenched.

"Is Susan Marks your client?"

"Not exactly."

"Is Susan Marks your client, Ruzak?"

"No. She's not."

"Is the Highly Effective—oh Christ, I can't remember how it goes—is the DIC a for-profit business?"

"Okay, Felicia. But I did promise I'd call Parker and ask if he saw anything that morning."

"Don't you think he would have told you already if he had?"

I shrugged. "Memory's funny."

"No pro bono work, Ruzak," she reminded me. The phone rang and I heard her say, "The Highly Effective Detection & Investigation Company. How may I direct your call?" even though there was only one place to direct it.

It was Deputy Paul.

"Teddy, I've got an answer on that partial tag for you."

"Hey, that's terrific," I said, digging in my desk drawer for my mechanical pencil.

"Well, it's probably not the answer you're looking for. You sure you got the letters right?"

"Hernando Radio Tango," I said, trying to sound very law enforcement.

"What?"

"HRT, that's what I saw," I said firmly.

"Well, there's no match, at least not to a Ford Expedition."

"Stolen tag?" I asked.

"I thought the same thing," he said, and I felt myself go warm with pleasure that I was thinking like a cop. Maybe I couldn't be one, but I could think like one. "But there's no record in the database. You sure it was a Tennessee tag?"

"One hundred percent."

"Okay. Huh. Well, sometimes not every number gets keyed in correctly. I could check the actual paper, but that takes time, Teddy."

"Look, I can't tell you how much this means to me . . . and to my client."

"Don't mention it, buddy."

I took a breath and said, "Does the name Lydia Marks mean anything to you?"

"No, should it?"

"She went missing around the same time the goslings were killed."

He didn't say anything for a second.

"Okay," he said. He was waiting for the punch line.

"Maybe it's connected."

"What?"

"Lydia Marks's disappearance and the killing of the geese."

"What was her name again?"

I spelled it for him. He said, "Who's the detective assigned to the case?"

"I don't know. I've been dealing with . . . an interested third party."

"A confidential informant?" There was a smile in his voice.

"Yeah, confidential informant, something like that."

"I'll ask around."

We expressed our mutual admiration and hung up. Felicia spun around the half wall as if on cue, as if this were a play and we had to keep the action moving.

"Three things," she said. "I hate our company greeting. It's too long and I refuse to say 'You've reached THE DIC.' We've got to change the name before it's too late. Also, Parker Hudson is holding for you, and what are you doing for lunch?"

"You're asking me to lunch?" I felt gut-punched.

"Relax, Ruzak, it's not a date. It's a working lunch."

"I didn't think it was a date," I said, but my tone probably gave me away. "What are we working on?"

"You," she said, and spun back around the wall. I was glad peasant blouses were making a comeback; I had always liked them.

I picked up the phone and asked Parker Hudson, "Have you ever been hypnotized?"

"I beg your pardon?"

"You know, where somebody puts you in this altered state. . . ."

"Teddy, I know what hypnosis is. And the answer is no, unless you include the spell placed on me by my beautiful wife thirty-five years ago." She must have been in the room with him; that's something you'd say if your wife was standing nearby.

I pulled the flyer about Lydia Marks out of my pocket. "She's thirty-seven, five six, a hundred and thirty pounds, auburn hair."

"Who is?"

"The woman you may have seen the morning the goslings died, maybe on the trail, maybe in the SUV itself. Her name is Lydia Marks and she's your neighbor, I guess."

"I've never heard of her. Or seen anyone like that. What's this got to do with hypnosis?"

"I figured you didn't have a memory of her or you would have mentioned it when you hired me. What I'm thinking is that they have that regression-type hypnosis therapy where you can reach suppressed memories. . . ."

"You want me hypnotized?"

"Totally voluntarily."

He laughed.

"You never know what might turn up," I went on. "Even if it isn't Lydia, maybe you'll remember the tag number, because my lead's not really panning out, or something else that'll crack the case."

"Why do you want me to remember Lydia Marks?"

I told him. He waited so long to say something, I had to ask if he was still there.

"I'd really like to help, Teddy. But I don't think I'd be comfortable undergoing hypnosis."

"What about your wife?"

"You want my wife to undergo hypnosis?"

"No, what if it was your wife who was missing? What would you think of a potential witness who refused to be hypnotized?"

"Now you're trying to manipulate me, Teddy."

"I'm just in the field, turning over stones."

He laughed. "Oh Teddy. You know what lives under stones. All sorts of nasty things."

He promised he'd think about it and we ended the call before I remembered to ask him about his golf game. I looked out the window behind the desk. My office was in the back of the Ely, so my view was totally blocked by the building behind me. It was 11:30, but it looked like dusk out there in the alley with the light rain falling straight down, making whispering sounds against the glass. I turned on my dictation machine and recorded a reminder to research hypnotherapists in the area in case Parker Hudson changed his mind. It had occurred to me during our conversation that maybe a shot of sodium Pentothal might open up his mind a little, but I doubted he'd go for it, since he was so hesitant about hypnosis, which was a lot less intrusive than an armful of truth serum, so I didn't bring it up. I also made a note to look into those psychic criminal investigators who the police bring in when they're desperate. I'd seen a special about them on A&E and, although I went in a skeptic, some of the stuff they came up with was pretty impressive. Thinking of psychics reminded me of another show I saw once, maybe on Animal Planet, about a pet psychic who could telepathically talk to animals, sort of a New Age Dr. Doolittle; maybe I could dig up one of those to mind-meld with the geese, because, apart from Parker Hudson, they were the only witnesses to the crime. I wondered if I was being creative or just getting desperate.

I called the number Susan Marks had given me and left a message for her to return my call. Her voice was very calm on the recording, very smooth, as if she recorded voice-mail introductions for a living.

Felicia came into the room and asked, "Did you drive to work this morning?"

"It was raining."

"So that means you did?"

"Yeah."

"Good, let's go."

"Where are we going?"

"Lunch, remember?"

I don't think I'd ever been as physically close to Felicia as when she slipped into the bucket seat beside me in the Sentra. I caught a whiff of peaches and thought of summertime. I took Cumberland Avenue west into Sequoia Hills, with the mansions lining either side of the road and the big Greek Orthodox church where every spring they have their fund-raising Greek Festival with all the food and dancing in the back parking lot, all the little Greek kids in their traditional Greek getups, their arms wrapped around one another's shoulders, and I wondered as we drove past the church if line dancing in country music had its origins in Greek dancing. I wasn't really hungry when we set out from downtown, but thinking of baklava got my appetite up.

"Is Bob a good cook?" I asked Felicia. "I hear firemen are great cooks because they're cooped up in the firehouse all the time."

"He's not cooped up all the time," she said, which really didn't answer my question, but I didn't press it. Something about Felicia tightened whenever I brought up Bob.

"Where are we going?" I asked. "And don't say 'lunch.'"

"American Clothiers."

"Oh, no."

"Think of it as an investment, Ruzak."

"PIs aren't known for their couture," I said. "Look at Columbo and Tom Selleck in those tacky Hawaiian shirts."

"What about Sonny Crocket?"

"Who's Sonny Crocket?"

"Don Johnson, *Miami Vice,* come on, Ruzak!"

"Felicia, I don't want to look like Don Johnson."

"I don't honestly think there's a danger of that, Ruzak."

"American Clothiers is very expensive."

"How would you know, Kmart Man?"

"I happen to know because I rented my graduation tuxedo from American Clothiers and even the underwear was seventeen dollars a pair, and that was fifteen years ago."

"You priced the underwear?"

"Anyway, detective work can be grungy, dirty business, Felicia. You sleep in your clothes sometimes and—"

"What times?"

"Like on a stakeout. And—"

"Why would you be sleeping on a stakeout? Doesn't that defeat the purpose?"

"I was just using that as an example."

"What kind of an example is it that makes no sense?"

"Sometimes what I say makes both," I said.

"Makes both what?"

"Sense and no sense."

She laughed. Some women have very unattractive knees, but Felicia's were top-notch. Her brown skirt with the cowgirl-like ruffles on the hem had ridden up to mid thigh.

"Do you ever line-dance?" I asked.

"Do I what?"

"You know, that kind of country-music dancing."

"Never. I hate country music."

"I don't like it, either."

"So why were you asking?"

"I don't know."

We were on Kingston Pike and the traffic was bumper-to-bumper. I looked at my watch. When I was a security guard, everything was very time-oriented: when your shift started and ended, when you made your rounds, even when you took your potty and other breaks. Now I was self-employed, it felt weird working without a strict schedule.

"That deputy with the sheriff's department called this morning," I said.

"I know. I answer the phone."

"Yeah. Anyway, he can't find that tag."

"Maybe you got it wrong."

"Maybe."

"Or they've disposed of the car."

"That could be."

"Or maybe he just missed it."

"Another possibility."

"I don't even know how you can see to drive, Ruzak," she said. "How long has it been since you changed the wiper blades?"

"Now I suppose I don't have the right kind of car."

"You're about to bring up Columbo again and that clunker he drove on the show, but you can't use Columbo, Ruzak. Columbo was a police detective, not a PI."

"So was Sonny Crocket."

We were close to West Town Mall and the traffic inched painfully along. Kingston Pike was always bad this time of day and the rain only made it worse.

I said, "You ever notice how when you get a new car, all of sudden you notice the same make and model all over the road, when before you hardly did? Ever since I met Parker Hudson, I've been seeing black SUVs. Look, there're three in the right lane up there and two in our lane . . . and another one behind us."

American Clothiers was on the west side of the mall, in a strip center with a Korean restaurant, a print shop, and a store called the Candy Factory, where every year I used to pick up some hand-dipped chocolate strawberries for Mom for Valentine's Day. American Clothiers reminded me of my mom, too; she'd taken me there to help pick out my tux.

"My only point is," I said as we walked toward the door. "My only point is PIs are eclectic when it comes to wardrobe. I don't want to walk out of this place looking like a banker."

"You're not fooling me. This isn't about clothes. Sometimes change isn't a bad thing, Teddy."

The store was ten degrees cooler than outside, and since it was only in the seventies outside, it was damn cold in that store. A salesman dressed like a banker swooped down on us immediately, like an ER triager who knew a critical case when he saw one. For the next hour and a half, I stripped, donned, paraded, and pirouetted for Felicia and the salesman, a guy named Simon, who handed me his card when it was all over, because now he was my man at American Clothiers, my wardrobe guy. I bought—or my company bought, since everything was paid off the business account—three suits, four sport coats, five pairs of slacks, six ties, seven pairs of socks, and two pairs of shoes. The total bill was $4,576.98. Everybody seemed very pleased with the outcome, with the exception of one key person. Simon called into the back room and a little Lithuanian guy emerged with a tape measure around his neck. I was just assuming he was Lithuanian because he was short, swarthy, and spoke with that harsh accent of Eastern Europeans, and Lithuania was the first country that popped into my head. Simon asked the Lithuanian when my clothes would be ready.

"Two weeks! Two weeks!" he shouted back unnecessarily, and disappeared.

When we were back in the car, I sat for a minute staring at the storefront, the smell of leather and wool still lingering in my nose.

"People have a comfort zone," I told Felicia. "You know, a boundary that if they cross over it, they start to panic."

"What, are you panicking?"

"Next you're gonna tell me I need a haircut and manicure and a full body waxing."

"Well, you do need a haircut."

"When I was on the football team in high school, the night before the biggest game of the year, all the guys got together and agreed to shave their heads."

"How come?"

I thought about it. "It's a guy thing. Anyway, I went home that night and shaved myself completely bald, and when I showed up at school the next morning, I was the only one. Nobody else shaved his head."

She laughed.

"I looked like Kojack, another detective not known for his fashion sense."

She laughed again.

"Seriously, what do you think about the body-waxing thing? I've got some back hair."

"I could have lived without knowing that, Ruzak."

I asked her where she wanted to eat, because now it was past one o'clock and I was starving. We stopped at Don Pablo's, a Mexican chain that featured a flagstone floor and round tables beside potted palm trees and round, wide hacienda-type umbrellas. That way, you could pretend you were dining outside in Mexico while you ate inside in Tennessee. Felicia ordered a strawberry margarita and I had a Corona.

"Speaking of comfort zones, our killer must have one," I said. "The thing is, how do you bring him out of it?"

She thought about it. "Pressure. You put the pressure on. Like with the newspaper article."

I mentioned that I had called Paul Killibrew with my idea for a follow-up story.

"Call him again."

"Why?"

"Tell him it might be connected to the disappearance of Lydia Marks."

"How's that help?"

"If all the person did was kill the geese, he might come forward, because he sure wouldn't want to be connected to abducting somebody."

"Susan said they wired the phones and staked out the mail, but nobody contacted them for ransom."

"Not a good sign."

"Not if it was a real kidnapping. I'm afraid Lydia Marks is dead."

"Probably."

CHAPTER SEVENTEEN

IT WAS ON MY MIND THE REST OF THAT DAY AND WAY INTO the night, so the next morning I ran the numbers, and they did not look good. Felicia was late again. I paced the office until she got there around 10:30, and I almost didn't say anything because her mood was so bad. She slapped her lavender purse on her desk, kicked off her lavender heels, and flopped into the love seat ($3,125 plus tax from Drexel Heritage) across from her desk ($2,567 plus tax from Braden's), rubbing the soles of her feet and grimacing like she'd stepped on a sharp object. In fact, I asked her if she *had* stepped on a sharp object.

"I'm just not used to heels," she said, and I thought of those thick-soled white numbers she wore waitressing.

"Nice outfit," I told her. And it *was* nice, a three-piece ensemble—lavender skirt, white blouse, lavender half jacket, the kind with the sleeves that are cut short, like the jacket worn by the kid on the Cracker Jack box, whose name probably is Jack. "New?"

"Yes, it's new. Why?"

"I've been crunching some numbers and we're in trouble."

She rubbed her arches and said, "How much trouble?"

"Enough trouble that Parker Hudson's fifty bucks an hour plus expenses is not going to help."

"That's impossible. There's no way we could spend that much in two months."

"Look at this." I handed her my calculations. Her nose scrunched up and her tongue came out like when she was framing the newspaper article.

"Well," she said finally. "Looks like you're going to have to postpone that body waxing."

"We need a cash infusion."

"You're meeting with two new clients today and one tomorrow," she said. "Up your fee."

"I canceled them."

She stared up at me. She was still sitting and I was standing a couple feet back, and for a second I was afraid she was going to come out of that love seat and coldcock me. Her tongue disappeared and her lips thinned out.

"Why did you cancel them, Ruzak?"

"I don't have a license, Felicia. I haven't sent back the application. I haven't taken the test."

"That didn't stop you from taking Hudson's case."

"I'm only comfortable pushing the envelope so far."

"Oh, what horseshit! You're kidding me, right?"

"And I took his case before I knew I needed a license. One of the requirements, Felicia, is you've got to have a good moral character. And anyway, the more clients I get, the greater the risk the state's gonna catch me, and then I'll never get my license."

"I lost my driver's license for six months and I didn't stop driving."

"You lost your license? What did you do?"

"That isn't the point. Sometimes you gotta play the odds, Ruzak."

"I'm in the accountability business, Felicia."

"The what?"

"My job is holding people accountable for their actions. That's what a detective does. It wouldn't be right for me to make a buck out of that while I'm not."

"While you're not what?"

"Accountable."

"Are you firing me?"

"Huh?"

"Is this where this is going? You're gonna fire me?"

"Of course not."

"Because I can save you the trouble, Ruzak."

"Felicia, look—" We were like a married couple fighting about household finances. I knew what that was like; Mom and Dad used to fight about it all the time. The worst fights they had were over money, the main issue being that there wasn't enough. There was never enough. Even rich people will tell you that: There's never nearly enough.

"But you just need to keep in mind you wouldn't still have your one client if it weren't for me."

"I'm not going to fire you, Felicia. I was going to say we need to cut back a little on the, um, I don't know what to call them. The stuff like here, in the office. Is it too late to return any of it?"

"Of course it's too late, Teddy. It's used office furniture. It lost half its value the minute it came through the door."

I whistled. "That's like when you buy a new car and—"

"Oh please," she said. "Spare me the Ruzakian riff on depreciation or relative resale values or whatever the hell you're about to go off on. You're like the neighborhood bar know-it-all without the drunken charm. Are you always so goddamned *earnest?*" She heaved herself off the three-thousand-dollar love seat and began to pace around the little area in her stocking feet. I could see the red paint of her toenail polish through the nude mesh. After pacing awhile, she stopped and said, "You're going to have to take those clients, Ruzak."

"Felicia, I told you—"

"You're going to take them and charge them a hundred bucks an hour to be their 'investigative consultant.' You want to play Mycroft, now you can. You'll sit your wide ass in that chair in there and noodle their problems and give them possible avenues to explore, and every minute the tiniest thought crosses that complicated brain of yours—I don't care if you're sitting on the can—you're charging them for it."

I thought about it. "That seems dishonest."

"Oh Christ!"

She flopped back down on the love seat and proceeded to jam the lavender shoes back on her feet. Again I could see the pink tip of her tongue, and all of a sudden I wanted to cry.

"Don't leave, Felicia."

"I'm not leaving, you bonehead! I'm putting on my shoes!"

"Good," I said, meaning the "not leaving" part. She went to her desk. "What are you doing now?"

"I'm calling the people you canceled and I'm uncanceling them."

"But what about—"

"Do you want to be a detective or not?"

"Of course I do."

"Then leave it to me, Ruzak. Have I ever let you down?"

I went into my office and sat my wide ass down in my $850 leather chair. It groaned a bit. I mean the chair groaned, not my wide ass. *Wide ass. Bonehead.* Guys are willing to take a lot more from a pretty woman than they would from a homely one. A homely one would be on the street right now, looking for a new job. Thinking that and thinking about morphing in a nanosecond from detective to "investigative consultant" made me feel like I had betrayed something precious or violated some solemn vow I never knew I'd taken.

She spent the next hour on the phone, getting my ex-clients back and rescheduling their appointments. I listened to her explaining my fee—$150 for the initial consultation, $1,000 retainer, $100 per hour—and saying how if they checked around, they'd find my rates very reasonable. When I couldn't take it anymore, I motioned to her that I was going out for a walk. She had slipped off her shoes again and had both feet on the desk as she talked. I noticed a tiny hole in her stocking, on the pad of her right foot, and for some reason the sight of that hole broke my heart and I wasn't sore at her anymore.

When I got back, Felicia delivered the good and bad news that of the three prospective clients, two had balked at my rates, refusing to make an appointment. This was good news for the maintenance of my moral character and bad news for my business. The third wanted to think about it, so the end result was that for now, I still had only one client.

I called Susan Marks's number and got the voice mail again. I hung up without leaving a message. Twenty seconds later, I called the number again, and this time I left a message, giving her my home number and telling her to call anytime.

I pulled out the envelope containing the PI application from the state, which had been sitting in my top desk drawer for over a week. The thing that concerned me the most was the fact that it would take three to four months for the state to process my application—three to four months *after* I passed the exam, assuming that I passed it.

I had to make a grocery run after work. The nearest store to my apartment was down on Broadway, almost five miles. That's one of the problems with getting people to move into downtown Knoxville: There're no grocery stores or gas stations or anything very convenient except the bus station and the mission houses for the vagrants. I checked my messages when I got home, but nobody had called. Maybe if I joined a gym or took some Krav Maja classes, I thought, I'd make some friends and people would call me.

I was putting away the last can of Campbell's when the phone rang. I jumped a little, because I wasn't used to the phone ringing. She sounded even younger on the phone, a little breathy, and I could picture her biting that fat lower lip as she talked.

"Mr. Ruzak?"

"Hi, Susan."

"This is Susan Marks. I'm sorry I didn't call you sooner. . . ."

"That's okay. Don't worry about it."

"You said in your message you had some information for me."

"Yeah. That's right. Look, I talked to my client and he doesn't remember anything, um, specific about your stepmom . . . seeing her or anything."

"Oh."

"So I told him maybe we ought to consider some hypnotherapy. You know, sometimes that can bring out things."

"Do you really think so?"

I kind of really didn't, but I wasn't going to tell her that. Still, you want to be careful with giving someone hope. False hope is crueler than despair.

"You never know," I said. "He wasn't too hot on the idea. How're things going?"

"About the same. I'm real busy. It's exam week."

"Well . . ." I was trying to think of something else to say. "That must be tough, exams in the middle of all this."

"Yeah." It was barely louder than a sigh. I didn't know how to comfort her, though comforting her wasn't really my job, beyond the normal moral obligation to give comfort when pain comes

your way. I had no point of reference besides sharing her humanity. My mother was never abducted, except in the poetic sense,
and I had never taken a college exam. When I thought about it, I
had practically no life experience at all—never been to college,
never been married, never had a kid. I was over ten years older
than she was, but I might as well have been ten years younger.

"And a bad answer is better than no answer at all," I said.

"It's like your life just freezes, you know? You can't grieve. You
can't hope."

"Oh, you can always do that," I said. "Hope, I mean."

"Why?" She repeated the question, her voice cracking a little.
She seemed intensely interested in the answer. *"Why?"*

"Because when you think about it, that's what makes us human, besides speech. I watch a lot of the Discovery Channel and
Animal Planet, and let me tell you, there's not much that separates us from the animals." She was very quiet as I talked. I couldn't
even hear her breathe. I was relieved. Maybe my topic was just
right, since she was studying to be a vet. On the other hand,
maybe she was smirking on the other end because here was high
school graduate and Police Academy dropout Teddy Ruzak lec-
turing her on animals. "Take chimps. Now, biologically, they have
ninety-nine-point-something percent of our DNA; we're practically identical. Chimps don't talk, but they communicate. They
use tools like sticks to dig out termites from mounds. They play
games like people, and there's even that old saying about a hundred monkeys hitting typewriter keys for a hundred years to pro-
duce the complete works of Shakespeare. . . ."

"Shakespeare?" she asked.

"Sure, William Shakespeare. All his plays. Maybe not the son-
nets. I don't know. I had a high school English teacher who read
all of *Macbeth* out loud to us, and she played all the parts; I still

remember the ghost of Banquo and the witches: 'Fair is foul, and foul is fair!' "

Now I could hear her giggling a little. This only encouraged me. Sometimes "Ruzakian riffs" could serve a purpose.

"But anyway, they love and grieve and form tight social bonds and learn from their mistakes, but like those damn geese, they can't hope. If a baby chimp gets sick, they don't hope it gets better. If a drought hits, the chimps don't sit around hoping for rain. They just suffer. When those goslings got killed, their parents grieved for maybe a day, no more than two, I would think, and then it was forgotten. I guess my point is that hoping is human, and when you give up hope, you give up that one or two hundredth of a percent that makes you human."

"I guess so."

"It's all, um, you know, precious."

"What is?"

"Life. I mean, it's too important to be trivial. Even a virus like Ebola. It's kind of what you might call evil in that it really messes with you, but that's exactly why it's not trivial." I told her the story of the kids throwing rocks at the geese. "That's when it hit me that I was wrong to think of my case as silly or a waste of my time on earth. Life matters, and to give up hope for life is like—well, I'm not what you might call a religious person, but the only word for it is *sin*."

She didn't say anything, and I wondered if I had trespassed by slapping down my soapbox smack in the middle of her heartache. Plus calling her a sinner, in effect, was probably not such a good idea.

"I'm sorry," I said. "I'm talking too much."

"No, I like to hear you talk. I've never known anybody who talks like you. I've never known anybody like you period."

"I'm nothing special," I said, which was one of those self-serving things people who think they're special say.

She didn't say anything, and so I went on. "Would you like to have a cup of coffee with me sometime? Not anytime soon—I know you're taking exams and stuff—but maybe in a couple of weeks I could call you?"

"Yes," she said. "I think I'd like that."

CHAPTER EIGHTEEN

FELICIA CALLED IN SICK THE NEXT DAY. I WAS SURPRISED but not shocked. There really wasn't that much to do. I decided she had a good idea when she suggested staking out the scene of the crime to see if the killer was a regular, so for the next couple of weeks, I got up at 5:00 A.M. and drove west into Farragut, parked my car in a spot closest to the road in the park's parking lot, drank too much coffee, and ate too many Krispy Kreme doughnuts, but I never saw a black SUV with HRT on the plates, which made me think maybe Gary Paul was right and I'd gotten the letters wrong. I wrote down the letters of the alphabet and tried to see which ones resembled *H, R,* and *T* the most. I came up with so many different possibilities and combinations that I gave up. I started to doubt the whole thing had happened at all.

One morning, Parker Hudson saw me sitting in my car and came over to say hello and tell me that he was glad I was still on the case. I asked him if he had given any more thought to the hypnosis thing, and he just laughed and shook his head.

I visited Mom a couple times, picked up my new clothes from American Clothiers after arguing with Simon, my wardrobe guy, that I should be able to return them for a full refund, except there was the problem that they had been altered to fit me and all purchases for altered apparel were final, and generally moped around, waiting for a break in the case or a break in the monotony of my life.

Another morning, I came into the office and saw Felicia sitting at her desk, going through the want ads. She stuffed the newspaper in her desk drawer when I came in. When I accused her of looking at the want ads, she denied it, and when I checked her desk after she left for the day, I found it locked tight.

Speaking of the paper, I checked it every morning for a follow-up story on the possible Lydia Marks/dead goslings connection, but no story appeared. I called Paul Killibrew at the paper and he told me that his editor had killed the story because he didn't think there was enough of a story there. I hung up thinking it was pretty wonderful human beings weren't stories, because most of us would be dead. Thinking that made me think of Susan Marks, but I got her voice mail when I called. Finals would be over now, and maybe she moved back home with her dad for the summer.

The weather turned hot and dry. By midmorning, the temperature was in the eighties. I sat in my little Sentra and sweated, watching the joggers and the walkers and the baby strollers on the trail, hardly paying attention to the cars as they went by. I was pushing the envelope on this case; I knew that. Nobody had come forward and I had no leads left. How long would Parker Hudson pay me to sit in my car every day and sweat?

Then one morning, a cop car pulled in directly behind me and flashed its lights at me. My heart fluttered and the adrenaline made my ears sing. I was busted. The licensing commission had found out I was conducting a stakeout without a license and had issued a warrant for my arrest.

A sheriff's deputy got out of the car and came up to my window. It was Deputy Gary Paul.

"Thought that was you," he said, and showed me his bad teeth. "How ya doin', Ruzak?"

"Can't complain," I replied, the phrase used by most people who can.

"You working or taking a break?"

"Both, I guess."

He laughed. "Me, too. Let's go have breakfast."

"I just ate six Krispy Kreme doughnuts."

"Then you're ready for a real breakfast. Follow me."

He went back to the car and I followed him out of the lot.

He took Concord Road to Kingston Pike, then turned north onto Lovell Road, where he pulled into an IHOP parking lot. He hitched his belt when he got out of the cruiser and slapped me hard on the shoulder on the way to the door. He ordered a Rooty-Tooty, Fresh & Fruity, and I ordered two eggs and sausage with a glass of orange juice, since I'd already had about thirty-two ounces of coffee that morning.

"I ran that partial through the system again," he told me.

"Don't tell me. Nothing."

He shook his head. "So I had a clerk pull the paper."

"No match there, either."

"Nope."

"You have much experience with regression therapy?"

"I don't even know what that is."

"I was recommending it to my client, but now I'm thinking I should do it. Maybe I'd remember the tag right. Also, you should never recommend someone do something if you're not willing to do it yourself."

"I also spoke with Harvey Listrom."

"That's terrific. Who's Harvey Listrom?"

"The lead detective on the Marks case. They haven't developed any suspect who drives an SUV. They haven't developed any suspects period."

"What's his theory?"

"Random crime. Husband's been cleared. No evidence the marriage was unhappy. Stepkids have airtight alibis. Bank account overflowing. Health good. No sign of forced entry. Nothing missing from the house. Looks like she was taking her morning jog and somebody snatched her. She was just in the wrong place at the wrong time."

"And now she's probably dead."

"They usually are after this long."

Our food came, but my appetite had left.

"That sucks," I said. "I met her daughter. I mean her stepdaughter. A really nice girl."

"Too nice to have to deal with something like this."

I nodded. "But it made sense to me, HRT being connected to both things. First, it came flying down the road ten, maybe twenty miles over the speed limit."

"On the other hand, I pull fifteen to twenty speeders off that road every month. Doesn't mean they kidnapped somebody."

"And call me naïve, but I honestly think most people would have stopped if they'd done something like that—hit a gaggle of baby geese."

"You're naïve."

"I've got that habit," I admitted, "of thinking people are going to react to something the same way I would. Still, if it was the kidnapper, that would explain why he didn't stop."

"So would being an asshole."

"But what about HRT? Why would somebody who hit some geese come looking for me, unless they were the kidnapper, too, and thought I could connect them to Lydia Marks?"

"Maybe HRT wasn't stalking you. Maybe that SUV you saw had nothing to do with Lydia Marks or the geese."

"It just seems too much of a coincidence, the geese, the SUV, and Lydia Marks."

He shook his head. "Maybe it is all connected, Teddy, but you can't prove it. It's like a Rorschach test: You see in the blob of ink what you want to see."

"You know what the funny thing is? I've been out there every morning for the past two weeks, and even before the sun comes up, there're people walking and jogging that trail. I can't believe nobody saw what happened. And on the flip side, I can't believe Parker Hudson was the only one who saw the geese die."

"People don't like to get involved."

"Did Listrom talk to Parker Hudson?"

He shrugged. "I gave him the name."

I hadn't touched my food, but Gary Paul's plate was clean. He had wiped it clean with his last slice of toast and jammed the whole thing in his mouth. Most cops I knew were prodigious eaters and did their eating fast. At least I shared that with them.

"Could you get me a list of all black Ford Expeditions registered in the state?"

"Huh?"

I repeated the question.

He sipped his coffee. He took it with lots of cream and three of those little packets of sugar. I also noticed that he bit his fingernails to the quick. When you're a self-possessed, procedurally oriented kind of guy, like this Gary Paul obviously was, sometimes normal human anxiety leaks out in little self-destructive habits.

"Do you have any idea how many black Ford Expeditions there are in this state?" he asked.

"I'll pay for it."

"That's not what I meant, Ted. You'd be looking for a needle in a haystack."

"I don't know what else to do at this point. Does the department ever use psychics?"

"Ever use what?"

"Psychics—you know, people who get in touch with the spirit world to solve the case."

"Not that I know of." He was smiling. "Why?"

"Just wondering. Seriously, I can't think of anything else—I mean, getting that list is all I've got left."

"Sure. Give me a couple days."

He wouldn't let me pick up the check, reminding me that he had invited me. I followed his patrol car out of the lot. He turned right onto Lovell and I turned left and jumped on the interstate, heading back downtown. My stakeout of the jogging trail was over.

Felicia wasn't in when I got back to the office, but she had left a message that something had come up and she might have to miss work again the following day. For once, I didn't mind. I watered the plants and locked the place up, and I half-expected to see Susan Marks sitting on my stoop as I went out the door. Then I did a funny thing: I went to a movie. I'm not sure why I went to a movie, but it felt like I was on some kind of vigil; I was waiting for something, but I didn't know what I was waiting for. The atmosphere felt pregnant, like the air just before a summer storm or on the eve of a big battle, or that moment right before the batter leans back to unload on a big fat change-up and you *know* he's going to hit it out of the park. I ordered a large popcorn and a Coke, which together cost more than my ticket, and hardly paid attention to the movie, which I think was a comedy, only there seemed an awful lot of bloodletting and cursing for a comedy, but the movies have changed a lot even since when I was a little kid, which might explain why I watch the old ones on AMT or Turner Classics. After the movie, it was time for dinner, so I went through the drive-thru at Buddy's Bar-B-Q and had a pork dinner with corn on the cob and coleslaw. I drove home, checked my messages (I didn't have any), and then settled down to *Biography* on A&E.

When I got in the next morning, Felicia was waiting for me, standing by her desk in lime green shoes, slacks, and jacket over a satiny black blouse, holding a newspaper. I felt something contract in my chest when I saw the expression on her face, but it wasn't my heart; it wasn't something physical. It went deeper than that.

"What is it?" I asked.

"Have you seen this morning's paper?"

I took the paper to my desk and read the entire article, then picked up the phone and dialed the number. Her voice mail picked up. I hung up and Felicia set a cup of coffee by my elbow and then went to her desk. I could hear her typing something on her computer. I stared out the window into the alley, where two pigeons sat on the windowsill directly opposite mine. I watched the pigeons for a few minutes, then called over to Felicia to say I needed a phone book. She came in and placed a single sheet of paper with Susan Marks's address and directions there, which she had pulled from the Internet. She had also printed out the address for Kenneth Marks in Farragut.

I passed the dry cleaner's at the bottom of the stairs. They were already at work, and it flashed across my mind that for weeks on my way up to my office, particularly when things weren't going well, I would think at least I didn't run a dry cleaner's, with all those chemicals and the smell and customers complaining I had lost their clothes or lost one of their buttons, that at least I didn't have to work over those steaming machines pressing shirts all day. And thinking that always made me feel fortunate, until I thought about it too hard and realized my good fortune had depended on my mother dying.

She was sitting on the bottom step, the same step I first saw her on, wearing shorts and a sleeveless white shirt. Her brown hair was pulled back and held by a pink scrunchy, which made her face look even younger and more boyish—that and the fact that she wasn't wearing any makeup.

I sat on the step beside her and we didn't say anything at first. Then she turned toward me and put her head on my chest and I put my left arm around her. She cried until I could feel the wetness from her tears against the bare skin beneath my new oxford shirt and undershirt. She said something that I couldn't hear, but I didn't ask her to repeat it. I just kept my arm around her and rubbed her bare shoulder with the palm of my hand.

Then she said something else, and this time I understood.

"You told me to hope."

"I'm sorry," I said.

She cried some more—not your wailing kind of crying, the kind you see on the news practically every night when the story is from the Middle East, but a soft, quiet crying, pressing her face against my chest. Her shoulders and arms were covered in freckles.

"Help me," she whispered.

"I'll help you," I said.

CHAPTER NINETEEN

Two hikers from New Jersey found the skull of Lydia Marks high on a ridge in the heart of the Great Smoky Mountains. The rest of her bones had been scattered by the wild animals that had feasted on her. One of the hikers slipped the skull in his backpack and they descended nine hundred feet down the mountain to the nearest ranger station, bringing the skull with them because, they told the newspaper, they were afraid no one would believe them.

Within hours, the forensic pathologist with the Tennessee Bureau of Investigation determined the skull belonged to a female between the ages of thirty-five and forty and that the quarter-size hole in her cranium had probably resulted from a massive blow to the head with a blunt object. Dental records confirmed it was the skull of Susan Marks's stepmother.

The article said the TBI and the Sevier County and Knox County sheriff's departments had formed a joint task force to investigate the abduction and murder of Lydia Marks. They had set up a tip hotline and were asking the public for any information that might aid in the investigation. A spokesperson for the TBI told the reporter they had no suspects at this time.

I asked Susan if she wanted to go up to the office for a few minutes, but she told me she had to get back home; her father needed her. I walked her to her car and asked if she needed a ride; I thought maybe she shouldn't be driving. But she told me she was okay to drive, so I went back to the office. Felicia told me both Deputy Paul and Parker Hudson had called while I was outside with Susan. I called Deputy Paul first.

"This is a huge break," he said.

"How so?"

"It's not a missing person's case anymore. It's a homicide. Top priority. And now there's physical evidence. Something to work from. It's terrible. It's shitty. But the odds were always that she was dead, and now that we have a body, we've got a better chance of finding the son of a bitch."

"I don't think the Marks family considers it a huge break."

I called Parker Hudson.

"I wish to God I had gotten a better look," he said. "But I was focused on the geese. I didn't even think to get the license number."

"We don't know it's connected," I said. "But you should call the task force."

He said he would. I said, "And I'll get hold of a hypnotherapist."

"Really, Teddy, I don't think that's necessary."

"It won't hurt to try."

"I won't do it."

"You will do it, Mr. Hudson."

"What did you say?"

"I said, 'You will do it.' When something like this happens, doing anything less puts you on the wrong side—the bad guy's side. You understand what I mean?"

When I hung up, Felicia was standing in the doorway. Her arms were folded over her lime green chest.

"I'm going to help her," I said.

"How much is she paying you?"

I didn't answer. She said, "Why are you going to help her?"

"Because I promised I would."

"Is there a reward?"

"A reward for what?"

"Finding the killer."

"Sometimes it isn't about money, Felicia."

"So you're willing to break the law for honor. It's just at money you draw the line."

"It's not a bad place to draw it."

"Aren't you noble."

"What's that supposed to mean?"

"Come on, Ruzak. You know the real reason you want to help this girl."

"She asked me to help her and I promised I would."

"And why did you promise that?"

"She asked."

Felicia laughed. "Okay, whatever. You want me to find a hypnotherapist for you?"

"That would be great."

I picked up the phone again and, after getting transferred a couple of times, spoke with the head of the joint task force, a detective with the TBI named Janet Watson, which was the same last name as Sherlock Holmes's sidekick. I told her about the black SUV that hit the geese around the time Lydia Marks disappeared and about the partial tag I spotted when a black SUV that might or might not have been the same one that hit the geese tailed me on Gay Street. Deputy Gary Paul of the Knox County sheriff's office had run the partial for me and hadn't found a match, but he was checking it again, I said. Then I asked her if she went into law enforcement because she had the same last name as Dr. Watson. That was a mistake, asking her that, because after she told me she didn't know what I was talking about, she treated me like you would a crank.

Felicia came back in after I got off the phone and handed me a piece of paper.

"Parker Hudson has a three o'clock appointment for next Tuesday. You want me to call him?"

"I'll call him."

"Address is on the paper," she said, and turned on her heel without saying another word.

There was something else I wanted to do, someone else I had made a mental note to call, but now I couldn't remember, so I got up and watered the plants and waited to remember. The best way to remember something is not to think about it, but to think about or do something else, and then it always comes to you. Try it next time you lose your car keys or can't remember somebody's name. I was misting the fern on the windowsill when I remembered, and I got on the phone right away to Paul Killibrew, the guy at the *Sentinel.* I told him his editor might be interested in running the follow-up now that Lydia Marks had been found murdered. He said he'd check again. Then I called Parker Hudson, told him about his appointment, and hung up before he could argue with me. Sometimes doing the right thing makes people uncomfortable, which is why the right things don't get done more often.

Felicia told me something had come up and she had to take the rest of the day off.

"What's come up?" I asked.

"It's personal."

"Is somebody sick?"

"Didn't I just say it was personal?"

"Technically, it's a business question, Felicia. I mean, I guess I kind of need a reason before I let you take off."

"Okay, *boss.* I'm not feeling very good, if you must know."

"That's all I need to know." She didn't look sick, but women have problems men don't see easily.

"Good, because that's all you're gonna know."

After she left, I took out my mechanical pencil and began a to-do list.

The door opened and a man's voice called out.

"Hello? Is anyone here?"

I went around my desk and saw a tall man standing by the love seat. He was easily halfway to thirteen feet tall, dressed in an expensive gray suit that might have been purchased from American Clothiers, and fairly sparkling with diamond jewelry: watch, two rings, and a stud in his left ear. His hair was fashionably long and swept back from his massive forehead, which jutted out like the brow of a warship over a very long, very straight nose and full, sensuous lips. It was the lips, particularly the lower one, which gave him away.

"I'm looking for a man named Theodore Ruzak," the man said.

"I'm Teddy Ruzak. And you're Kenneth Marks."

"How do you know my name?"

"I see the family resemblance. Come on in. Sit down. Can I get you anything? The coffee isn't fresh, and I keep meaning to get one of those watercoolers, but Felicia, my secretary, might have something stashed in the filing cabinet, not that she drinks on the job, but she did have a margarita once when we had lunch."

"No thank you," he said, slipping into one of my visitor's chairs. "I haven't much time."

"No, I didn't figure you would—not have a drink, I mean, but have much time. I gotta tell you how sorry I am about all this. . . ."

"No sorrier than I, Mr. Ruzak. We are preparing to leave for Ireland in two days."

"Ireland?"

"For my wife's funeral."

"You're burying her in Ireland?"

"As per her wishes, yes."

There went my surveillance of the funeral.

"I feel really bad about all this," I said. "Like I said before. I didn't know your wife, but I do know your daughter, which I guess you know I do, since she was here this morning and now you're here."

He didn't say anything for a second. Then he said, "My daughter tells me you have promised to help us find my wife's killer."

"Something like that."

"You're aware the authorities are also investigating her death?"

"Well," I said, "it certainly isn't a competition. They've got me outgunned in terms of manpower and experience and the ability to make an arrest."

"Then what do you suppose you can do?"

I shrugged. "Who knows?"

"Indeed."

He put his elbows on the armrests and laced his perfectly manicured fingers together. Now, this guy radiated charisma and power. I'd never asked Susan what her father did for a living, but whatever it was, he was very good at it and he knew it. He was not somebody to be messed with on a financial plane, not that I had any intention of messing with him on *any* plane. Still, the spouse is the first person you look at, so I looked at him and wondered if he'd had anything to do with his wife's murder. If this was a movie, I would have said Mr. Marks was suspect numero uno: rich, arrogant, smart. A guy you love to hate. He certainly wasn't playing the part of grieving widower very well, but these business-genius types are pretty cold fish, pretty ruthless, like those takeover guys who move in and fire half a company in order to save it. I really didn't have a head for finances. I was past my twenties and nearly midway through my thirties, and I still didn't know what I did have a head for. I certainly hadn't proved myself in the detective line. I couldn't even solve the murder of a gaggle of geese.

"Perhaps you would be interested to hear what I'd like you to do?" he suggested.

"That would be great. But I see my role as an adjunct to the police. Sort of an advisory position, because, see, technically, I don't have my license. I'll be taking the test next month, but as of right now I'm not a PI."

"If you're not a PI, what are you?"

"I'm an ex–security guard who lucked into some money and didn't have the brains or maturity to think things through before stenciling 'THE DIC' on my door."

He laughed. It was a bled-white kind of laugh, a social formality he observed, like shaking hands in the West or kissing cheeks in the East or bowing in the Far East.

"How did you luck into money?" he asked. I must have touched on his favorite topic.

"My mother died."

"You consider that luck?"

"I didn't say it was good luck."

"My daughter told me you are the most unusual man she has ever met. I begin to see what she meant."

He had such a formal way of talking, I wondered if he was a foreigner, too, like his second wife. Maybe he was naturalized, but he didn't have an accent, as far as I could tell. But I wasn't very good at accents.

"She brought your name up several weeks ago, after she read an article in the paper about your case of the dead geese. I told her at the time I didn't think talking to you would lead anywhere, but perhaps it has, or might, and that is why I'm here."

Now was the moment to pull out the ol' checkbook and write Teddy Ruzak a big number, one with lots and lots of zeros, but he didn't. He just studied me over his folded hands, his very light blue eyes taking everything in. Maybe German or Swiss. He was a big-bodied, stolid kind of guy, which fit the German theory; plus, the name could be an Americanized Marx, like the guy who started communism and made Ronald Reagan's second career possible. But he also was precise in the way he talked, clipping off the end of each word very neatly and organizing his thoughts, and even in the way he held himself erectly in the soft chair without so much as twitching an eyelash. There was a stoicism about him that might be Swiss, plus my belief, not based on anything really, that the Swiss were very good with money. Maybe it's all the talk about Swiss bank accounts, and you never read about Swiss poverty or them running to the World Bank for some debt relief. You never hear much about the Swiss period.

"I want the person who murdered my wife," he said.

"Sure."

"And toward that goal, I am offering half a million dollars for the arrest and conviction of her killer."

I gave an appreciative whistle. "Gee, thanks for letting me know. I've been cautioned against pro bono."

"That money is for anyone who comes forward with information that leads to an arrest and conviction."

"You bet, I understand. We see eye to eye on that."

"However, I am prepared to offer you twice that amount."

His proposal didn't make much sense, but I was sure the blame for that didn't rest with him. I wasn't getting it.

"There is another proviso to my offer to you, Mr. Ruzak, and that is if or when you discover his identity, you do not tell the police. You tell me."

He hadn't moved a muscle. I was moving a lot of them, mostly the internal ones.

"Mr. Marks," I said. "Wouldn't I have to tell the police to fulfill the arrest and conviction part of the deal?"

"Our deal does not end with arrest and conviction."

"You know," I said, "when my mother died, I was pretty torn up. She died of cancer, and my first reaction was, Somebody by God's going to pay for this. Like, Look how long cancer has been around, and we still can't lick it? I wanted to mow down the entire medical community and maybe the government, too, for dropping the ball on the whole cure issue. I mean, we can put a man on the moon and build bombs that can blow up half the planet, but we can't cure cancer? Anger is pretty natural—I think it has its roots in our genetic history, something to do with the fight-or-flight response, and sometimes it's pretty useful, but it's always been my opinion that revenge is anger misdirected in an unproductive way."

"Then you are declining my offer?"

"All I ever wanted to be was a detective," I told him. "If I take you up on this and somehow I succeed, that makes me an accessory to a serious crime, and I don't think the licensing bureau would look too kindly on my application. Of course, it would also stink morally, ethically, and, besides, could land us both in prison for a very long time."

"You don't believe I could protect you?"

"What could you do to protect me?"

"Safe passage to a country of your choosing. A new identity. Or, in the alternative, my word that if things do not turn out as planned, I will take full responsibility and never reveal how I came upon the information."

"How's that protect me from my own conscience, though? What about the moral and ethical part—you know, the evil?"

"Don't presume to lecture me about the nature of evil, Mr. Ruzak. I am intimately acquainted with it."

"Mr. Marks, I wouldn't presume to lecture a dog, much less somebody like you. I understand you're something of a world traveler and I can only imagine some of the things you've seen in your travels. There's an awful lot of bad out there, which is fortunate for my business but unfortunate for the species at large. I was only saying, all things being equal, I'd prefer to be on the side of light—you know, a bulwark against the darkness."

"One-point-five million."

"Gee, that shows a lot of confidence in me. It's flattering as hell, but I really don't—"

"Two million, then. My final offer."

"I'm glad of that, because this sort of reminds me of a parlor game me and my buddies used to play in high school. Well, I called it a parlor game, but it wasn't played in a parlor. We usually played in my parents' basement. You know, where you'd challenge each other to see how far you'd go for money, along the lines of the old saying that everybody has a price. Like, Would you eat a bowl of dog crap for five thousand dollars? I just grabbed that number out of the air, but usually the dog crap fetched a price closer to a million. I believe I said I'd do it for five hundred thousand. I was in high school, you understand, and when you're that age, you're pretty materialistic. I remember I was ready to give up a foot for two million. Some people never grow out of that stage; otherwise, we wouldn't have so much insurance fraud, like those people who stage car wrecks."

He blinked several times, like he had something in his eye, or it may have been just the sting of the dry-cleaning fumes.

"Mr. Ruzak, you are either the most facetious man I have ever met or the most facile."

"You mean you can't figure out if that was a yes or a no. One of my problems is that I've got a restless mind, probably a result of spending most of my adult life sitting by myself in the dead of night listening to too much late-night talk radio. They didn't allow televisions, so that was really the only media outlet available to me."

"I don't think your problem is too much talk radio," he said.

"Well, that's a relief. That would be something you can't undo."

"So your answer is no?"

"See, that's the thing."

"What is? What is *the thing*, Mr. Ruzak?" he fairly barked at me.

"Am I hesitating because I don't know who did this to your wife? In other words, is my moral character predicated on my lack of knowledge or on a truly righteous underpinning? See, it's like that game I told you about. It's all abstract because I don't possess the key to the treasure chest. That said, I made a certain promise to your daughter that I'm going to do everything I can to help find Lydia's killer, but I'd be happy to settle for the half million and forgo the jackpot."

His hands came apart and spread wide in a vaguely European gesture of surrender.

As I walked him to the door, I said, "You know, I probably don't have to tell you there're maybe a couple dozen guys in Knoxville alone who would jump at your offer."

"And what would you do, Mr. Ruzak, if some unfortunate accident befell this person who murdered my wife?"

He meant would I rat on him.

"I don't know. I'd feel pretty lousy for everyone involved, but we all have choices to make, Mr. Marks. I don't have to live with anybody but Theodore Ruzak. That's tough enough."

CHAPTER TWENTY

FELICIA CALLED IN SICK THE NEXT MORNING. I GOT OFF the phone with her, called the downtown fire station, and asked for Bob. When he came on the line, I hung up. Then I felt crummy for checking up on her like that. Most people are honest and all have problems. You can't get cynical. Cynical people aren't a happy lot and they have tight mouths.

I was so deep in thought, I didn't hear the door open and didn't notice I wasn't alone until my guest was halfway to my desk. We needed a bell over the door or one of those buzzers like they have in retail outlets. When I saw who it was, I went around the desk and held the chair for her.

"Hello, Mrs. Shriver," I said.

"Will you call me Eunice?"

"If you'll call me Teddy."

Her hair looked shorter and less blue, perhaps her summer do. She was wearing a pair of those orthopedic shoes with the thick heels over the knee-highs and was carrying the same big handbag. I sat behind my desk, smiled at her, and waited.

"I shall call you Teddy, but only on the condition that you call me Eunice."

I told her we had a rock-solid deal. She asked, "How old are you, Teddy, if I may ask?"

"Thirty-three."

"My youngest son is thirty-four."

"Well, we're practically contemporaries."

"Samuel is thirty-four, Rachel is thirty-seven, Kirk is thirty-nine, and Vernon, my eldest, is forty-two."

"Wow, you must have waited to have them."

"On the contrary, I couldn't wait to have them. I love children, though more abstractly when I was younger."

"That's probably pretty common."

"Do you have any brothers or sisters?"

"My parents decided one little Ruzak was plenty for them."

"Are you close to your parents, Mr. Ruzak?"

"They're both dead."

"Oh, goodness. Ruzak, what sort of name is that?"

"Polish. I'm Polish on my father's side, German, English, and maybe a little Dutch on my mother's."

"I am third-generation Knoxvillian," she said proudly. "My great-grandfather Martin Sparks founded the first full-service laundry facility very close to here, in the Old City."

"That's something," I said. "You know, I've got a dry cleaner's right below me."

"He was also a bootlegger, but the family doesn't talk about that."

"Every family has a few skeletons."

"Tell me, Teddy, do you speak to your parents often?"

"Not anymore. They're dead," I told her again. "But I do visit them and talk to Mom, or at her grave anyway, though sometimes I throw a word or two at Dad. I wasn't that close to him. He worked hard and I didn't see him much growing up."

"It's never too late to mend fences," she said.

"You think so? I guess I always assumed death put the kibosh on patching things up, but hearing that really helps, Eunice. It lifts my spirits. You know, my mom died recently, leaving me a little money, and now any success I have will owe a lot to the fact that she had to die for me to have it, and that's been weighing on me."

"Oh, I know all about that weight. The weight of death."

Here it came. She paused, tears welling in her eyes. She seemed to be waiting for something. I dug in my desk drawer for my mechanical pencil and found my yellow legal pad under a pile of papers.

"I suppose you know why I've come," she said.

"I think I have an idea."

"Must I say it, then?"

"I guess you need to, Eunice."

She nodded, running her palms along the straps of her purse. Both feet were planted firmly on the floor and her back was straight. She had pretty good posture for an old lady.

"I am a murderess, Teddy."

"I thought so," I said. "Did you kill Lydia Marks, Eunice?"

She burst into tears, but her back remained straight, her feet planted firmly on the floor.

"Eunice," I said. "How could you?"

"I wish I could say it was an accident, a horrible accident, but that isn't the truth. I killed her. I killed that poor woman and left her body in the mountains as carrion. Oh, Teddy, what shall become of me?"

"How did you kill her, Eunice?"

"Stabbed her with my sewing needle."

"Really? The coroner said she was bludgeoned to death."

"Oh, yes, yes." She gave a little wave with her mottled hand. "That, too."

"So you killed her and then dragged her up the mountain to leave her for the carrion?"

"Yes. Yes, oh God forgive me, yes."

"Well, I gotta say that's impressive. A woman of your age dragging a corpse nine hundred feet up a mountain."

"I didn't say I acted alone."

"No?"

"You remember I mentioned my son, my eldest, Vernon."

"Sure. Vernon."

"He helped."

"Why?"

"Because the last thing he wants to see is his eighty-six-year-old mother sitting in the electric chair!"

"That would be the last thing anyone would want to see," I said. "What did the police say?"

"They told me to go away. They told me they didn't want to see me anymore."

"You see them a lot, Eunice?"

She didn't answer. She was dabbing her eyes with her white handkerchief.

"If the police won't arrest you," I said, "what is it you want me to do?"

"Help me," she whispered.

"This Vernon, he lives in Knoxville?"

She nodded. "He came over last Sunday and found that woman's body in my basement, covered with an old blanket. He said, 'Mother, why do you have a body in your basement?' So I told him I had killed her and he said, 'Mother, we must not leave this body here. It's begun to stink.' So we put it in the trunk and drove into the park and Vernon carried it over his back up the mountain. I stayed in the car, as a lookout." She looked away. It was hard to tell, but she might have been pretty in her day. Not a stunner, but pretty, and despite her wackiness, there was a dignity about Eunice Shriver, like with a lot of very old people, the pride of having outlasted so much pain and heartache.

"That's a horrible story, Eunice," I said.

"I know it's a horrible story. And what makes it more horrible is nobody but Vernon believes me."

"I believe you, Eunice."

She swung her eyes back in my direction. The hope in them was palpable and heartbreaking.

"Do you? Do you, Teddy? That's all I want. You asked what I wanted, and that is precisely it. I want somebody to believe me."

"Why wouldn't I believe you?" I asked. "You haven't lied to me yet."

"Then you'll help me, Teddy?"

"Sure I'll help you, Eunice."

CHAPTER TWENTY-ONE

THROUGH SOME ACE DETECTIVE WORK, I DISCOVERED THE
name of Susan's brother: Matthew. Matthew Marks. It sounded
like some kind of joke, a biblical play on words. I discovered his
name by calling Susan and asking her for her brother's name and
phone number. He agreed to meet me on the Strip for lunch, a
Mexican fast-food place called Moe's. You ordered your food and
then watched them create your meal in assembly-line fashion.
Moe's was famous for its huge burritos, which were long, stuffed
to overflowing, and extremely bland. I didn't like Moe's—the
food reminded me of myself.

He was a big guy, like his dad, with roughly the same haircut,
except the kid wore his combed forward instead of back, like a
bloated version of an Abercrombie & Fitch model. His face was
wide and pockmarked with acne scars and he had a sort of hooded
look around the eyes that reminded me of a lizard, though I'm not
sure lizards have eyelids.

"I'm only talking to you as a favor to my sister," he told me
after we carried our trays to a table by the window. The sky was
overcast and therefore the world was shadowless, which always
made me feel a little disoriented.

"Sure," I said. "I appreciate it."

I asked him about school. It didn't seem right diving right into the gruesome circumstances of his stepmother's death as we stuffed our mouths with beans, rice, and chunks of greasy ground beef. I also wanted a chance to size him up before getting down to brass tacks. He had a chip on his shoulder, I could tell, like a lot of rich kids who never want for anything. But I figured that chip might come from Lydia being murdered and left as a meal for wild animals.

He said he was just a freshman and hadn't decided on a major. "What about business?" I asked. "You're the only son, right? Maybe your dad would—"

"My dad," he sneered. "Don't start with my dad. I hardly know the guy. He was never home when I was growing up. I was raised by my mother."

"Yeah, your mother . . ."

"Not Lydia. Lydia was never my mother."

"You and Lydia didn't get along?"

He shrugged. The shrug is a gesture we lose as we get older, reaching its peak usage when we're around twenty-five. I'm not sure why that is. Maybe there's less to shrug about, which is ironic, because you think you know it all at twenty. I have a theory the shrug was born with the advent of organized sports, because, no matter the sport, players always do it after a penalty's called against them. The shoulders hunch, the arms come up, hands palm upward, like, What? *What?*

"I didn't know her very good," Matt said. "You wanna know how all that happened? One day, Dad comes walking in the door and says, 'Kids, here's your new mother.'"

"What happened to the old one?"

"She died, man. When I was fifteen."

"That's tough. My mother died just recently."

"Yeah, but you're what, forty? I was fifteen."

"Actually, I'm thirty-three, but a lot of people think I'm older."

"You don't have the baby face like a lot of fat guys."

I set down my burrito and sipped my diet Coke.

"How'd your mom die?"

"Car accident."

"Bummer."

"What did you say? Did you just say 'bummer'? What is this, Ruzak? You trying to relate to me or something?"

"No. I honestly thought it was a bummer. Bummer was my first reaction to the news your mother died in a car accident. I thought, Bummer. So that's what I said. What happened?"

"A truck ran her off the road. She hit a tree. She died."

"I'm tempted to say 'That sucks.' "

"What are you talking about? It does suck."

"How did your father and Lydia meet?"

"Why don't you ask him?"

"Was it in Ireland?"

"No, it was in fucking Afghanistan. Of course it was in Ireland. She was Irish, for Christ sakes!"

"So he travels a lot on business."

"I think I said that. You're not much of a detective, are you? Yeah, he travels all the damn time. England, Ireland, the Netherlands, Russia, Turkey, South Africa, you name it, wherever the almighty dollar leads him."

"How's he make it? The almighty dollar?"

"Didn't Suze tell you? He's a smuggler."

I laughed.

"I'm serious, man. He smuggles. You name it—drugs, weapons, even people. Human contraband, Ruzak. You know, slavery. My dad is a slaver." He laughed. I wondered if he was putting me on and decided he probably was. I was wasting my time, but I told myself I wasn't always going to be dealing with a cooperative witness.

"Why do you think Lydia's dead?"

"Because somebody killed her. What do you think?"

"I mean, do you think somebody she knew—"

"Man, Lydia didn't know anybody over here. She refused to make any friends. She spent about two thousand dollars a month in phone charges to the Emerald Isle to talk to her family over there. I always wondered why the hell she married my father and moved here if she loved it over there so damned much."

"Susan said she loved your father. Adored him."

He shrugged again. "I guess it's easy to love somebody who isn't there."

I said, "Why didn't she travel with him? What kept her in Knoxville while he jet-setted all over the world?"

"What did my sister say?"

"I haven't asked her."

"If anybody would know, it'd be Suze. Really, I never hung around Lydia much."

"Well, that's understandable. I mean, it's hard to accept a step-parent in the best of circumstances."

"Oh, it wasn't that. That woman gave me the creeps."

"Why did she give you the creeps?"

"She never talked much. Just stared at you all the time with this stupid smile on her face." He gave his best imitation of the smile, but I didn't think he was very good at imitating attractive Irish women. "You know? And when she did say something, it was always . . . oh, shit, I don't know, always so calm and almost whispery, almost like she was putting on an act or was doped up or something."

"When your dad was around—were they real affectionate with each other?"

"Man, why would I notice something like that? You think I'm some kind of pervert?"

He finished his burrito in one awe-inspiring face-stuffing orgy of sauce and dripping hamburger juice.

"So . . . ," I said, knowing this was a signal my interview was almost over, "Lydia wasn't having an affair or anything of that nature . . . as far as you know?"

"Ruzak, that woman was about as sexy as a telephone pole. No personality at all, you know? Kind of pretty, though she didn't have any shape. I never got what my father saw in her, but to each his own. I never saw the mailman hanging around, if that's what you're asking. But like I said, I wasn't around much. Maybe she was screwing the whole neighborhood."

He stood up. I kept sitting.

"One more question," I said. "Who do you think killed Lydia?"

He leaned over the table, bringing his face so close that I could smell the spices on his breath.

"The British secret service. She was IRA, Ruzak. Dad's a sympathizer and the marriage was a sham to get her out of the country. But the Brits found out where she was hiding and took her out."

"You think so?"

He just laughed and shrugged. "I gotta go back home and pack."

"Thanks for talking to me, Matt."

"Thanks for the burrito, dick. That's what they call detectives, right? Dicks?"

He sauntered out the door while I sat there watching his shoulders give a little roll—the same way his father walked. I didn't feel as if I'd learned anything, and now I had a very bad case of indigestion. What bothered me about where Lydia Marks was found was that it would take a pretty big guy to haul a dead body up a mountain through dense woods. Matt was big enough. But then she might have been marched up that mountain at gunpoint, and practically anybody can point a gun, even me. I just can't shoot one with any accuracy.

CHAPTER TWENTY-TWO

THE WHOLE MARKS FAMILY LEFT THE NEXT DAY TO BURY the remains of Lydia in the family plot in Dublin. Now, the first Mrs. Marks was buried right in Knoxville, which raised the vexing question (at least to me) of where Kenneth would spend eternity—beside his first wife in Tennessee or his second across the pond?

"Say you were married," I told Felicia.

"Why say I was married?"

"I'm posing a hypothetical."

"I love it when you talk like a college professor. How're you able to do that, Ruzak, seeing you never went to college?"

"I read the dictionary."

"Really? How often?"

"Every day. Usually while I'm in the john."

"Did anybody ever point out to you the dictionary's not the kind of book you *read*."

"It goes back to my Dictionary Ruzak days. When I was a kid living in St. Louis, this group of neighborhood boys invited me to join their club, which met over one of the kids' garage, and I went to one meeting where they swapped these mysterious hand signals and spoke in code words that meant nothing to me but a great deal to them, and they laughed the whole time at inside jokes that nobody bothered to explain to me. They told me I had to pick a handle only the club members would know—it was sort of a benign gang—and I told them to call me 'Dictionary,' because I was going through my *Encyclopedia Brown* phase. That cracked them up. For the rest of the meeting, they asked me to spell words like *xylophone* and *oxymoron*. It was the first and last meeting I went to."

"You know what, Ruzak? You're the kind of guy who gets asked what time it is and then tells the person how to build a watch."

"Can I finish my hypothetical?"

"Sure, I can't do anything anyway until my nails finish drying." The polish was bloodred, to match her dress. She might have been sick the past few days, but she had managed to drag herself out of her sickbed to visit the salon. Her hair wasn't quite so blond anymore and I detected a hint of auburn. Women in general are restless when it comes to their appearance. There may be a Darwinian component to this, but I never really took the time to think it through.

"So you get married and something happens to your husband."

"He dies."

"Or runs off on you or—no, let's just say he dies and at the time he dies, you love him."

"Okay. Husband. Dead. Love him. Go on."

"A few years go by and although you can't imagine ever falling in love again, you do, and you get married a second time."

"For what?"

"For a second time."

"No, I mean for what reason am I marrying a second time? Love? Money? Blackmail?"

"Love. Deep, deep love."

"Okay. I could see that happening."

"So then he dies."

"He dies, too?"

"Or you die—that really doesn't matter."

"We both die?"

"Not at the same time. Well, it could be at the same time for the purpose of the hypothetical."

"All this is going somewhere, right?"

"Right. So here's the hypothetical . . ."

"You love saying that word, don't you? You should see your lips when you say it, especially the 'po' part." She pursed her lips at me. "Hy*po*thetical."

"Can I finish?" I was just acting sore. Inside, I was glad she was in a better mood. "So, which one would you want to be buried next to—your first love or your second?"

"This is important?"

"It's been vexing me."

"I don't know, Ruzak. It sounds like one of those questions the Pharisees threw at Jesus. Probably the first husband."

"Why?"

"He had dibs."

"So it's a question of first come, first served? What if you loved the second guy more?"

"You didn't say that in your hypo. You just said I loved him, too, which implies I loved him equally. Of course I'd want to be next to the one I loved the most."

"What do you think the odds are, one wife getting killed in a freak auto accident and the other murdered by some psychopath?"

"Pretty damn long."

"That's what I thought."

"You think that's what the cops are thinking?"

"But Marks was out of the country."

"People like him don't get their hands dirty, Ruzak. He hired somebody to do it, the same way Parker Hudson hired you to find the goose killer."

I thought about telling her of his offer to give up the killer for two million dollars, then decided not to. One hypothetical was enough for one morning.

"What's his motive, though?" I asked. "Susan said he was nuts about her and her him, and besides, even though I'm sure there was life insurance, the guy's already richer than God."

"Really? What did you say his phone number was?"

"Money really does overcome everything," I said. "This guy might have killed two wives and you're jumping in line to be number three."

"Maybe he didn't kill her to get money, but to save it."

"She was threatening divorce? But Susan said—"

"Okay, then. Money and jealously aren't the only motives for murder, Ruzak."

I thought about it. "Blackmail?"

"Maybe the kid was right in a way. Maybe the marriage was a sham, like she made him marry her and get her to America because she had something on him, and the only way to remove the threat was by removing her."

"But what could that be?"

She stuck her tongue out at me. "You're the investigative consultant."

I went to my desk and called Deputy Paul's number. The dispatcher told me he was on patrol and couldn't be reached. I left my number. Then I called Parker Hudson to remind him of our appointment with the hypnotherapist.

"You're really going to make me go through with this," he said.

"Well, I guess the only thing that could make you is your conscience," I replied.

"You know what I like about you, Teddy? On the outside,

you're just a cuddly big ol' bear, but on the inside, you're a scrappy little bulldog."

"Makes for a lethal combination," I said.

I told Felicia I was going out for some legwork and she said it looked like I needed it. I walked out the door with downcast eyes, like a puppy scolded by its mistress. Verity comes at you that way: Parker Hudson described it; then Felicia encapsulated it.

I walked one block west to the Lawson McGee Library and took the stairs two flights up to the periodicals room. Matthew Marks was a freshman in college and his mother died when he was fifteen, which meant the accident happened no more than four years ago. I told the lady at the desk what I needed and she disappeared down an aisle that was marked EMPLOYEES ONLY. She came back after a minute with four microfiche cartridges, sat me down in one of the little booths against the wall, and showed me how to use the reading machine. Not to propagate stereotypes, but she was in her mid-fifties, wore no makeup, and smelled of old paper.

She left me alone. My eyes were pretty worn-out by the end of it, but I finally found the story two hours later in the September 17, 2000, issue of the *Sentinel.* I located the obituary that ran three days later and asked the periodicals lady to make copies. I paid her for the copies, fifteen cents per page, and made the remark that at fifteen cents per page, you wondered where all your tax money was going. She curtly asked if there was anything else she could help me with, and from that, I gathered she was trying to show that my tax money paid her salary. I told her yes, there was something else, and asked for a receipt.

I walked back to the office. Deputy Gary Paul was standing at Felicia's desk and they were both laughing, but they abruptly stopped laughing when I walked in. It was clear to me by that point that Felicia had a thing for guys in uniform—firemen and cops and probably military types—but drew the line at security guards.

"Teddy!" Deputy Paul said, and we shook hands. He followed me into my office and sank into one of the visitor's chairs. Like Barbara Eden sans the bare midriff, Felicia appeared at his elbow with a fresh cup of coffee. She left without offering me any.

"So what's up with the goose killer?"

"Parker Hudson is getting hypnotized tomorrow. We're gonna regress him to the day of the killing. It's a long shot, but—" I shrugged. I had noticed I was shrugging more after my meeting with Matthew Marks. I am very impressionable where tics and mannerisms are concerned.

"Kenneth Marks's first wife was run off I-Forty five years ago, going about eighty miles per hour," I told Deputy Paul. "Her car flew over an embankment and smashed head-on into a tree, killing her instantly. The other driver kept going and, as far as I can tell, was never caught."

"Okay."

"Witnesses described the other vehicle as a white delivery truck with no identifying markings."

"And?"

"And four years later, Kenneth Marks's second wife disappears into thin air."

"Yeah," he drawled. There were dark circles under his eyes. I wondered if he had been rotated to the night shift. Then I remembered the dispatcher telling me earlier that he was on patrol. "I'm sure the task force is looking very carefully into the affairs of Ken Marks."

"But if he's our perp, there's one thing I don't understand." I told him about Marks's offer to pay me two million dollars to find Lydia's killer and forgo telling the police. "Isn't that a crime?"

"Not the offer. It becomes one if you actually did it."

"But my point is, if Marks is our man, why would he make an offer like that?"

He shook his head. "No idea. If I had an idea, Teddy, I probably wouldn't be a patrol officer."

"Should I tell the task force?"

"That's up to you."

"Would you?"

"You bet I would."

"Where are they with all this? Do you know?"

"They believe Lydia was alive when she was taken into the Smokys. Killed where the hikers found her."

"How do they know that?"

"Logic, Ruzak. It would be next to impossible to hike twelve miles from the nearest road, up a mountain, and through dense woods carrying deadweight like that, unless you're Paul Bunyan."

That had been my theory, and I felt a flush of pride that I was thinking along the same lines as professional law enforcement.

"How was she killed?"

"Multiple blows to the head by a heavy object. Still working on what that object might be, but that and the kill zone pretty much rule out a professional job."

"How come?"

"Professionals don't operate that way—too much risk. A professional kills on first contact, quickly, and disengages ASAP from the kill zone. If Lydia Marks was a contract job, she would have been taken in her house in the dead of night, one shot through the head as she slept, or something like that. The way she was taken and killed—way too many opportunities for witnesses and mistakes."

"So they think it was somebody she knew."

"Or it still could be some psychopath, a stranger killing her."

"Which is another point for Kenneth. He was in Brussels when she died."

"Some people just have crappy luck, Ruzak."

"His luck isn't so crappy. At least he's still alive."

CHAPTER TWENTY-THREE

PARKER HUDSON MET FELICIA AND ME AT THE THERAPIST'S office on Wiesgarber, between Kingston Pike and Papermill Drive, within walking distance of the Krispy Kreme place on the Pike. As we drove past, I pointed out to Felicia the HOT sign was lighted.

"We can't stop, Ruzak," she said. "We're late as it is."

"I like to sit at the counter and watch the conveyor belts in the oven room with all the rows and rows of fresh doughnuts going down the line."

"Maybe you should work a second job at the Krispy Kreme."

"But then I'd weigh about four hundred pounds."

Parker Hudson was not late. He was standing by his Mercedes in the parking lot, wearing a windbreaker over a polo shirt and tan slacks.

"What's that?" He pointed at the recorder I was carrying.

"A tape recorder. This has evidentiary potential."

"'Evidentiary potential'?"

"Teddy reads the dictionary in the john," Felicia said.

"Old habit," I told him. "What do you read?"

"*Field & Stream* and *Golf Digest*. Sometimes *The Wall Street Journal.*"

"Seems too heavy."

"Depends on the bathroom I'm in."

Felicia laughed, for some reason. She was wearing a navy blue pantsuit with a white blouse and only moderately high heels. Parker Hudson eyed her backside appreciatively as we went through the door. It doesn't matter how old you get; the procreative drive stays with us to the grave. They say Picasso fathered children well into his old age. But being an artist, of course, he never really grew up, and responsibility wasn't high on his list. Not that he couldn't afford a stableful of progeny. I saw somewhere that his signature on a check for a million dollars would be worth more than the check for a million dollars.

It's probably hard to make a living solely practicing hypnotherapy, so Dr. Stephanie Fredericks also practiced your regular type of therapy. The diplomas on her walls said she had a Ph.D. and an M.D. from Michigan State. The receptionist gave Parker Hudson a stack of forms to fill out, including a medical release form stating he couldn't hold Dr. Fredericks liable if she regressed him to memories that drove him crazy. Under the question of who was financially responsible for the account, he wrote, "THE DIC." I guessed this was his way of registering his protest to the whole hypnosis angle.

"You should do it, too, Ruzak," Felicia said.

"How come?"

"Maybe you'll get the tag right, even a description of the driver."

"Yeah."

" 'Yeah,' you might if you did, or 'yeah,' you're gonna do it, too?"

"Our appointment is only for Parker. Maybe I'll come back."

"I don't see how I can be morally obligated and yet you have a choice," Parker Hudson said. He was clearly nervous.

"Memories usually get repressed only if they're involving some kind of catastrophic event," I said. "Like the dead baby geese."

"You've done some research into repressed memories?" he asked.
"I've looked into it."

"Oh, he talked to the shrink about five minutes," Felicia said. "Don't listen to him."

I gave her a look. Whose side was she on? My palms were sweating at the thought of being hypnotized. I'd never been what you might call a control freak, but the thought of entering some kind of altered state that included the danger of quacking like a duck unnerved me.

"Personally, I think it's all a bunch of hogwash," Parker Hudson said. "I don't think it works, and haven't there been studies that show a lot of repressed memories aren't really memories at all, but manufactured to fit someone's expectations?"

"No stone unturned," I said.

"Unless the stone is resting on your big fat behind," Felicia said.

"You know," I said, "I'm getting pretty tired of the remarks about my butt. I know I have a big butt. You don't have to point it out every five minutes." The receptionist was staring at me, but I didn't care. "I don't point out your pug nose to you."

"I beg your pardon? You don't point out my *what?*"

"Are you two married?" Parker Hudson asked.

"Good God, no," Felicia said, and that broke the tension—at least for her—and she laughed.

The inner door opened and Dr. Fredericks leaned out and smiled, waving us in. She was an attractive lady in her middle fifties, maybe, dressed in a conservative business suit with sensible heels. She led us to her office and I made the introductions. She explained how the procedure worked and what we could expect. Parker might remember more details, she said, or he might remember nothing new at all. She admitted she might not even be successful at putting Parker under; a lot depended on the patient.

Parker sat directly across from her and rubbed the pads of his thumbs against his palms.

"Where do we do this?" he asked.

"Right here," Dr. Fredericks said. She had a very melodious voice, which probably came in handy in her line of work. "Just remember, hypnosis isn't magic and it has nothing to do with mind control. Our goal is to lower your normal inhibitions and let what bubbles to the surface bubble."

Her voice and manner seemed to calm Parker somewhat, and he followed her obediently to the sofa.

"How would you be most comfortable, Mr. Hudson? Lying down or sitting up?"

"I might fall asleep if I lie down." He sank into the sofa and closed his eyes, folding his hands over his stomach. Dr. Fredericks gave a little smile in our direction.

"What do you want us to do?" I asked.

"You can stay, if that's all right with Mr. Hudson. Just be quiet, please. If you have any questions you want answered, write them down on that pad right there and pass it to me. Once we begin, the only voice I want him to hear is mine."

She turned the lights down and pulled a chair close to the sofa. Soft music was playing through hidden speakers and I wondered when she had turned the sound on. I expected her to pull out a watch or hold up her pen, like on TV or in the movies, but she just started talking. Her spiel was very repetitive; she told Parker to relax and imagine himself completely at ease, in a place of his choosing, maybe on a little boat on a lake or, if he didn't like water, lying on the shore in the shade. She went on like this for maybe five or ten minutes, and Parker Hudson didn't move a muscle. For a second, I was afraid he had fallen asleep.

Then Dr. Fredericks said, "Parker."

"Yes."

"I'm going to take you back now. I want you to imagine there's a doorway in front of you. The door is closed right now. Can you see the door?"

"Yes."

"Parker, on the other side of that door is yesterday. I want you to go to the door and open it. It isn't locked."

"Open the door?"

"Yes. Go ahead and open it."

"Okay. I'm opening the door."

I realized at that point that I had forgotten to turn the tape recorder on. I hit the record button and it sounded very loud in the space. Dr. Fredericks gave me a look over her shoulder and Felicia jabbed me in the side with her elbow.

"What do you see?" Dr. Fredericks asked Parker Hudson.

"Yesterday . . ."

"Now you aren't just watching, Parker. You are really there, in yesterday. What are you doing?"

"Making a BLT."

"You're in the kitchen?"

"Yes. The lettuce is going bad. She should have picked up some fresh lettuce."

"Your wife?"

"Yes. Damn it. She always forgets something, though she walks out the door with her purse stuffed with coupons and a list half a mile long. Always something. Then she'll pick up a jar of pickles, when we have five jars sitting in the pantry. Or mustard. We'll be out of milk but have sixteen bags of M&M's lying around."

"How is your sandwich?"

"Good, except the lettuce is wilted."

Felicia looked at her watch. At this rate, we'd be on the lake with Parker by early fall.

"Parker, I want you to look up. Right in front of you is another door. Do you see it?"

"I'm not finished with my sandwich."

"Do you want to finish your sandwich?"

"No." He sighed. "I guess not."

"Do you see the door?"

"Yes."

"On the other side of that door is last week. I want you to go to it, open it, and tell me what you're doing."

"I'm playing golf. I'm losing. The rest of my foursome are drunk."

"You're not?"

"I never drink and play. But I'm losing, so maybe I should."

This went on for another twenty minutes or so. She led him through door after door, until they came to the last door. I glanced down at my tape. It was sixty minutes per side and we were already halfway through side A. I wondered if I'd wake him if I had to stop and flip the cassette.

"Do you see the door, Parker?" Dr. Fredericks asked.

"Yes, I see it," Parker said. His voice had been calm, but now there was an edge to it, the same edge as when he'd talked about the wilted lettuce.

"This is the last door, Parker. On the other side is the morning of April sixteenth. Does that date mean anything to you, Parker?"

"Yes. It's the day the goslings died."

"How do you feel? Would you like to go through this door?"

"Yes." He sighed. "Yes. I guess I do."

"Then open the door, Parker, and walk through."

She waited while he walked through.

"Where are you, Parker?" she asked.

"The trail."

"You are walking on the trail?"

"Yes."

"What do you see?"

"The park. The lake. The old fence. The field. Railroad tracks. The sun is just coming up. Mist on the water. I love that."

"You love what?"

"The way the mist rises over the water in the early morning. The lake is perfectly calm and mist rises on the surface. Beautiful . . ."

"Do you see anyone else?"

"No, I'm alone. It's very early. Dawn. Not a soul. I love this. My favorite time of day. Just me. Just me."

He was smiling, content as a Buddha.

"Can you take a picture for me?"

"I don't have my camera. . . ."

"No, but try freezing what you see."

" 'Freezing'?"

"Stop it. Like you're watching a movie at home. Pause the movie."

"Okay."

"Did you pause it?"

"Yes. The mist isn't moving now."

"Good. Start it again. Remember you can pause the movie whenever you want to. Whenever I tell you to stop the movie, will you stop it for me?"

"Yes."

"Good. Are you still walking?"

"Yes."

"Which direction are you walking, Parker?"

"East."

"And you're walking the trail on the north side of the road, so the road is on your right. And across the road?"

"The park and the lake. Oh, there're some geese."

I straightened in the chair and checked my tape. Felicia was leaning forward, her elbow on her knee, her chin on her fist.

"You see geese?"

"They nest here every year. I've seen these geese. I know these geese. Oh, it's a family! The babies have hatched!"

"Where are the geese, Parker?"

"Right on the trail, about a hundred yards in front of me. Two adults and—let's see—one, two, three, four, five goslings—no, six! I didn't see that little piker behind one of the adults."

"And still no people? Nobody on the trail?"

"No one. Oh, I wish I had my camera."

"What are the geese doing?"

"They're coming out of the field, crossing the trail. Going toward the road."

"They're leading the babies back to the water?"

"They must be . . . yes, there they go. The big male, he's leading, and there they go! How orderly they are, in a perfect line. He's leading the babies and she's in the rear."

"Now, Parker, I want you to stop the picture but keep the sound going. Can you do that?"

"Yes."

"What do you hear?"

"He's honking, just braying to beat the band. It's like he's saying, 'Watch out! Get out of our way! Geese crossing!' "

"What else do you hear?"

"Other birds. The sound of cars, very far off. My own breath. Oh, now there's something else."

He fell silent with a small sigh.

"What else do you hear, Parker?"

"A car. It's loud . . . getting louder . . ."

"Where? In front of you? Behind you?"

"Behind me . . . coming up behind me . . ."

"Okay, now I want you to start the movie again. You're walking on the trail toward the geese; the geese are crossing the road toward the lake. And now you hear a car coming up behind you. . . ."

"It's going very fast. . . ."

"You see the car?"

"No, but its engine . . . very loud . . . revving up."

"Do you turn toward the sound, Parker?"

"No . . . I'm watching the geese . . . middle of the road . . . stretched all the way across, like a cordon of geese. . . . Oh God! Oh no!"

"Freeze the picture!" Dr. Fredericks raised her voice slightly. Parker was breathing heavily now and I could see a sheen of sweat on his forehead.

"What do you see?"

"Black. Big. Middle of the road. Son of a bitch!"

"Describe it, Parker. What kind of car is it?"

"Oh God, it's going to hit the babies!"

"Focus on the car, Parker. Is it still frozen?"

"Yes."

"Then the babies are okay. Don't worry about the babies right now. Look at the car."

"It isn't a car. It's one of those gas-guzzling SUVs. It's big. Big tires. Black."

"Can you tell what make it is?"

He mumbled something and she repeated the question.

"I don't know cars very well . . . makes of cars. . . . It's big and black and it's very loud. . . . Don't they hear it? *Do* they hear it? Oh, they don't know. They don't know what's going to happen. Do they know?"

"Parker, you are in control. You can stop the movie anytime you want. Do you understand?"

"Yes. I am in control."

"Do you see the license tag? Can you see what state the car is from?"

"Oh, yes. Tennessee. It's a Tennessee tag."

"Are you certain?"

"It's very clear. . . ."

This was it. I knew what she was going to ask next. I held my breath.

"Can you see the numbers on the tag, Parker? Can you read them?"

"Oh dear God . . . dear God, those babies . . ."

"Parker, you're looking at the SUV now. The movie's stopped and you can study the car as long as you like. Are you looking at the tag?"

"Yes. Yes, I'm looking at it."

"What are the numbers?"

"It's letters . . . letters and numbers."

"Ah, come on," Felicia whispered. "I can't take it anymore."

"H . . ."

"The first letter is an *H?*"

"Yes. I see it very clearly now. HRT. Those are the letters."

I felt my heart thumping hard in my chest. I was going to solve this case. I was going to hand a terrific lead to the task force and maybe collect half a million dollars. Most importantly, I was going to keep my promise to Susan Marks.

"And the numbers? What are the numbers, Parker?"

"Seven . . . one . . . nine . . ."

"Seven one nine?"

"Yes. Yes. I see it very clearly. HRT seven one nine."

Dr. Fredericks looked over at us and gave a thumbs-up. Then she turned back to Parker.

"Now, the movie is still frozen. Can you see inside the car, Parker?"

"No. Black windows. Tinted. I can't see inside."

"Can you look around for me? Do you see anyone else? Is there another car on the road? Anyone walking on the trail?"

"There's no one . . . no one but me. . . . I'm going to start the movie."

"Parker, you don't need to—"

"No, I'm going to start it again. . . ."

"Parker, don't start the movie."

"It's moving. Oh my God! My God!" His body stiffened and his right hand gripped the couch's armrest. "He's going to hit them! Get out of the way! Clear out of there! He isn't going to stop! Oh, for the love of Jesus! Feathers! Feathers! Blood and feathers! And oh God, he didn't even slow down, the son of a bitch! He didn't even swerve! Oh God, they're flat as pancakes, but look—one's still alive! Half its body is smushed and it's crying! 'Mommy! Daddy!' And they're screaming. Mommy and Daddy are screaming and flapping their wings and their necks are stretched as far as they'll go, and oh, the rage! The rage and loss! Bloody road! Oh, the babies! The little itty-bitty baby birdies!"

I heard a sound beside me. Felicia had a hand over her mouth. Tears glistened in her eyes, but the sound I thought I heard coming from behind her hand was the sound of suppressed laughter.

CHAPTER TWENTY-FOUR

Dr. Fredericks slowly woke Parker Hudson from his movie memories, and when she asked him how he felt, he said, "Very thirsty," and she left the room to fetch a glass of water. He was a little breathy and sweating pretty hard.

"Well, Teddy. I suppose you were right and I was wrong."

"You remember what just happened?"

"I remember everything now. HRT seven one nine. That was the tag."

"You're sure?"

He nodded. Dr. Fredericks came back with an Evian. She turned up the lights, went to her desk, and sat down.

"There's something we all need to remember," she said. "Hypnotic regression has not been shown to be one hundred percent reliable. I'm sure you've heard about cases that have gone to trial, particularly cases of past sexual abuse, where the victim has not actually accessed repressed memories, but invented them out of whole cloth, usually through the hypnotic suggestion of the therapist. I was very careful not to ask Parker any leading questions, but the danger remains that he is taking postevent information and inserting it into the event."

"Wow," I said. "What's that mean?"

"For example, after your encounter with a black SUV near your apartment, you told Parker you thought the letters on the tag were *HRT*. Obviously, since these letters were on the same type of car Parker saw, you assumed it was the same vehicle. You planted both the letters and the connection to the event in Parker's mind. Just now, as he was reliving it, it is possible he overlaid that information on the event matrix."

"So he could have seen different letters?"

"The likelihood, if that is what happened, is that he saw no letters at all, and his mind supplied the missing detail with information provided by you."

"But what about the numbers? I didn't see any numbers."

"He might have seen the numbers that day and they very well may have been seven one nine, just as he might have actually seen the letters *HRT*. But they could also represent any number of things—a date that's significant in his life, or numbers from a tag he casually glanced at in traffic two weeks ago. Or they may be completely random. The point is, you have to take any information gathered in hypnosis with a grain of salt."

"No," Parker said firmly. "I know what I saw. I saw them as clearly as I'm seeing you right now."

"This is terrific," I said, trying to stay upbeat. Dr. Fredericks had practically killed the party. "It gives us something to work from. It might be nothing, but it could be everything. Thanks a lot, Doc."

We said good-bye to Parker in the parking lot.

"That woman is wrong," he said. "I remember now. HRT seven one nine. That was the tag number."

"Well, there's still no proof it's connected to Lydia Marks, but if you're right, we've got your goose killer."

"And it's been worth every penny. I want that SOB prosecuted to the full extent of the law."

I told him I'd have an answer for him in a few days. I could get the name from Deputy Paul, but I wanted to talk to the driver first, to see if I could wrest a confession out of him. Parker Hudson agreed that probably was the best course of action. He didn't look good. He looked like somebody who had been laid up in bed with the flu for a couple of weeks.

I drove back to Kingston Pike and made a left toward downtown.

"You know," I said to Felicia, "we could grab half a dozen to celebrate."

"Are you always thinking about food?"

She started to laugh.

"What?" I asked.

" 'The babies! The itty-bitty baby birdies!' "

"Felicia."

"Well, I'm sorry. It's funny."

"It's grotesque."

"Your first case solved. How's it feel, Ruzak?"

"It isn't solved yet."

CHAPTER TWENTY-FIVE

I CALLED GARY PAUL'S NUMBER THE MINUTE I GOT BACK TO the office. The dispatcher told me he was off duty and refused to give me his home number, even after I told her it was a matter of the utmost urgency. I managed to wrest a promise from her that she would page him and give him my message. Felicia was staring at me as I hung up.

"Are you done? I have to make a phone call."

"I had a couple more calls, but go ahead."

She disappeared around the half wall and I leaned back in my big leather chair and congratulated my big bulldog self. My PI exam was coming up and I was sure I'd ace it with flying colors. Though there were lots of questions about Tennessee law. I had gotten hold of a sample exam from the administrating company, but I had no idea what some of the questions meant. I was brimming over with confidence, though. The newspaper article might have been Felicia's idea, but hypnosis had been mine, and it looked like hypnosis was going to be the hammer that cracked this case wide open.

"I'm changing my name to Teddy 'the Hammer' Ruzak!" I called out to Felicia.

"I'm on the phone!" she shouted back. Then she came into the room and said, "I have to go."

"Is something wrong?"

"No, nothing's wrong. I just have to go."

"Felicia, wait. . . ."

"What is it, Ruzak? I'm in a hurry."

"It's just that—well, you've been missing a lot of work lately. . . ."

"You're not going to try to fire me again, are you?"

"I didn't try the first time. I was going to ask if everything was all right. I mean, you've been pretty upset and distracted over the past few weeks. . . ."

"It's nothing. Okay? Everything's fine. I don't need anything from you, Ruzak, just a paycheck, which, by the way, has been sitting on your desk for two days and you still haven't signed it."

"Really? It has?" I dug through the papers on my desktop. "Jeez, I'm sorry. Here."

She snatched the check from my hand.

"We had a deal, Ruzak. Personal lives stay personal. Maybe if things ever got busier around here, my being gone would matter more."

"I get a feeling they will now."

"You and your feelings."

"Look, it isn't personal. I'm not trying to pry; I just want you to know if there's anything I can do."

"There's nothing anyone can do. I'll see you tomorrow."

I thought there was maybe a fifty-fifty chance of that, but I didn't say anything but good-bye. As usual, I felt smaller when Felicia wasn't around. The office got bigger and I got smaller. I went back to my desk and started to dial the number for the task force, then set down the receiver before I hit the last number. I really didn't have anything yet, and Detective Watson already thought I was a borderline kook. It would be better for the case and better for me if I waited till I had a name.

I set the tape recorder on my desk and played back the tape of Parker Hudson's hypnotic session. He whispered in some parts, but the part about the tag was very clear, because he was nearly shouting by that point. I turned it off before it reached the part about the itty-bitty babies. That was too tough to listen to. Parker Hudson had lived a long time, by statistical standards, and it was reassuring to know that not all of us go completely numb by the time our hair's white. The lives of six goslings still matter to some of us.

The phone rang. It was Deputy Paul.

"You've got the killer," he said.

"Hey," I said. "Sorry to bother you on your day off."

"I'm always happy to hear from my favorite detective."

"Thanks, but technically I'm not a detective yet. Still working on getting my license." I told him about Parker Hudson's revelation during the hypnosis session. I repeated the tag number twice for him.

"Looks like we might have him," he said. "Did you call the task force with this yet?"

"The therapist said it might be a blind alley—you know, a false memory or something like that. I couldn't exactly follow everything she said."

"Right. And we still don't have a connection between ol' HRT and Lydia Marks. Better to wait. I'll call my contact with the DMV and call you right back, okay?"

"That'd be great."

"Okay. And Ted? Good work on this, bud."

I hung up, my cheeks positively glowing. Maybe this detective thing wasn't such a dopey idea after all.

"HRT seven one nine, here I come," I said aloud in the empty room.

CHAPTER TWENTY-SIX

I SPENT THE REST OF THE AFTERNOON STUDYING FOR MY PI exam and waiting for Gary Paul to call back with the identity of HRT 719. At 4:45, he still hadn't called, so I watered the plants, shut down Felicia's computer, and locked up for the night.

I went downstairs to the street. The lights were still on inside the dry cleaner's and I could hear the machines humming through the walls. When I first leased the place, I thought renting above a dry cleaner's was a savvy move on my part. Your businessmen and other professional types—who else would be dropping off dry cleaning downtown? Every time they came by, they'd see my sign on the side of the building, and who else except a professional could afford to hire a PI?

I didn't feel like driving home to my empty apartment. As I was waiting for Deputy Paul's second call, I was thinking I should celebrate solving my first case and figured I should eat at the Old City Diner, where I'd celebrated getting my first case. Technically, there was nothing to celebrate yet, but I was still hungry, the diner was close and, after studying for hours for an exam I had no prayer of passing, I didn't have the mental capacity to think of another place.

I ordered a steak, medium-well, a baked potato, and a house salad with Thousand Island dressing. Freddy, the owner of the diner, must have seen me sitting there, because he came around the counter in his white smock and thick-soled running shoes and walked to my table.

"Ruzak," he said. Freddy had bright red hair and a face full of freckles. "Haven't seen you in a while."

"I've been pretty busy with my new business."

"Oh, yeah. Detective, right?"

"Investigative consultant—at least until I get my detective license."

"Well, that's terrific. Good for you. How's Felicia doin'? She went to work for you, didn't she?"

"Yeah." I averted my eyes. He might be sore for me taking her away from him. He didn't act sore, though.

"She's a good little girl. Did you know she was about a semester shy of getting her nursing degree at UT before she dropped out?"

"I didn't know that. I just thought—well, I thought she was just a waitress."

"There's always more to folks than meets the eye, Ruzak. But you're an investigative consultant now; you know all that."

"We don't discuss personal issues in the office," I said. "Why did she drop out?"

"Never said."

"Can I ask you something, Freddy? Did Felicia miss a lot of work?"

"Called in sick a lot, but she always found somebody to cover for her."

"Was she? Is she? Sick, I mean."

"I don't see her anymore, Ruzak."

"Is something wrong with her, like some kind of disease she doesn't like to talk about?"

"There's a lot Felicia don't like to talk about."

"Like what?"

His small blue eyes narrowed at me.

"Maybe she wouldn't like me telling you things."

"I'm not being nosey."

"Sounds like you are."

"It's just—well, I don't know what I'm going to do. She's in only three days a week at most, and then those days she does come in, she usually ends up taking off early."

"Here's a radical suggestion: Fire her."

"She keeps daring me to."

"I know you got a kind of thing for her—"

"Freddy, I don't have a thing for Felicia. . . ."

"You always did. Got those puppy dog eyes for her. Everybody around here saw it. Hey, Lacey!"

She yelled back, "What?"

"Didn't Ruzak here have the hots for Felicia?"

"You bet he did. Everybody knew it."

"Everybody except Ruzak!" he yelled back, and that cracked everybody up, including strangers who were staring at me as they chewed.

He turned back to me triumphantly.

"It's business, Ruzak. You can't let your feelings get in the way. Fire her and tell her if she needs a job, I could always use a good waitress."

He walked back behind the counter, wiping his hands on his filthy apron before slapping a couple more burgers on the grill. My face was burning and I was sorry I had brought the whole thing up. He was hiding something, probably to protect her. Or maybe he was trying to get me to fire her so he could hire her back.

I ate my meal faster than I should have; you always eat faster when you eat alone. It sat like a brick on my gut as I drove home.

I didn't really want to go home, but I had no idea where else to go. That's pretty lousy, home being the place you go when you have no place better to go.

You should feel good, Ruzak, I told myself. Why don't you feel good? You would think living alone would free me from all the normal burdens of responsibility that people complain or worry about, but all living alone does is increase your psychological weight, as if your soul were living on Jupiter. It tends to make you more important to yourself and exaggerate your problems to the point that they're insurmountable afflictions. This was probably what was behind my wanting a dog. It wasn't just about companionship; it was about responsibility, too. There wasn't a damn living thing that depended on me, except the plants in my office.

There was a message from Felicia the next morning, saying she wouldn't be in. She didn't offer an explanation. I dialed her number, thinking that when she picked up, I'd ask for one, but she didn't pick up and I hung up without leaving a message. Hiring her may have been premature, as rash as opening a detective agency without having a license or quitting a job without having the slightest idea how to run a business or actually solve crimes.

Parker Hudson called around ten and asked, "So, who is HRT seven one nine?"

"When I know, Mr. Hudson, you'll know."

"Why so testy, Teddy?"

He was a chipper old codger. Life will grind you down to a bitter nub if you let it, but Parker Hudson had come to terms with his. Of course, having lots of cash lying around in his old age didn't hurt. As that old saying goes and even some scientific studies have shown, money doesn't bring happiness, but the poor people I knew didn't seem any happier than your average millionaire. I'd take the cash and risk the misery.

"Do you have a dog?" I asked him.

"Yes, we do. A golden retriever named Prince."

"I've been thinking about getting a dog, but it's forbidden in my lease. When my mother died, I thought about subletting and moving back into the old homestead, but too many ghosts, you know? I don't mean my parents. I'm not too concerned with the paranormal, though that's been all the rage—I guess because we're living in such uncertain times. Like those TV psychics communing with dead relatives and bringing back messages from beyond. Everybody's looking for some reassurance, and to me, it all boils down to justice. You know, that life's so screwy and messed up, there better be a payoff when it's over."

"Oh," Parker Hudson said. "I firmly believe in justice, Teddy. Otherwise, I never would have hired you."

"What would you like to see happen to this goose killer, assuming HRT seven one nine is our man?"

"I've been thinking some sort of restitution, perhaps a generous donation to the World Wildlife Fund."

The door swung open and Gary Paul stepped into the room. He was dressed in his civvies—a pair of crisp, brand-new blue jeans and a plain white T-shirt that accentuated his pectorals.

"That's terrific," I told Parker Hudson. "I'll call you back. . . ." I gave Gary the eye as he slipped into a visitor's chair.

"Soon?" Parker asked. Gary nodded. "Soon," I told Parker Hudson. I hung up and Gary broke into a big smile that reminded me I hadn't been to the dentist in over two years. If there were no evident disparity between the rich and poor, we wouldn't have half the wars in our history. Maybe no wars at all, but that was old thinking. Theodore Ruzak, the Bolshevik detective.

"We got him," I said.

"We got him," he replied.

CHAPTER TWENTY-SEVEN

GARY PAUL OFFERED TO GO WITH ME TO CONFRONT OUR suspect.

"Right now?" I asked.

"Why not?"

"Well," I said. "It's a question of thoroughness. I haven't been too thorough in my thinking up to this point—I mean in my life, not just with this case—and I don't want to go off half-cocked without a firm POA."

"POA?"

"Plan of attack."

"Detective lingo?"

"I wouldn't know. I just made it up."

"I thought we'd just drive over there and ask him," he said.

"That was my first instinct. It's direct and exploits the element of surprise, but that assumes this is unconnected to the murder of Lydia Marks."

He slowly shook his head. "I'm not following you, Ted. That's not unusual, but I'm thinking this is one of those times when I really should."

"If this guy's our goose killer, he might also be her killer, and I don't want to be mucking that up. I don't want to blow it for the task force. What if this guy takes off or destroys key evidence on the basis of our visit?"

"I don't think you go anywhere near that. Like I said, there may be no connection at all, but on the off chance there is, you don't bring it up. You stay on-message with the geese."

"Still, it might spook him."

"So it spooks him. I don't see how you can avoid it, if you want to solve this case. Besides, I'll be there."

In the end, that settled it for me. How badly could I screw up with a member of law enforcement at my elbow? Plus, in the back of my mind, I really did want to kill both birds with one stone. *All right, all right, you got me, Ruzak! I did them both, the goslings and the Irish dame! Take me away!*

The address was on the northwestern edge of the county, north of Farragut and just south of Oak Ridge, where they work on nuclear bombs or the technology for nuclear bombs—I was never quite sure which and didn't really want to be. Oak Ridge was sometimes called "the Secret City" because during World War II nobody knew about it, or if they did, they didn't know what they were doing up in those hills outside Knoxville. Gary offered to drive, but I told him it was my party, so he rode shotgun in my Sentra. Our perp, if he was our perp, lived in a newer subdivision, in one of those stucco two-story cookie cutter–type houses on a postage stamp–size lot with saplings still staked to the ground and straw still visible on the freshly seeded lawn. The house had a two-car garage, but the Ford SUV was parked in the driveway, and I saw the tag as we pulled in. At the sight of that tag, my heart rate picked up.

"Look familiar?" Gary asked.

"That's it," I said. "That's the car that tailed me."

I parked behind the SUV, blocking any possibility of a getaway, and Gary stopped me as I started up the walk to the front door.

"Hang on a sec," he said. I followed him to the front of the Ford. He squatted down and ran his hand under the front bumper, frowned, then lay flat on his back and reached underneath again, feeling along the edge of the front license plate holder. He pulled something free and held it up: a goose feather—or rather, a downy minifeather, a baby's feather.

"Bingo," he said.

He handed me the evidence and I slipped it into the money compartment of my wallet, between a five-dollar bill and an old gas receipt, which I was saving for tax purposes. On our way to the door, he said, "Maybe you should let me take the lead here, Teddy. The Marks thing does complicate matters, and I've got experience with dealing with these lowlifes."

"Sure," I said. "That's terrific. I really appreciate it, Gary."

He answered the bell right away, which made me wonder if he'd been standing on the other side of the door waiting for us. He was younger than I expected, maybe in his mid-twenties, and better-looking, though I really didn't know why I expected someone in his mid-forties, balding, and with a middle-age paunch. I guess my expectation was based on my assumption that whoever smashed those goslings was either a shallow housewife bent on getting to the mall before it opened or a midlevel executive late for his flight to New York to close that big deal. He was wearing Bermuda shorts and a Ron Jon Surf Shop T-shirt. His hair was wet, like he'd just stepped out of the shower.

"How ya doin'?" Gary said. "My name's Gary Paul and I'm with the Knox County sheriff's office. This is Teddy Ruzak. He's a private investigator."

"Investigative consultant," I said.

"We're looking for Michael Carroll," Gary said.

"I'm Mike Carroll," the guy said.

"You got a second, Mike?"

"Am I in some kind of trouble?"

"Well," Gary said, "let's just say we're not here to solicit donations for the Benevolence Fund."

"Ah, jeez. Okay. I'm kinda running late for something, but come on in." He asked us to slip off our shoes by the door because the hardwood was brand-new and cost sixty-five dollars a square foot installed, and we followed him into the living room. The house was sparsely furnished and had a Rooms-to-Go feel. There were some built-in bookcases against one wall with no books in them and a glass-topped coffee table with a lava lamp set in the middle, maybe as a conversation piece.

"Nice lamp," I told Mike Carroll as we sat down, in case it was. Gary and I took the sofa and Mike sat on a rocking chair without any padding on the rails, which made me wonder how much he really cared about the hardwood.

"Isn't it cool? Those got hip again a couple years back, but now they're waning again. I can't help it, though, I just love 'em."

"You probably have some memory attached to it," I said. "That's what usually happens."

He shook his head. "I've got nothing attached to it at all." He looked at Gary and wet his lips. He had the classical features of a Greek statue and very blue eyes. If his hair had been lighter, it might have been possible to mistake him for Brad Pitt or an Aryan god, like Thor, only I wasn't sure Thor was Aryan, being a Norse god. Weren't the Norsemen from Norway? And I was pretty sure Brad Pitt had brown eyes, and your classic Aryans were blond, all of which would mean Mike Carroll did not resemble Brad Pitt, or an Aryan, or a Norse god.

"Hey, Mike," Gary said. "We're gonna cut right to the chase here. For a couple weeks now, Teddy and I have been trying to hunt down the owner of that Ford in your driveway."

"Well," Mike Carroll answered. "I guess your hunt is over. That's my Expedition."

"Mike, we have reason to believe that vehicle was used in the commission of a crime." Then Gary added quickly, "Not a very serious crime as far as the statutes go, but in terms of human decency."

Mike slowly shook his head. "I have no idea what you're talking about, Gary."

Gary looked at me and nodded. I pulled out my wallet and drew out the gosling feather. Mike barely glanced at it.

"It's a feather," he said.

"We found it stuck under your front bumper, Mike."

"My client saw a black Ford SUV with your plates hit a gaggle of baby geese by Anchor Park in Farragut a couple months back," I said. "There was a big write-up in the paper about it. Maybe you saw it."

"Look," Gary said after the silence dragged out and no confession was forthcoming. "I'm gonna be straight with you, Mike. Nobody's here to arrest you or slap a fine on you and nobody will in the future, but we would like you to fess up so Teddy's client can have some peace of mind. He's kind of an old liberal tree-hugger type and he's been giving Ted here fits about this hit-and-run. All we want is some honesty and a willingness to stand up like a man and admit you made a mistake. We know you didn't intentionally kill those babies. It was an accident, right? You were in a hurry, didn't see them until it was too late, and who really gives a shit about six little baby geese?"

Mike nodded. He wet his lips again and ran his fingers through his damp hair, and in that moment I hated Michael Carroll like I'd never hated another being in my entire life. I wanted to grab that lava lamp and smack him over the head with it. He didn't have to open his mouth for me to know he was our perp. Gary had it nailed: Mike probably hadn't meant to hit the geese, but he didn't care that he had. And here it was midmorning and he had only now taken his shower, and he was dressed casually, so I guessed he didn't even have a job and lived off the largesse of his parents or maybe a girlfriend (he wasn't wearing a wedding ring). He drove a nice car and lived in a brand-new house, and this is what tore me up, the callousness born of privilege, like the rules didn't apply to him. And I knew, too, even without any proof, that he wasn't alone in that SUV that morning; that Lydia Marks was with him, maybe struggling, maybe not. Maybe I was sitting across from her boyfriend, who got mad when she wouldn't dump her sugar daddy for him, so he took a hammer to her head high on a ridge in the Smoky Mountains.

"Okay," he said softly. Then he laughed. "Okay, I guess I'm busted. Yeah, I saw the article," he said to me. "And I guess you know I went downtown that day looking for you. I'm not sure why I did that. I was kind of pissed, to tell you the truth. Like, Who does this fat ass think he is? Like, What's the big friggin' deal?" He spread his hands wide, then slapped his palms on his shorts and rubbed his thighs vigorously, like he had a circulation problem.

"You hit the geese," Gary said.

"Yeah, didn't I just say that?"

"Not in so many words."

"Well, what the hell do you want? A written confession? You said you weren't here to arrest me or ticket me. What the hell are you here for, then?"

"A check," I said.

"A . . . a what?"

"Made out to the World Wildlife Fund. I'm thinking maybe three hundred bucks."

"Three hundred bucks!"

"That's fifty per gosling."

Gary smiled. "Seems fair."

"You're kidding, right? Jesus, man, it was just a bunch of friggin' geese!"

"Gaggle," I said. "And tell that to the parents of those friggin' geese."

"No, why don't *you* tell them, Ruzak? You're out of your damned mind if you think—"

"Hey, Mike," Gary said. "Mike, Mike. There's no need to get all excited about it. I think Teddy's suggestion is terrific. Three hundred bucks isn't going to bring those geese back, but it tips the scales in the right direction."

"I don't give a crap about any scales," Mike said. "What the hell are you talking about with these scales? Look, I'm sorry I hit them, okay? And yeah, I should have stopped I guess and I definitely should have come forward when that story hit the papers, but it's not like it was a group of schoolkids crossing the road."

"You know, Mike," Gary said. "You say you're sorry, but your whole attitude lacks any kind of remorse whatsoever. It's troubling to me and I'm sure it's troubling to Teddy here and I have no doubt Parker would find it even more deeply troubling. So troubling he might decide to press charges against you."

"Charges? Like what charges? This is bullshit, man. Okay, okay, what do you want me to do? I sure as hell don't want to *trouble* anybody."

"Teddy's already told you. A three-hundred-dollar donation to the World Wildlife Fund."

"Tax-deductible donation," I added.

"You bet," Gary said. He was smiling broadly now at Mike, who was smiling back with perfectly even, perfectly white teeth, which were made even more perfect by the juxtaposition to Gary's.

"And an apology to my client," I said.

"Apology for what?"

"For hitting the geese."

"But that was an accident."

"I think he could have lived with that," I said. "Anybody can have an accident. It was the driving away part that got to him."

"I was in hurry. Didn't I say that? Jeez, am I the only one who sees the ridiculousness of this?"

"The only one in this room," Gary said.

"What if I don't have three hundred bucks to give to the World Wildlife Fund?"

Nobody said anything. Nobody needed to. Everything about Gary Paul's aura said, I don't give a flying flip about your excuses, pal.

Mike sighed, his smile faded, and he stood up. "Okay, I'll get my checkbook. It just blows my mind when I pick up the paper and see all the shit happening in this town and here's a guy who cares more about *geese*—I mean, these are fucking geese we're talking about, and here you two are banging on my door, kind of strong-arming me because I made a *mistake*. Why should I have to pay up if it was an accident?"

"Everything has a price, Mike," Gary said softly. "Even accidents. Especially accidents."

I had an idea as he started out of the room.

"You don't need to get your checkbook right now," I said. They both looked at me, a little surprised. "I'm sure my client would prefer the check and the apology straight from the horse's mouth."

He gave a little frustrated roll of his shoulders, as if the situation was slipping outside all bounds of normalcy. He looked at Gary as if to say, Save me from this freak.

"You have my personal guarantee I'll do everything in my power to keep him from popping you in the nose," I said.

"Oh, sure, that makes me feel a lot better," he said. "But that's not going to happen, Ruzak. First you come in here demanding three hundred bucks and now you tack on a personal apology. You guys keep upping the ante. What's next? Taking out a billboard?"

"I'm thinking more along the lines of a written apology." Gary said. "With a copy to the newspaper."

"I'm sure he'd prefer it in person," I insisted. "A letter to the newspaper isn't bad, either; I'll run that by him when I set up the meeting."

"I'm not meeting with him, Ruzak," Mike Carroll said, but he was looking at Gary. He had Gary pegged as the rational one, the good cop.

I said, "Is tomorrow, say four o'clock, good for you?"

"Didn't you hear me? I'm not meeting with him."

"Parker would prefer it."

"I don't give a shit what Parker would prefer. He gets a check and note, 'Dear Mr. Hudson, I'm sorry about killing those fuck-ing baby geese.' If that's not good enough for you, then slap the cuffs on me now. I'm not a bad person; I'm a decent human being. And I really resent the hell out of you two showing up at my door like this, acting like I'm some kind of serial killer or something."

"I don't have my cuffs, Mike," Gary said. "But I'm afraid you're going to have to go along with this, or I'll come back with them."

"You're kidding me."

"No."

"Yes, you are."

"No, I'm not. You'll do this, or I promise you I will come back, and when I do, I'll be wearing my badge, Mike."

CHAPTER TWENTY-EIGHT

PELLISSIPPI PARKWAY WAS ONLY A MILE OR SO FROM MIKE Carroll's house, so I swung onto it, heading south toward the interstate.

"You in a hurry?" Gary asked, and I eased up on the gas, thinking maybe my speeding seven miles over the limit disturbed his cop sense.

"I guess not," I said.

"Let's have a beer, then."

"A beer?"

"To celebrate."

He directed me off the Kingston Pike exit, then west toward Farragut, then into a little strip center anchored by a Harley-Davidson shop called Biker's Rags. At the corner of the L-shaped center was a sports bar with a big screen on every wall, a pool table, a couple of dartboards, and a tired-looking waitress with dyed-blond hair and a tattoo on her shoulder that said BITCH. Gary ordered a Michelob lite and I had a Budweiser. We shared a bowl of stale pretzels, and the waitress ignored us after she asked if we wanted some wings or a slice of pizza and we said no.

Gary raised his frosty mug and said, "To Teddy Ruzak, ace detective, first case in the can."

I clinked mugs with him and said, "Investigative consultant."

"What's the difference?"

"One's legal and one isn't."

He shook his head. I wasn't sure what the shake of the head meant, but I didn't ask. Something was bugging me, and I couldn't put my finger on it. I should have been flush with pride, overjoyed at my perfect batting average, relishing my victory, but there was a shadow over me, or it was more like a thorn in my head, pricking my brain.

He laughed suddenly. "Did you see the look on his face when he realized we knew?"

"Hand in the cookie jar."

"This gives me incredible satisfaction, Ruzak. I just can't tell you. So many times I've sat there in court and watched these jerks walk and there was absolutely nothing I could do about it. It's a pretty frustrating job, being a cop. The pay is shit, the hours are lousy, and, five times out of ten, after all the shit work you get the pleasure of watching the perp walk. It can make you cynical, you know? Pretty down on everything. It's nice to see something come out the right way once in a while."

"Oh," I said. "You bet. But what's your gut tell you, Gary? Is he the one?"

"A black Ford Expedition with the same license plate that both you and Parker saw, a goose feather caught in the undercarriage, and a confession. Yeah, I'm pretty sure he's the one."

"I don't mean the geese."

"Ruzak, the only thing I know about Mike Carroll is that he's a very careless driver, a very casual dresser, and a very poor decorator. But you can bet the task force is gonna know his name."

"He never said," I said.

"He never said what?"

"Why he was there that morning. Why he was driving so fast. Why he didn't stop."

"Maybe he didn't because we didn't ask."

"I was nervous," I admitted. "Thanks for coming along, Gary."

"Oh, no, you did great, Teddy. My only criticism would be this setup with Parker. He was about to write you a check and you stopped him. What makes you think he's going to show?"

"I don't know."

"You're a trusting son of a bitch, you know that?" Then he laughed and finished his beer.

I dropped him off in front of the Ely Building. It was almost one o'clock and I hadn't eaten lunch. I doubted Gary Paul had, either, but for some reason I wanted to be alone. I thanked him again, we said good-bye at the steps, and I watched him walk down to Gay Street and disappear around the corner toward Jackson. Gary had that *High Noon* saunter affected by a lot of cops, like a toned-down version of the Mick Jagger strut, which I always thought had something to do with the gun slapping on the upper thigh—not Mick's, the cops'.

I ate a quick lunch at the Crescent Moon, a little bistro-type place half a block from the Ely Building. It was run by a couple of ladies I suspected were lesbians. My clues were the lack of makeup, the butch haircuts, and the brusque way in which I was always treated. They had terrific iced tea, though, and I drank about a gallon of it. Beer in the afternoon makes me extremely sleepy, and this didn't help the fog or shadow over my soul or the thorn in my brain, or whatever it was. When I got back to the office, the mail had come, and I carried it upstairs. I had closed the windows and shut down the fans before I left, and the place reeked of fumes. I rolled my big chair over by the window and went through the mail as I leaned on the sill, breathing through my mouth like a fish. I was trying to take my mind off the brain sliver, but reading the mail wasn't a mindless-enough exercise, so I tossed the pile on the desk and decided to water the plants. The ferns especially were looking a little droopy. I was thinking about a scientific study I had read about years ago, about how plants might actually feel pain, when the sliver in my brain slowly drew out and light burst through the fog. I picked up the phone and called Parker Hudson.

"Know anybody named Michael Carroll?"

"Never heard of him," he said.

"Well, he's heard of you."

"Who is he?"

"I'm not sure, but I'm going to find out."

"Don't tell me we finally have a suspect."

"I think maybe we do."

"I told you it wasn't a false memory," he said. "I can't tell you how grateful I am that you made me go through with that hypnosis, Teddy. I'm an old man and new things don't come easy for me, but you pushed and I'm glad you did, not only because now justice will be served but because I feel as if I've got a whole new lease on life. I am a bona fide believer, Ruzak."

"Everybody should be about something."

"In fact, I have an appointment with Dr. Fredericks next Tuesday."

"Next Tuesday? Why?"

"To do it again! That session was one of the most exciting, vivid experiences of my life. And let me tell you, Teddy, you don't get to be my age without having your fair share of exciting, vivid experiences. It felt more real than the real event, if that makes any sense."

"Sure."

"I highly recommend it. Tuesday, I'm going to ask to be taken back to 1974."

"Good year?"

"One of my best."

"Gee, that's terrific, Mr. Hudson."

"I figure I have fifteen, maybe twenty years left—plenty of time to relive practically my entire life, particularly since I'm skipping over the bad parts. By doing that, I'm actually living an extra forty years, by my calculations. Virtually speaking."

"Wow."

He must have noticed the lack of enthusiasm in my voice. "Are you feeling all right? You don't sound like yourself."

"No. No, thanks for asking, Mr. Hudson, but I'm myself. I'm myself."

He laughed. "That's good to hear. I would sorely regret your passing."

This struck me as creepily prophetic. "So would I," I said. "I'll call you back in a couple of days."

I hung up to the sound of him chuckling. My hand was shaking. Must be the tea, I thought.

I made three more calls: one to the Department of Motor Vehicles, one to the Knox County Tax Assessor's Office, and one to Harvey Listrom, detective with the Knox County sheriff's office.

Then I went home and took a nap. I was pretty tired.

CHAPTER TWENTY-NINE

FELICIA CALLED IN AROUND TEN THE NEXT MORNING.

"You're not coming in," I said.

"How badly do you need me to come in?"

"Are you sick? You don't sound sick."

"I'll be there tomorrow; I promise."

"Is there anything I can do?"

She started to cry. This took me aback. I had never heard her cry before.

"Sometimes," I said. "Sometimes it helps to talk."

"What are you, Ruzak, my mother?"

"Just trying to be your friend. I've pretty much demonstrated I suck at being your boss."

"What does that mean?"

"Even Freddy would have fired you by now."

"Do what you want, Ruzak. I didn't come to you, remember. You asked me to take the job."

I'm not sure how that applied to her questionable work ethic, but I let it go. It was probably Bob. In fact, I was sure it was Bob. In general, firemen are obnoxious, chauvinistic jerks, or at least that was my impression, based on nothing really, since I had never actually known any firemen. Stereotypes and prejudices flourish in the experiential vacuum of my own head. Although Felicia was probably not the easiest person to get along with—like a lot of strong-willed people—she was a seawall against which weaker wills crashed and collapsed. So maybe it was Bob and maybe it was Felicia; one thing I was certain of, it was the relationship that was the problem.

"I know who HRT is," I told her, to change the subject.

"Who is it?"

"Not at all the kind of person I expected."

"So the case is over?"

"Um. Don't know."

"How could you not know, Ruzak?"

"Like most things, there's an ambivalence there, a delicate shading. . . ."

"You're not going to tell me, are you?"

"Not yet. I'm pretty sure, but not completely. I've got this working theory though, finally, which is more than I had twenty-four hours ago."

"Maybe you're just drawing the whole thing out to bill Parker more hours."

"That would go back to my moral character," I told her. "Don't impugn my moral character."

" 'Impugn'?"

"What's wrong with *impugn*?"

"You have the vocabulary of a college professor without the intellectual and educational underpinning."

"Well," I said, "you just used the word *underpinning*."

"I'm hanging up now, Ruzak."

I hung up after apologizing for impugning her underpinning. It occurred to me I was too softhearted for this line of work. If somebody challenged me to name the chief characteristics of a successful private eye, being softhearted would not be at the top of my list. It certainly wasn't anywhere on the state of Tennessee's list. Additional cottony softness was located due north of my plushy heart, in the region between my ears. What if I was wrong? Sure, things as they had been presented to me didn't add up, but was that because I wasn't good with math? You read about genius and epiphanic moments, like the apple falling on Newton's head. I had the sort of head that would cry, Damn that apple! and then I'd go home to complain to my wife about my terrible luck, which only goes to show that geniuses are just like the rest of us, only more so.

In addition to being a very casual dresser and a very poor decorator, Michael Carroll was also very punctual: He arrived at four o'clock on the dot. He was wearing the same Bermuda shorts but had changed into a Tennessee Volunteers orange-and-white T-shirt. I offered to make a fresh pot of coffee, but he seemed in a hurry or upset by something, or maybe both. He sat on the edge of the visitor's chair, working his fingers through his damp-looking hair, and I decided I'd had it wrong the day before; his hair hadn't been wet, just gelled to saturation.

"I've got the check," he said. "Where's Parker Hudson?"

"Oh," I said. "Today's his foursome."

He blinked those gorgeous baby blues at me and said, "He's not coming?"

I shook my head no. If I had expected him to act relieved, I would have been disappointed. He slid the check onto the desk blotter and sat back. He had folded it in half and maybe was waiting for me to unfold it. I didn't unfold it. I didn't touch it. I watched his eyes as I asked, "Who is Lydia Marks?"

"Lydia who?"

He didn't blink; he didn't hesitate; he didn't fidget. He gave no indication he was lying, but I had no training in the area of lie detection—as I had none in any area of private detection. But it wasn't like I'd let that stop me.

"How do you know Gary Paul?"

"What's that mean? What are you talking about, Ruzak? Look, you've got what you wanted. There's your check, and now I'm gonna—"

He started to stand up. I told him to sit down. He stood anyway. I said, "That wasn't your car in the driveway. And that wasn't your driveway, either, because that wasn't your house." He sat down. He scrunched low in the chair because he was a young guy and that's what young guys do: They scrunch in their chairs or tip them back on their rear legs.

"The black Ford Expedition in your driveway yesterday, the one with the baby bird feather stuck to it, is registered to Deputy Gary Paul of the Knox County sheriff's department. And the house with your lava lamp on the coffee table is deeded to a man named Kenneth Marks, who happens to be the surviving spouse of Lydia Marks, who was murdered around the time that car hit those baby geese."

Mike Carroll wet his lips. Since that was a classic gesture of guilt or, at the very least, unease, I figured I had taken the right tack.

"So?" he asked.

"So, it's one thing to borrow a buddy's car and smush some waterfowl. It's something altogether different to smush a human being's head and dump her body in the mountains as fodder for the indigenous wildlife."

"Look, Ruzak. Look . . ." He gave a little laugh that tended toward a giggle. "I don't know anything about any murder, okay?"

"Then maybe you can help me out, Mike. Maybe you can help me and that way I can help you."

He wet his lips again and I fought an almost overwhelming urge to scream at him, And stop wetting your lips like that, pretty boy!

"Okay," he said.

"Yes or no, were you the one who hit the geese?"

He shook his head no.

"Gary hit them?" I asked.

"I have no idea who hit them," he said. "Look, okay, here it is. Gary and me go back aways. He . . . I . . . see, when I was a kid, I got into some trouble and Gary, he helped me out, okay? I don't know, he thought maybe there was some hope for me or something, but he arrested me when I was a junior in high school, marijuana possession, and I did my time, but not as much as I would have if Gary hadn't gone to bat for me. So I owed him one. A couple days ago, he calls me out of the blue and tells me he wants me to admit to this goose-killing bullshit because this pal of his— you—had this client who was all over his ass over this stupid thing and he wanted me to 'confess' to it to get him off your back. But you had to buy into it, too."

"Why?"

"He didn't say why, okay? He just offered me a thousand bucks, and what the hell was I going to say to a thousand bucks?"

"I guess you said yes."

"You're damn right I said yes."

"Awful lot of money just to boost my spirits," I said. "Especially on a deputy's salary."

"Man, I didn't ask him where the money came from."

"But why the meeting at a rental owned by Kenneth Marks?"

"How the hell should I know? He didn't say and I didn't ask. He said be at this place at this time and that's what I did."

"Where do you really live?"

" 'It's none of your damn business where I live, Ruzak."

"Probably nowhere near Farragut. He was being thorough— wanted to make sure everything fit—car, location. And it almost worked."

"Why didn't it?"

"You knew Parker's last name," I told him. "It kind of imbedded this splinter into my thinking, so I checked with DMV, which is something I guess I should have done a long time ago, but I'm too trusting and maybe a little lazy, to be perfectly honest."

He stared at me. "Whatever. So what happens now?"

"You don't tell Gary about this conversation."

"What's gonna stop me?"

I sighed. "How about a thousand bucks?"

"You got a thousand bucks?" he asked. I made a mental note to tell Felicia she was wrong: After I had poured thousands into this cramped, crappy space and thousands more in clothing for my rotundity, people still couldn't believe I was solvent.

I wrote him a check for a thousand dollars and told him the bank was right down the street and that he could go straight there after leaving and cash it. Then I took his check and slipped it into my top desk drawer.

"Hey," he said. "Give that back."

"Why?"

"I shouldn't have to pay it now. I didn't hit those goddamned geese."

"Well," I said. "I doubt there's going to be any other justice in that regard, so I'm keeping it."

"Then you should give me thirteen hundred to offset my loss."

"You already got a thousand from Gary," I pointed out, though I was sure the money had actually come from Kenneth Marks.

"I made him give me three hundred more to cover that check."

"Gee, you're a tough negotiator," I said. "You've got potential, and that heartens me. It reaffirms one of my core beliefs: that the book's never closed on us until the casket lid is."

"What the hell does that mean?"

"It means I'm not giving you three hundred dollars, since Gary already has."

"I'll stop payment on the check."

"That seems a pretty low gesture. Don't you care about nature?"

"You're an asshole," he said, getting up and staying up this time.

"And you might be an accessory to murder," I said. "So far, I have only a working theory, but there's room in it for you, Mike."

He slammed the door on his way out and, even though I saw that coming, I jerked in my chair. I've always been sensitive to loud noises. As a kid, I hated the Fourth of July. I pulled the tape recorder from its hiding place under the desk and checked the sound quality. My voice sounded much louder than Mike's, but you could still make out what he had said. I thought about following him to wherever he'd gone next, then thought better of it and decided to have a cup of fresh coffee, water the plants, and think instead. I doubted the plants were doing a damn thing to improve the air quality in the office, but they did seem to improve my thinking.

I had finished watering the plants and was shutting down Felicia's computer when the door opened and Eunice Shriver walked in.

I followed her into my office and offered her a cup of coffee.

"Do you have any Earl Gray tea?"

"Celestial Seasons. I think it's herbal."

She wrinkled her nose at the thought of herbal tea and settled for a bottle of Evian. I sat behind my desk and wished that, like every movie detective in history, I had a bottle of scotch stashed in my bottom drawer.

"So what'd you do this time?" I asked.

"What, murder isn't enough?"

"And conspiracy," I said. "You and Vernon."

"Are you mocking me, Theodore?"

"Mocking's not in my nature. Occasionally, I tease, but that's a whole different animal. Mrs. Shriver—sorry, Eunice—I know for a fact you didn't run over those geese and I also know for a fact you didn't kill Lydia Marks."

"And what is your proof?"

"I don't need to prove you didn't do it."

"Then who did?"

"I'm working on that. It's a process of elimination. I'd show you my list, upon the top of which your name has been crossed out, but I've lost it."

"Some detective," she sniffed. "I actually am not here about either killing."

"You've robbed a bank."

"That bordered on mockery."

"Sorry."

"Teddy, I would like to hire you for a job."

"A detective job?"

"Is that not your business?"

"Actually, I'm an investigative consultant."

"But the sign on your door . . ."

"Well, that's just a marketing tool. Like the way chiropractors call themselves doctors."

"Chiropractors aren't doctors?"

"You never see an M.D. after their name."

"I love my chiropractor."

"That's terrific. I've noticed your posture. It's very good for somebody of your years."

"I'll give you his name."

"Mine's a slouch," I said. "Nothing to do with spinal pain."

"I have money," she said. "To pay you, of course."

"That's good," I said. "But I don't want your money, Eunice. I'm pretty sure I don't want your case, either."

"But you haven't even heard what it is yet."

"I'll guess. Somebody's trying to kill you."

Her eyes widened. "How on earth did you know?"

"A lucky guess. See, a real detective wouldn't admit to guessing, but a consultant guesses all the time. Who's trying to kill you?"

"That's what I want you to find out. I have a list of suspects." She dug into her enormous purple purse and fished out four pages of typewritten single-spaced names, which she handed to me.

I whistled. "You've got quite a few enemies, Eunice."

"If I could narrow it down further, I wouldn't need to turn to you, Theodore."

It made me feel funny, old Mrs. Shriver calling me Theodore. Only my mother ever called me by my full name.

"Who are these people?"

"Neighbors, my children, of course, the ladies from my prayer circle, the postman, the mayor, among others."

"Why would the mayor . . ."

"Now, *that* is a long story."

I laid the paper on the desk, sighed, leaned back in my chair, and folded my hands behind my head.

"I'd love to hear it," I said.

CHAPTER THIRTY

It was close to seven o'clock when I left the office. I was hungry, but I drove home. The nesting instinct was strong upon me, and as I drove, I wondered if I faked some kind of illness, my landlord might let me keep a dog, like if I could provide a note from a competent physician or maybe somebody like Dr. Fredericks, who could vouch my lack of companionship was slowly driving me mad. Of course, I could simply bring a dog in and hope one of my neighbors didn't turn me in, but that reflected on the moral character issue I was trying to work on or work out.

I went straight to the refrigerator, but there was not so much as a slice of bologna, and all I had in the pantry was Campbell's cream of tomato soup and a can of sardines. I was checking out the fridge again, sniffing various containers, when the floorboards creaked behind me. I closed the door and without turning around, because I knew who it had to be, said, "Hey, Gary."

I turned around. He was sitting on the sofa in his full uniform, including the gun and the walkie-talkie strapped to his shoulder, and for some reason I thought of my old job. We'd had walkie-talkies, too, but working the night shift, there was nobody to communicate with, so I didn't even know how to use mine.

Walkie-talkie is one of those archaic terms that's funny when you think about it.

"Hello, Ted."

"Guess I've blown a thousand bucks today."

"Probably not all you've blown, Ted."

"Maybe I'll sit down."

"Maybe you should. I'm waiting for a call and I thought it'd be best to wait for it here with you."

"Sure, Gary," I said. "You bet."

I sat on one of the bar stools by the counter.

"You want anything?" I asked. "I'm fresh out of just about everything, but there're a couple of Buds with good born-on dates."

"No thanks."

"Okay." I sat there for a second and thought, Maybe I should take up smoking so I would have something to do with my hands in situations like this. But there was a downside to smoking, of course, and I had enough vices for two people. Plus, odds were this was the last situation like this I'd ever have.

"I knew the second that dumb-ass said Parker's name that the thing was fucked," Gary said.

"You give me too much credit, Gary," I said. "I almost missed it, though the shadow of it was heavy upon me, like a splinter in my brain. It was like one of those *Encyclopedia Brown* moments— you know, like, 'Encyclopedia realized Mike couldn't have known Parker's last name, since Ruzak never mentioned it!'"

Gary Paul laughed. "You skipped to the back of the book."

"Is that where we are?"

He nodded. "Nearly."

"Are you going to kill me, Gary?"

His small eyes widened. "Why would I kill you, Teddy?"

"That's a good question. I don't have any proof, nothing that could get anybody in any kind of serious trouble. If I did, I would have called the task force. But there are a couple tapes. Hope I'm not being premature telling you that."

"Tapes?"

"Yeah. I've got a tape of Parker Hudson remembering your tag number under hypnosis and I've got a tape of Mike Carroll confessing to your setup at the Marks's rental. That might be a little difficult to explain to the task force."

"Oh," he said. "You mean *these* tapes." He then pulled them from his pants pocket and held them up.

"You broke into my office," I said.

"Right after you left tonight." He slipped them back into his pocket and adjusted the volume of his walkie-talkie. "You probably have a couple questions. Some loose ends. A couple extra splinters in your brain."

"That story in the paper—about the geese—that bothered Ken Marks?"

He hesitated, then nodded. "I guess it did."

"So he sent you to me, to find out what I knew and when I knew it. To throw me off or keep me close, or both, and when I got the tag number, you set up this deal with Mike to wrap my end up and keep me from nosing around and mucking things up worse than I already had. That's why you pretended to talk to Detectives Listrom and Watson. I don't know about Watson, but I know for sure you never talked to Harvey Listrom. Harvey doesn't even know who you are."

"Right on the money, Teddy."

"Only Mike blew it, and this puts you in an extremely awkward position."

"Bingo."

"It was you on the road that morning, wasn't it, Gary?"

"You really think I'm going to answer that question?"

"Oh, I only have one tape recorder, and that's at the office. But you know that already."

"I probably know just a little more right now than you do."

"I have a working theory. You want to hear it?"

"You bet. We've got a few more minutes."

I thought about asking him, A few more minutes till what? But I decided against it.

"Okay, here's my working theory. It still has some rough edges, and maybe since you're here, you can help me smooth them out. I think you're the goose killer. I think you grabbed Lydia that morning, probably just as she was starting out on her jog. She knew you, though, somehow, or maybe you were wearing your uniform; at any rate, there was some measure of trust there, but she realized at some point something was up, and I think there was a struggle going on when you hit those geese. You weren't watching the road and you couldn't stop, obviously: You had a job to do for Kenneth Marks. I think he paid you to kill Lydia like he paid you or somebody like you to kill his first wife."

He didn't nod or shake his head or make any expression at all while I talked. He just stared at me.

"I don't know why he wanted them dead," I went on. "I guess maybe it's the old money thing. As in it doesn't matter how much you have, because what you have is never enough. I don't know exactly what he does for a living, but my guess is that he lives pretty high on the hog and hiring someone to kill his wives was a way into some quick liquidity."

" 'Liquidity'?" he asked, smiling.

"Liquidity. And I don't know how he hooked up with a sheriff's deputy willing to go to the chair for a few dollars, but somehow he did—right? See, these are some of the rough edges in my theory, but not even Darwinism fits together completely, you know?"

"Gosh, that's one helluva theory, Ted. I don't suppose you've

gone to the task force with it yet. They already think you're a -
nut—I've made sure of that—and what do you have? Without
the tapes, what do you really have?"

I was about to say, I have Parker Hudson, but at that moment,
like a cosmic turning of the wheel or clicking of the karmic gears,
his walkie-talkie squawked to life and he pulled it to his right ear
to listen. I couldn't make out what the dispatcher was saying, but
it sounded pretty urgent. He stood up and said, "It's time, Ted.
Let's go."

"Where are we going?"

"You know where we're going."

"No, Gary, I honestly don't."

"Okay, you don't know where, but you know what and why."

"You've been hanging around me too long," I told him, but because of that or in spite of it, I knew exactly what he meant.

CHAPTER THIRTY-ONE

I RODE SHOTGUN IN GARY PAUL'S CRUISER, AND IT occurred to me that it was my first time in a police car since my Academy days, racing around the track in a mock pursuit, orange cones and life-size cutouts of pedestrians flying everywhere, the instructor, a little redheaded Irishman named O'Roark, screaming in my ear, "Accelerate through the curve, *through* the curve, you big dumb Pollack!"

Gary jumped on the interstate, heading west, and I knew the minute we mounted the entrance ramp where we were going. I didn't know precisely where, but I knew generally where. He turned on the siren and we roared west going ninety-five miles an hour till he reached the Lovell Road exit, which we took practically on two wheels.

"But here's the roughest edge," I said, raising my voice to be heard over the screaming siren. "Why would Ken Marks offer me a boatload of money to find out who was responsible if he was the one responsible?"

"Gee," Gary answered. "That *is* rough."

"Maybe it's like Jane Goodall and the chimps."

"What is?"

"You know, she hung with those monkeys for so many years,

she started to act like them, think like them, even look a little like them as she got older."

"What you just said makes no sense to me, Ruzak. Sorry."

"He had to come see me, and why else would he come see me? He had to have a reason to come, a reason that would make sense to me. He wanted to know what I knew without tipping his hand, so his only choice was to play the part, the only part, I would expect him to play."

We pulled into the parking lot at Anchor Park. There were four other cruisers in the lot, which had been roped off with the yellow crime-scene tape, an ambulance, a fire truck, and a mobile crime-scene lab. Cars lined the other side of the street, parked illegally against the curb, and gawkers stood on the walking trail, moms in unflattering jogging shorts and baggy T-shirts and retirees in bright green shorts and sandals over white athletic socks. I followed Gary past the picnic tables and horseshoe court, down to the water's edge. The first thing that caught my eye was not the men in black wet suits wading toward the shape floating in the middle of the lake, but the two geese swimming nonchalantly near the shore. The water was sparkling in the last rays of the setting sun.

"Who is it?" I asked Gary.

"Who do you think it is, Ms. Goodall?" he asked.

"It's Parker Hudson," I said, and as if on cue, one of the geese gave a loud bray and ducked its head under the surface of the lake.

I turned away, leaned against a tree, and my empty stomach heaved. Gary put a hand on my shoulder in an obscene parody of sympathy and condolence.

"I think you're beginning to understand you're in way over your head on this one, Ted. Your reach has exceeded your grasp."

I nodded, head down, my arm wrapped around the tree, knees slightly bent. I wished I had eaten something; this dry retching really tore at your gut and burned your throat. This was the moment to pull free from Gary Paul's grip and run to the water's edge, shouting, "I've got him; I've got him right here! The killer's standing right over there by that tree!" But I didn't run anywhere or shout anything. Without the tapes and the only witness, what did I have? The guys in the black wet suits brought the body to the shore and laid it about fifty feet from us, and the people from the medical examiner's office hovered over it, taking pictures and gingerly touching, prodding, and poking Parker Hudson's body. He was dressed in shorts, sneakers, and a red polo shirt. I wondered what the hell was in that old man's head that he'd cared about what happened to six insignificant baby geese. Hadn't he realized the species would survive regardless? And why, if he'd cared so much, had he hired a hapless buffoon like Teddy Ruzak, who barely possessed the intellectual wherewithal to tie his own shoes?

"Let's go sit in the car, Ted."

He opened the back door for me and I slid into the seat behind the wire mesh. Gary got behind the wheel and slammed his door. His eyes were upon me in the rearview mirror.

"You agree, right? Way over your head?"

I nodded.

"Good," he said. "Now we've got to come to an understanding here, Teddy. I hope you appreciate the fact that I'm doing everything possible to keep you in one piece here. I'd like to hate your fat guts, but I can't, and believe me, I've tried. I took a big risk with that whole farce with Mike Carroll, and now I'm gonna have to ask you to think clearly for a second. What would be the easiest way to resolve this?"

"Kill me," I whispered.

"Kill you. You bet. What's the next easiest?"

"I don't know."

"Think, Ted. Come on. *Think.*"

I tried to think. "Oh, crap, I don't know. Buy my silence?"

"That opens a can of worms, though, don't you think? Marks offered you a ton of cash and you turned it down. Maybe you can't be bought. Or I pay you off and down the road you change your mind or decide it wasn't quite enough. It's too open-ended. There's no closure."

I thought some more. I felt the answer floating in the ether but couldn't pin it down. Since there were no plants around to water to distract myself, I chose my usual method of distraction.

"That's something I've always been curious about, personally and professionally," I said. "Does it get easier? My mother always said lies were that way, and I've wondered if the same applies to your mortal sins—say cold-blooded murder. I mean, was it easier to kill Lydia than his first wife? Or maybe his first wife wasn't the first person you killed, I don't know, but even if she wasn't, was killing Parker Hudson easier than killing Lydia? Or is killing people one of those things that never gets easier, but something in which you find a comfort zone, like maybe flying an airplane, not easier or harder per se, just more relaxed?"

He smiled. "No, killing people isn't like flying an airplane."

"So you enjoy it?"

"Stop it, Ruzak. I know what you're trying to do."

"It is a little ridiculous," I admitted. "Trying to expand your understanding of the world while somebody's seriously considering putting a bullet in your head, unless you buy into the afterlife. How about that, Gary? I was never too religious myself, but you were born and raised in the buckle of the Bible Belt. Any qualms in that area?"

"You asking if I'm afraid I'll go to hell?"

"Well . . . yeah."

"I don't think about it."

I nodded. "I've got the opposite problem. I tend to think about everything, only I don't have the requisite wattage upstairs to accomplish it with any thoroughness or to bring anything to a conclusion. Like walking in circles: I get the exercise but never arrive anywhere. . . ."

He laughed, and as he was laughing, it hit me. In a way, the best alternative to killing me was worse than actually killing me. The answer was obvious, of course, and maybe it was slow coming to me because it was so obvious.

"Ah, come on, Gary, that's like . . . well, it really is beyond the pale."

"Then suggest a viable alternative."

I didn't say anything.

"There's really no way to protect her, you know," Gary said softly. "You try to hide her, I'll find her eventually. Do you really think I won't be able to find her? I'll know if you so much as breathe in the direction of the task force, Ted. You do anything, *anything,* and she dies. I know you're upset, and sometimes when people are upset, they miss subtle details, so my goal here is not to be subtle with you. I want the understanding between us to be crystal clear. Cross me and Felicia dies."

Neither of us said another word. He drove me home, pulling to a stop in front of the Sterchi. I stepped out of the car onto the curb and closed the door. He rolled down the passenger window and leaned over to call out, "You okay?"

I nodded, he gave a little wave, the window rolled back up, and he drove away. I watched him turn up Summit Hill; then I climbed the three flights to my apartment. It looked the same but not the same. I'd had a similar feeling right after Mom died, where everything familiar looked unfamiliar and strange. My insides felt hollow and my legs weak, and I realized I better eat something or I was going to have a major episode. Plus, I needed to think, and you should never try thinking, if it's of the serious variety, on an empty stomach. So I ordered a pizza, and while I was waiting for it, I went into the bathroom and washed my face and hands. My reflection in the mirror made my stomach give a slow roll and I bowed over the toilet in an attitude of abject prayer, but nothing came up. When the feeling subsided, I paced around the two rooms, moving aimlessly, and for some reason, I remembered the time I'd slipped in the shower, cracking my head against the tile as I went down. You hear those stories of people who die alone in their apartments and nobody finds them for days. There was nobody who would check on me if I went missing, and maybe in a week or two, Felicia might come by and find me bloated and stinking—you read about such things. When I left the security company, I lost my company benefits, including the life insurance. Now I had no life insurance, and if something happened, there'd be no money for the expenses and they'd throw me into a pauper's grave. But I had nobody to leave money to, so I wasn't too concerned about it.

At one point, I stopped dead still in the middle of my mindless circuit around the apartment and said out loud, "He's lying. He's just buying time till he can kill me without causing a ruckus. He can't afford the risk of me changing my mind or getting too big for my britches and running to the task force, thinking they'll protect me."

Then I thought, No, he really doesn't need or want to kill me. With each death, the risk escalated, and like he'd implied, I was a pussy. I didn't have the guts to do the moral thing, the thing that was right by Lydia, because doing the right thing conflicted with my self-interest. I had passed muster on every state qualification to get my license except that one, the one about moral character.

It had thrown me for a loop because in thirty-three years, my moral character had never really been tested. It was a pretty scary thought, so I pushed it out of my head as quickly as I could. People in general spend a lot of their time worrying about wasting money or time, but the thing most squandered is thought. We waste a lot of it. The biggest successes in life are those people who are economical with their thinking. Losers like me are fooled into thinking that thought is cheap because it doesn't cost anything. But real thought, true thought, costs dearly.

My buzzer rang. The pizza. I punched the intercom button.

"Just bring it on up!"

"Mr. Ruzak?"

"Susan?"

"Hi. Can I come up?"

"Uh. Sure."

She came up wearing a black dress and dark hose with sensible low-heeled sandal-type black shoes, her dark hair pulled back in a severe-looking bun. I held the door for her and caught a hint of lilac as she passed.

"It's not too late, is it?"

The question was so ironical, I almost laughed.

"I didn't know you knew where I lived," I said, because I didn't.

"I looked it up in the phone book."

I threw the dead bolt on the door because she might have been followed or someone might be staking out my building, and what I was suffering from seemed to be exceedingly contagious: the pathogen of extreme violence. Parker Hudson had already succumbed to it.

She sat on the sofa. Her dress was sleeveless and terminated about two inches above her knees. Except for the shoes, she looked like she might be dressed for the theater. I offered her something to drink and she said Coke if I had it, which I did, and I poured her a glass with lots of ice in it, because I had heard in Europe they go easy on the ice—maybe two cubes at the most. You wonder why refrigeration is such an issue over there or if it's just a cultural thing, like not being able to get sweet tea above the Mason-Dixon Line.

"How was the funeral?" I asked. Bad topic for small talk, but it was really the only thing we had in common.

"Catholic and very, very Irish. The wake was incredible. I never laughed so hard—or cried so hard—in my whole life."

"I hear those Irish Catholics know how to throw a burial."

"It makes me wish I had known her better."

"Me, too. Not you, but me, I meant. How well did you know her, Susan? Did you meet before the wedding?"

"I didn't even go to the wedding. They were married in Ireland, honeymooned in Morocco, and flew to Knoxville six weeks later."

"You had no idea?"

"It was a total surprise."

"Matthew seemed to think there was some kind of fix involved."

She shook her head and again I got a whiff of lilac. "There was no fix," she said. "Matt's got a chip on his shoulder, that whole 'absent father' thing. Dad loved Lydia."

"He offered me a couple million dollars to hand him the killer so he could take care of things extrajudicially."

"Sounds like my father. Please don't report him or anything, Mr. Ruzak. He didn't really mean it. My father is the kind of man who always looks for the shortest distance between two points."

That was for sure. "I didn't report him," I said. "And I really wish you'd call me Teddy. Even the mailman, who I hardly know, calls me Teddy."

She nodded and sipped her Coke. "This is good. Thank you. I still have some jet lag, I think."

She slipped off her shoes and put her stocking feet on the coffee table, pulling the hem of her dress down demurely as she did.

"Speaking of Matt," I said. "He pretended he didn't even know what your dad did for a living."

"He's an investor. Real estate mostly. He started here in the States, of course; he's got half a dozen houses around town and some condos, but after a while, he got into the overseas market. He buys it, develops it, and sells it at a huge profit, I guess, because two million dollars is nothing to my father."

"I guess your dad's very economical in his thinking."

"What's that mean?"

"Nothing. I'm working on a theory of the economics of thought."

"Are you really?"

"No, not really. Sometimes things cross my mind that are beautiful but fleeting, like a shooting star—though more overwhelming. More like fireworks than a shooting star, I guess. So I get all excited and think I'm onto something profound, until I find out somebody else thought it or said it a few hundred years ago. It's hard to have a truly original thought anymore—I guess because we've been around for so long. Kind of like the monkeys typing Shakespeare."

She laughed. "Oh no. We're back to Shakespeare's monkeys."

"I'm not sure about that hypothesis, though. It's like that mathematician's theorem about the arrow never hitting the target."

Her eyebrows came together, creating a fine horizontal line that hovered over her nose.

"You know, anything that travels must cover half the distance before it can arrive at its destination. But before it can travel half the distance, it has to travel half of that half, and so on, and if you calculate that, always dividing by half, the arrow never gets anywhere."

"Sort of like our conversations."

"Sorry."

"No, I meant it as a compliment."

"You probably mean you never get any answers from me about your stepmom. I guess that's why you've come, but honestly, I don't have anything. Not a blessed thing." Even to my own ears, I sounded sincere as hell. I was a better liar than I thought I'd be, and I remembered Mom's saying each lie gets easier. "I thought I had something, but that fizzled out, so now your best bet is the task force. I guess you're in touch with them, too. You've got to remember that these people have access I don't. You know, forensics and databases and years of experience in this kind of deal."

She nodded. "I don't like that Detective Watson. She talks to me like I'm a moron or a little kid."

"Oh, I'm sure she's a crackerjack detective, though. You don't reach her level in a place like the TBI without having something on the ball. Did she tell you their theory?"

"Yes. That Lydia was jogging on the trail and a stranger pulled her or lured her into his car."

"So, um, they've ruled out somebody Lydia might know?"

"I guess that was pretty easy, since she didn't know many people."

"Why is that? Did she have some kind of psychological disorder or—"

"I think America was a little overwhelming to her. She wasn't an outgoing person at all, Mr. Ruzak. She told me once that when she was growing up, all she wanted to be was a nun. Why do you think she didn't marry until she was in her thirties? At the wake, her family said they used to tease her about being an old maid."

"So what was she up to when she met your dad? I mean, did she have a job?"

"Yes, but I don't know what it was."

"What's that story? How did they meet?"

"In a restaurant. She was at a table with some friends and Dad went over and introduced himself. He told her he had never seen a more beautiful woman in his life."

"Turned her head."

"He was good for her. He brought her out of her shell some— not a lot, but some. And she was good for him."

"How so?"

"She made him laugh. She was a very funny person, but her sense of humor was very subtle. Some people missed it, like Matt."

"Maybe he resented her. You know, that happens when a kid thinks his parent is trying to replace the original."

She lowered her dark eyes. "Maybe," she said softly.

"I looked into that a little," I said. "Your mother's death."

"I'm sure you did," she said. "I'm sure Detective Watson did, too."

I agreed she probably had.

"It sure is an odd coincidence."

"Exactly," Susan Marks said firmly. "And that's all it is."

My buzzer rang. She gave a little jump and I said, "I ordered a pizza."

Veggie lovers' supreme, heavy on the olives. I was being half-heartedly conscious of my weight. Susan said she wasn't hungry, but, like a lot of slight girls, she had the appetite of a horse. I fetched her another Coke and we ate sitting cross-legged on the floor, with the pizza on the coffee table between us. I was pushing the envelope even having her in my apartment. What if someone was staking me out? Was Gary already on his way to Felicia's?

Susan picked the olives off and dropped them one by one onto my slice.

"The stranger theory doesn't work," I said.

"Why?"

"Location for one, if she really was snatched from the trail. A kidnapping like that is a crime of opportunity. She would have been taken from the house, which everybody agrees she probably wasn't."

She nodded. A piece of cheese clung to her plump lower lip and this produced a sensation in my gut that was pleasant and uncomfortable at the same time.

"They found remnants of her jogging shorts in the woods," she said.

"So she was either on the trail or in the neighborhood on the way to the trail, a little early for rush hour, but people might have been around anyway."

"Like the man who saw the geese."

The reference to Parker made my throat close up and completely killed my appetite. I set down my slice of pizza.

"Right. The second thing is, I don't know much about her, but from what you've said, Lydia wasn't the kind of person who would just jump into some stranger's car."

"No way."

"Would she have fought with him?"

"She was Irish."

"Okay. Let's try to imagine this. She's jogging along and this SUV pulls over and a stranger jumps out and grabs her. Does she holler? Kick? Punch?"

"Probably all those things."

"Or the car pulls over and the stranger asks her something, maybe tells her something, that would make her come over at least, close enough for the grab. Could that have happened?"

She shook her head. "She wasn't distrustful, but I can't imagine anything somebody could say that would have made her stop and go to the car. She thought America was a very violent place."

"That means a lot, coming from somebody from Ireland. So an organized killer like this one—and we know he's the organized type, based on how easily he got her in the car and how he killed her—just wouldn't have picked her randomly like that. Too much risk."

"But if it wasn't a stranger . . ."

"It could be somebody *she* knew, not necessarily somebody *you* knew she knew."

"Like a neighbor?"

"I'm sure the task force has covered all the neighbors. But it could have been somebody she met at a store or a restaurant, maybe even the bag boy at Fresh Market. I'm just using the bag boy as an example. She knew this person in passing at least; there must have been a germ of trust there, a note of familiarity. Or maybe even someone in law enforcement. Or, um, maybe even pretending to be in law enforcement, though not every cop is a saint—we're all human—but you know everybody trusts cops. I'm just using that as an example, too. I'm not saying it was a cop or somebody pretending to be a cop. Did she know any cops? Mention any cops to you? Maybe not, if it was a casual acquaintance, maybe even a mutual acquaintance—you know, of hers and your dad's. No? Well, you wouldn't necessarily know her casual acquaintances. I don't care how close you are to somebody, and it looks like Lydia wasn't close to hardly anybody, you don't know everybody they know."

I was spinning this and I knew it was all a bunch of hogwash, since, after all, I knew the truth, or most of it at least. And there was something terribly obscene about me hypothesizing about it, dropping hints and asking leading questions like some dime-store pettifogging shyster. But Susan Marks needed something to cling to. She was young; she wanted answers to life's horrors. There was also the seductive fact that she was one of the few people who seemed to hang on my every word. When somebody finds you interesting, you try to be even more interesting.

The cheese still hung to her bottom lip and it took everything in me not to reach out and pull it off.

"Maybe I don't know everybody she knew, but I know most of the places she went. I know where she shopped for clothes and groceries. I know where she had the car serviced, where she got her hair done. She managed Dad's rental properties here in town when he was away. Collected rents, dealt with tenant complaints, things like that. I could make a list for you and you could work from that."

She must have seen something change in my expression, because she said, "What?"

"Susan, I don't know how to tell you this, but . . . but I've got to let this go." I cleared my throat. "I don't want to let it go, but the truth is, I have what you might call an ethical dilemma."

"What's your ethical dilemma?"

"I don't have a license to practice detection."

"I don't understand."

"I rushed into hanging up my shingle before I even looked into the requirements. I'm taking the test in a couple of weeks, but as of now, I can't work on any cases."

"But I'm not paying you anything. Is that what you want, Mr. Ruzak? You want me to pay you? Okay, what do you charge? I didn't realize this was about money. . . ."

She had started to cry. I passed her a napkin and said, "If it was about money, I would have taken your father's when he offered it."

"You couldn't take it because you don't know who did it."

She had a good point. She had wrapped the napkin around her index finger and was dabbing the corner of her eyes with it. Prep school, horseback-riding and tennis lessons, and long afternoons at the country club sipping iced tea and gossiping with the girls. We might as well have been from different planets.

"Okay, maybe it's more accurate to say I don't have the experience to help you. It's more like someone asking you tomorrow to remove a cat's gallbladder. Only I'm not sure if cats even have gallbladders. My point is, my reach has exceeded my grasp on this one."

"Okay, Mr. Ruzak."

"Please call me Teddy. Why won't you call me Teddy?"

"I understand. I guess I'll have to find somebody else to help me. . . ."

"The task force—"

"You just said the task force had it all wrong!"

"I was speaking from the exuberance of inexperience."

"What?"

"Well, it's like when—"

"Oh, no, no, no. Don't tell me what it's like. Everything you say is like something else. When is something just what it is and not like something else?"

I tried to think of an example, but just thinking of an example proved her point. She stood up and her hem fell down. When she said, "No, no, no," she had shaken her head violently and a thick strand of her dark hair had pulled free from the bun and fallen against her cheek. Audrey Hepburn, that's who she looked like. Another simile; there really was no escape.

She jumped up and went to the door.

"Susan . . ."

"I just want somebody to help me," she said. "Why won't somebody help me?"

She pulled at the knob, not realizing I had thrown the dead bolt.

"Susan," I said. "There are some things I can't tell you. . . ."

This stopped her, giving me time to cross the room.

"What things?"

"I'll be frank," I said. "Frankly, I'm really torn up right now. I'm trying to figure out what's the right thing to do, and that isn't always clear."

"You don't think finding who killed Lydia is the right thing to do?"

"It's more complicated than that."

She slowly shook her head and another strand came loose.

"That's not complicated, Mr. Ruzak," she whispered. She had started to cry again. "You don't know what it's like . . . what it's like to lose somebody . . . to lose two mothers. . . ."

"No," I said. "I lost only one."

I don't remember who moved toward who first. The next thing I knew, she was in my arms and the smell of lilacs was all around me. Then I was kissing her. Our mouths came open and I could taste cheese.

CHAPTER THIRTY-TWO

SHE BROKE THE KISS FIRST. THIS WASN'T SOMETHING NEW in my experience, so my feelings weren't hurt.

"I don't know why I did that," she said.

"Why did you?"

"I just said I didn't know." She sounded cross. "I have to go. I think I really need to go." She looked at her watch.

"I'll walk you to your car," I said.

"Why? Am I in danger?"

"No. At least, I don't think so. You'd like to think there's a limit to evil—you know, a line or a barrier that can't be crossed—but the ancient Greeks didn't buy that and I'm not too sure I do, either. Let's just say the longer you're here, the more somebody else is in danger."

"You?"

"No. Maybe. Probably, in the end."

The line deepened between her eyebrows. "You're trying very hard to tell me something without telling me anything." She waited for me to say something. When I didn't, she said, "That's okay. I understand. Well, I don't understand, really, but that's par for the course with you, Mr. Ruzak."

"Stay here till I get back," I told her.

"Where are you going?"

"I'm going to walk around the block. I won't be long."

"There's something about Lydia you're not telling me. You know something."

I knew just about everything, but how could I tell her that? I trotted down the stairs and into the night. I walked a block east toward the river and back again, but I didn't see any suspicious persons hunkered in cars, or any persons whatsoever, for that matter. I spotted her car parked across the street from my building. It was the only car parked on that side of the street.

Upstairs, she had to go to her tiptoes to kiss me good-bye.

"Thank you, Mr. Ruzak," she said softly.

"Wait," I said. "I'm walking you to your car."

I escorted her across the street, her small hand resting on my forearm as we walked.

"What's the matter?" she asked. "Why are you so jumpy?"

"It's a personality trait. Can you call me whenever you get where you're going?"

"Okay."

"Where are you going, exactly?"

"To my apartment. Why?"

"Matt staying at home with your dad?"

"Matt's staying in our condo at Riversound. Are you going to tell me what's going on?"

"Maybe later. I've got to . . . I've got some very keen thinking to do."

She laughed, threw her arms around my neck, and kissed me again. I stood on the sidewalk and waved as she made a left onto Summit Hill before disappearing from view. I stood there another couple of minutes, then went back upstairs, took a shower, sat on my unmade bed afterward for about thirty minutes, and cried.

CHAPTER THIRTY-THREE

I woke up the next morning with the sun shining in my face. The last thing I remembered before falling asleep was the conviction I would never fall asleep. The phone was ringing.

It was Gary Paul.

"Hey, sleepyhead. It's rounding ten o'clock. Rough night?"

"It's been a rough twenty-four hours, Gary."

"No doubt. But, you know, I'm not entirely to blame for that, Ted. I just got off the phone with Felicia. What a nice gal. Is she married?"

I pressed the tips of my forefinger and thumb hard into the corners of my eyes. I had cotton mouth bad, but the phone wasn't cordless and I was trapped in the bed.

"She has a boyfriend, a firefighter boyfriend. Big guy, heavy into weight training and Krav Maja."

"What the hell is Krav Maja?"

"It's this hand-to-hand street fighting technique developed by the Israelis. Very deadly stuff."

"Seriously?"

"Oh, I kid you not."

"Sometimes I get the impression you're kind of putting me on."

"You wouldn't be the only one. Anyway, I've never met him, but I hear he's got a hair-trigger temper; you know, a real hothead."

"Hmmm. And he's a firefighter, you said?"

"Yeah. He's a fire-fighting hothead."

He laughed. "Look, Ted, the reason for my call. Two reasons, really. First, I was curious after our little conversation yesterday to know how you're gonna handle things from here."

"Well," I said. "I have no tapes, no witness, no client, and no money. Like you said, even if I went to the task force, they wouldn't believe me. I can't see any way to proceed except to shut my doors and try to get my old job back."

"Gee, that's really good to hear, Ted. I know you loved being a private eye, but sometimes things don't work out."

"Oh, I'm not sure how much I loved it. It certainly wasn't what I expected, but how many things can you say turn out to be the way you expected? You should never really trust your expectations. For example, there's about eighty percent of me that actually expects you to keep up your end of our bargain."

"Why wouldn't I?"

"Gary, you've lied to me from the day we met."

"Okay, but why would I make the offer if I planned to kill you? That's what you're concerned about, right? That I plan to kill you?"

"It's crossed my mind."

"Believe me, Teddy, if that was the plan, you'd be dead already."

"That's crossed my mind, too."

I washed up in the sink, brushed my teeth, and drove straight to the office without consuming so much as a slice of toast. It was a bright, sunny day with a forecasted high of eighty-seven degrees.

Felicia was there, standing by the sill behind my desk, staring at the brick wall of the building through the window.

She was wearing a clingy gray sleeveless dress with matching gray heels and no hosiery. Her legs were nicely tanned and I wondered if

she used those tanning sprays or if that was what she'd been doing yesterday, maybe lying out by a pool.

She barely glanced at me. "Where have you been?"

"I overslept." I sank into one of the visitor's chairs. "Felicia, we
have to talk."

She nodded and sank into my executive chair. She looked
tired, the skin on her face not as tanned as her arms and legs. It
had kind of a saggy, worn look to it, and there were dark circles
under her eyes.

I got up, poured myself a cup of coffee, and sat back down.

"That cop friend of yours called," she said. "He said he was off
duty last night and didn't know till he picked up the paper this
morning."

"Okay," I said.

"Then he asked me for a date," she said, and laughed.

"What about Bob?"

"I didn't say yes, Ruzak. To tell you the truth, he kind of gives
me the creeps."

"How come?"

"He's too . . ." She gave a little wave of her hand. She was wearing a charm bracelet and the charms tinkled against one another as
she waved.

"Nice?"

"No. Yes. I don't know."

"He has bad teeth."

She laughed. "And Paul Killibrew called."

"Who's Paul Killibrew?"

"The reporter from the *Sentinel,* remember?"

"Oh, yeah."

"Jesus, Ruzak. Anyway, he wanted to talk to you about what
happened yesterday."

"I don't know anything about what happened yesterday."

"You called him after the first story ran, remember? After you saw HRT. He's thinking of doing a story on it now."

"On what?"

She sighed loudly. "On HRT seven one nine, the geese, and Lydia Marks. Whether there's a connection."

"Boy, it would be a helluva coincidence if there wasn't."

"What's the matter with you? Why are you talking like this? Tell me what's going on, Ruzak. You know something."

"Did you tell Paul about HRT seven one nine? I mean, did you give him that number?"

"No—why would I do that?"

I sipped my coffee. Felicia made it too weak for my taste. I figure if you're going to drink coffee, you might as well go for the high octane. It's like those people who smoke low-tar cigarettes. It kind of defeats the purpose of indulging in the vice in the first place.

"The real question is," I said, "Where do we go from here? My only client is dead."

"What about the reward?"

"What reward?"

"The reward for finding Lydia's killer."

I almost laughed aloud.

"I'm dropping it, Felicia."

"You're dropping . . . what? What are you dropping?"

"Everything. This." I motioned to the room.

"You're not quitting, Ruzak."

"I don't have a choice, Felicia."

She folded her bare brown arms across her chest, leaned back in my executive chair, and asked, "Because?"

"Because? Because for one thing, I'm way over my head and, like a panicked swimmer, I just keep flailing around in the water, sinking deeper the harder I try to stay afloat. Let's face it, I'm all wrong for this kind of work. I'm disorganized, I'm sloppy, I don't have a logical mind, and I tend to get too personally involved with my clients." My cheeks were hot. I was close to telling her about Susan Marks and our impromptu pizza party. I sipped some coffee to steady myself, but coffee isn't known for its steadying influence. "Plus, most importantly of all, I've bottomed out. I've got no evidence, no witnesses, no leads, no case, no license, and no money. I've come up against it, Felicia. I've hit the wall pretty hard."

"What wall, Ruzak?"

"You know, reality."

"So," she said. Her lips had gone thin. "That's it. You're done."

"I think I'm done."

"You asshole. You come into my life . . . you make these wild promises . . . you drag me into this deal so you can act out your childhood fantasies, and now when things get tough, you throw up your hands and say, 'Oh, well, guess that didn't work out. Good luck to you, Felicia.' "

"Look, it's not that bad. . . ." I fumbled in my pocket for a handkerchief, then realized I didn't even own a handkerchief, so I went into the bathroom and pulled off half a dozen squares of toilet paper and tried to hand them to her. She pushed my hand away.

"I'm not dabbing my eyes with toilet paper!"

"Right," I said, and stuffed the wad into my pocket. "Anyway, it's not that bad. I talked to Freddy, and he said—"

"When did you talk to Freddy?"

"Couple days ago."

"*Why* did you talk to Freddy?"

"He came over to the table—"

"You have no business talking to Freddy about me."

"Why not?"

"Because you have no business in my business!"

"And you have no business in mine!" I bit my lower lip hard, what I usually do when I've mouthed off and there's no way to take it back, so I guess biting my lower lip is a form of self-punishment.

"Well"—she leaned over the desk and hissed at me—"you wanna know something funny, Ruzak? I absolutely agree with you: You're not cut out for this line of work. You're probably the worst-qualified PI on the face of planet Earth, but that's not the point anymore. Whether you like it or not, you're in this thing, and now you've dragged me and . . . and my life into it with you, and throwing up your hands and walking away is not going to get either of us out of it. Before, maybe doing things half-assed was an option, but that option doesn't exist anymore, Ruzak."

I nodded, but I didn't say anything.

"So which is it?" she asked softly. "What are you going to do?"

I dropped my head. "I'm scared," I said. I raised my head. "I'm afraid, Felicia."

She nodded. "And I'm unemployed. Thanks a lot, Ruzak."

CHAPTER THIRTY-FOUR

WE ARGUED FOR ANOTHER HALF HOUR WHILE I SLUGGED down three more cups of the weak coffee and she clicked around the hardwood floor in her heels, but I held firm to my "I'm just a big fat pussy" defense, which came off convincingly because it dovetailed so well into everything she knew about me. What about justice? she asked. What about my promises? she wondered. Promises I'd made to Parker and to Susan and to her especially? The whole thing was leading into "What is your measure as a man?" territory and that was a place I'd be lost even with a map. Finally, when she realized I wasn't going to give in, she grabbed her matching snakeskin gray purse and pounded down the stairs to the street. I followed her outside, where I found her fumbling in her purse for a pair of sunglasses, which she jammed over her eyes with such force, I thought she must have bruised the bridge of her nose. I had drunk too much coffee, being fooled like those low-tar smokers who just smoke more, and, as usual when I drank too much coffee, I had the peculiar sensation of my legs being too long for my body; I seemed to lope.

"What are you doing?" she asked.

"I just wanted to say I'm sorry."

"Who cares about your 'sorry'?"

She shouldered her purse and set out toward the Hilton. She

parked there for seventy-five dollars a month, but that was paid for out of the company account. She could never say after that and all the paid time off and the free designer wardrobe that she didn't have her share of perks.

"I'm sorry, Felicia. I really am," I said, loping after her. "I never thought taking on a wild-goose case would lead—"

"Oh, save it, Ruzak. It's over. Now you can crawl back to the security company and beg for your old job and I can go plant a big fat wet one on Freddy's pimply ass. And whoever killed Lydia Marks will get away with murder."

I followed her into the garage, thinking you shouldn't assume just because a guy is on the large side that his ass is pimply. She asked why the hell I was following her into the garage. I didn't answer. When she slid into the car seat, that clingy gray number pulled up on her thigh and I saw a lot of bare tanned leg.

"Get in the car, Ruzak."

Her tone brooked no argument, so I climbed into her Corolla without any argument. Too much had happened in the past twenty-four hours to absorb in its entirety. The danger of life in general is that you get so worn down, there's not enough left of you to fight. You see this especially among the poor, but nobody's immune, even nations and whole civilizations. Everybody's gotten so tired, they get to the point where they just don't give a damn anymore. I'm not a big believer in the spiritual side of things, but I suspected I had disturbed some balance in the cosmos by calling myself "the Hammer." It flipped some kind of karmic switch.

Felicia took the Henley Street Bridge over the river, and a couple of boats were out, with young women lounging on the bows in luminescent bikinis. We passed Baptist Hospital, where my mother died, on the opposite shore, then continued south, now on Chapman Highway, heading toward Seymour. She didn't say anything and I didn't say anything, even when we passed Baptist Hospital and I was overwhelmed with memories of chemotherapies and biopsies and radiation treatments, of long silk scarves wrapped around my mother's bald head and how she seemed to shrink inside her gown as the cancer ate her from the inside. Sometimes it's not enough for life to wear you down; sometimes life just eats you alive. It cleaves you in two. A lot of people spend the majority of their lives running from that fact, but in life, death has a way of bringing you up short, grabbing you by the nape of the neck, and slinging you around to face the Big Dark.

Felicia made a left onto a little side road off the highway. We drove for about half a mile before she turned into the driveway of a small frame house, once white behind a white picket fence, but now both house and fence were badly in need of a paint job. She pulled in behind an older model Toyota truck parked beneath the corrugated overhang attached to the house and cut off the engine. Someone had removed the first two and last two letters of the make, leaving the letters YO on the tailgate. Felicia took a big breath and told me to come on, and so I followed her up the overgrown walkway to the door, and we went inside.

The blinds were drawn. A television provided the only light in the small family room, so everything had that blue TV tint, making it hard for me to tell even what color the carpeting was. A large shape rose from the sofa, and instead of being Bob's, like I expected, the shape was that of Lacey from the diner.

She stood still for a second, absorbing my presence. Felicia said, "Lacey, you know Ruzak."

Felicia dropped her purse on a straight-backed chair set by the front door and asked, "Where is he?"

"In his room," Lacey said. "Why are you here?" she asked me, or more in the direction of me.

"She drove me," I said.

She gave me a look that said she didn't care for smart-asses. A door slammed somewhere in the back and a kid came barreling into the room wearing shorts and a yellow T-shirt with Spiderman's red face on the front, and he flew into Felicia's arms as she knelt to grab him. She picked him up and spun once around with him.

"How's my captain?" she asked. "How's my little knight?" And he was all giggling and slobbering, and I guessed he was maybe four or five, but there was something wrong with this kid. His head looked too big for his body, and he was pretty hefty for a five year old, with small eyes and very short, fat fingers. He noticed me and the giggles stopped like a switch had been flipped. Felicia set him down and said, "Honey, this is the man Mommy works for. Or used to work for. Can you say hi to Mr. Ruzak?"

He kind of lunged forward on those thick legs and grabbed my hand and pulled me so that I lost my balance and almost landed right on top of him. Then he wrapped his arms around my knees and twisted his body back and forth, wiping his mouth on the leg of my pants.

"Okay, no wrestling holds on Ruzak," Felicia scolded him, and behind me Lacey was laughing. I was looking straight down at the top of the kid's head, and his hair was very fine, like a baby's hair, and I could see the irregular shape of his skull.

"Ruzak, this is Thomas," Felicia said.

"My name is Thomas!" the boy said, tilting back his head and shouting up at me. "Thomas Kincaid! Who are you?"

"I told you, honey. Mr. Ruzak," Felicia said.

"Ruzak!" the boy shouted. "Ruzak! Ruzak! Ruzak!" He let go of my knees and did a little dervish sort of dance in the space between Felicia and me. He was giggling again and a thick line of spit ran out of his mouth and trailed down his chin.

"He likes your name," Lacey said.

"Ruzak! Ruzak! Ruzak!" Thomas Kincaid shouted.

"Now you know why I dropped out of nursing school," Felicia said.

CHAPTER THIRTY-FIVE

FELICIA TOOK THOMAS BACK TO HIS ROOM AND AFTER A long time, maybe an hour, came back with red eyes, like she'd been crying, and told Lacey she'd be back after she ran me back to the office. While she was with Tommy, Lacey and I sat on the sofa with the volume on the TV turned low, and it was a long hour, because Lacey was the kind of woman who didn't like men in general, or maybe just me in particular.

"He's not right, you know," she had said after Felicia left the room. "He's got 'developmental issues.' A preemie—four pounds, six ounces when he was born. Doctors think the cord got wrapped around his neck in the womb or something like that, cutting off the oxygen to his brain."

"Who's the father?" I asked.

"Somebody Felicia met at the diner while she was working through school. He took off."

"Does he know?"

"Know what?"

"Well, did he take off when she got pregnant or after the baby was born?"

"What's that matter?"

"I guess it doesn't."

"Freddy was real good about it," Lacey said, implying I was

not. "Real understanding. Course, we were always willing to cover for her when something was going on with Tommy. She's all he's got, Ruzak."

No wonder she got so upset. Now either way things went, I had toppled the applecart. You never fully appreciate your effect on others. I was like a malevolent Jimmy Stewart in *It's a Wonderful Life*, screwing up the lives of everyone in my path.

When we got back in the car, I asked Felicia to forgive me.

"Forgive you for what?"

"Assuming you were, I don't know, a goof-off or something. Why didn't you tell me, Felicia?"

"What would that accomplish? I don't want pity, Ruzak, just a paycheck."

That made sense to me. Felicia was an awfully proud person, and awfully proud people never want special consideration. Unless they also happen to be rich—rich people usually want special consideration, based solely on the fact that they have more money than you. Like Kenneth Marks offering me the insider deal on finding his wife's killer. Money can make you arrogant, but it isn't the only thing that can. There's a certain kind of arrogance born of ignorance. Sometimes I felt like Rip Van Winkle: fifteen years on the night shift, awake when the world slept, sleeping while the world went on. I froze at the age of nineteen, when I took that job, and completely missed those life experiences that would have matured me. So in my arrogant ignorance, I had assumed Felicia was missing work because she was a goof-off or had some kind of nymphomaniacal dysfunction.

"It's Marks," she said.

"What is?"

"The killer."

"But he was in Brussels."

"He hired somebody, dummy."

"And that somebody followed me after reading the article, then killed Parker because he knew he was a witness?"

"Right. See, you're not such a bad detective, Ruzak."

"It fits the facts," I said. "But you don't need Marks in the picture for the facts to fit."

"What about the first wife?"

"That still could be a coincidence. And what about the fact of him offering me money to find the killer?"

"Done to throw you off. He knows you won't find the killer, so what's he got to lose?"

"How does he know I won't?"

"He thinks you can't. He thinks he's too clever."

"Maybe he is."

"Apparently for you."

She was trying to goad me. Appeal to my manhood. It wasn't going to work, but not for the reason she thought it wasn't. She dropped me by the front door of the Ely Building.

"Are you going back to the diner?" I asked.

"What do you care?"

"Well," I said, "I do."

"Maybe I'll take the exam and get my detective license. I don't know. Or maybe . . ." Her nose crinkled. "Maybe I'll marry Bob and he can support me."

"Has he asked?"

She rolled up her window and drove away. I thought about going upstairs to the office, but what was I going to do up in that office?

Instead, I drove to Wal-Mart and picked out a semiautomatic handgun. I filled out the application and was told I could pick up my gun after the waiting period. I told the clerk the clock was ticking but that on principle I believed in waiting lists and background checks and wondered if any exceptions were ever made based on dire circumstances. The clerk had never heard of any, and I didn't doubt that he was a highly trained professional, but still he was a Wal-Mart clerk, so I decided to look into the matter more thoroughly. You couldn't expect a Wal-Mart clerk to be an expert in all the ins and outs of federal law.

Then I drove north on Broadway until it turned into Maynardville Highway, about four miles into the Halls area, and Sharp's Ridge towered in the distance, its TV towers stretching like long fingers against the backdrop of the overcast sky. I hadn't been to Halls since the week after I buried Mom; her insurance agent was out there, Harry Conrack, a burly ex-marine with a crew cut. I explained what I was after, and Harry looked me up in his actuarial tables and told me if I lost twenty to twenty-five pounds and got out of my risky line of work, I could reduce my premium by forty-five dollars a month. Then he performed some calculations—burial expenses, plus outstanding debts, plus my last four years' income, plus the time remaining on my leases for the apartment and the office—and came up with a value on my life of $250,000. That struck me as strangely too much and not enough.

"Who do you want as the beneficiary?" He had been a drill sergeant in the marines and tended to bark his questions at you, looking down his nose over his little half glasses like you were a raw recruit just off the bus.

I gave him Felicia's name. He scribbled it on the form.

"Anybody else?"

I didn't answer at first.

"Listen! You can do it two ways, Ruzak," he shouted. "Co-beneficiary or contingent beneficiary, in case she's dead, too."

"Contingent," I said. "Thomas Kincaid."

He told me a nurse would be calling in the next couple days to arrange a physical. Then he sold me a rider that stated if I was ever hospitalized, I would receive a stipend of two thousand dollars a month. I thought that was a particularly sweet deal, since being healthy never brought in that much.

Then he asked if I had renter's insurance.

"No."

"You're buying some."

"I am?"

"Damn straight you are, Ruzak!" They say the best salesmen fit their pitch to their personalities. Harry had all sorts of awards on his walls and pictures of himself with celebrities and politicians and other important-looking people whom I didn't recognize. Harry's pitch was perfectly meshed with his military background.

So I left his office insured from the soles of my feet to the top of my head. He informed me I was an extremely lucky individual, since nothing horrible had happened since the hanging of my shingle, and gave me two coffee mugs, a calendar, some brochures on financing my next vehicle through him, and a prospectus on mutual funds. The burden of being a truly responsible adult felt new and strange to me, but at the same time I felt liberated from my childhood in a way my mother's death could not deliver.

I stopped for lunch on the way to the office, so it was after three o'clock when I finally walked through the door. The place was lonely without Felicia around. She had hardly ever been around even when she was around, but at least the potential for Felicia had been there. It was lonely and hot and smelled bad. I went through the mail, then checked my messages. There was just one, from Susan Marks.

"Hey," I said when she answered the phone. "I was going to call you. I probably should tell you I'm getting out of the detective business, too, but anyway, how are you?"

"Oh, I'm okay." She sighed into the phone, and for some reason, the cheese clinging to her bottom lip immediately leapt into my mind. "I'm starting my summer job, working for a vet full-time. Dad's planning another trip overseas and Matt's taking some summer classes because his grades were so horrible."

"You hear anything from the task force?"

"They don't talk to me. They talk to Dad."

"Does Dad talk to you?"

"What does that mean?"

"I mean about what's happening with the case."

"Oh. No. No, not much."

"When's he leaving?"

"In a couple days. Paris this time."

"Would you like to have a cup of coffee sometime?"

"That would be great," she said in a tone that told me it probably wouldn't be.

The call ended with both of us feeling a little relieved that no definite plans had been made. She was a nice girl, but our connection was based on death. It's always hard to forge something tender out of that.

CHAPTER THIRTY-SIX

THAT NIGHT I MADE THE MISTAKE OF FALLING ASLEEP TO
the Discovery Health Channel, which late at night airs very
graphic shows of operations. I dreamed I was in Mom's hospital
room when a Code Blue went off and the doctor decided there
was no time to get her into the OR, so they cut Mom open right
there and the doctor reached in and pulled out Lydia Marks's
head from Mom's stomach, and the head began to talk in a lilting
Irish brogue, only it was one of those dreams where you couldn't
make out the words, but it was clear enough from the head's attitude that I was a deep disappointment as a detective and an even
deeper one as a human being. I woke with the word *reword* on my
tongue. I stood in the shower a long time, wondering why I woke
thinking of *reword,* until it occurred to me that maybe what I
should have thought was *reward* and, to protect myself, my brain
turned it into *reword.* Of course, in some private depths, I must
have realized the day before what I had to do. It was really the
only option left to me, and why I'd decided to buy a gun and life
insurance at the same time I'd decided to quit. Timing was a
problem: Marks was leaving the country in two days and the waiting period on the gun was six. I guessed I could have borrowed a
gun from somebody, but the only person I knew who owned a

gun for sure was Gary Paul. On the other hand, I wasn't sure what I would do with a gun. I'd failed marksmanship in the Academy, but just the thought of having one made me feel better, like keeping an emergency kit of batteries and fresh water and nonperishable canned goods tucked in a closet in case of a terrorist or nuclear attack.

I looked up the address in the phone book, then got in my car and, instead of heading west, took Broadway to Central, to the cemetery where my mother lay.

"Well," I told her. "I guess I've solved my first case, but it looks like it also might be my last case, and the one thing I didn't plan for or tell anyone was where I want to be buried, which, of course, would be right here next to you and Dad, but both places are taken up by other families, so I don't know where they're gonna lay me. I guess Felicia will decide that. If I had any foresight, I would have told her or written a note, but my problem is that I can't think of everything. Of course, if I had any foresight, I wouldn't have taken up this whole cockamamy detective thing in the first place, but it's like you always said, Mom, you gotta play the cards that're dealt you, even in solitaire. I never told you this, but I don't much believe in heaven or an afterlife, but I like Whitman's idea that we become part of the grass and all the green growing things, even those dead goslings, though there're some schools of thought that hold animals have no soul. Then somebody close to you dies and you've got to justify your loss with the fact that you suspect it's permanent in the cosmic sense. There's also that whole question of suffering and why it happens if there's a big Someone absolutely great and good looking after us, so I suspect the whole reason I'm not more spiritual is my shorts in the brains department. You know when I was little how I loved those seek-and-find word puzzles? I think that deal was me trying to convince myself I was smart, as if finding *artichoke* out of a jumble of letters proved anything. I love you, Mom, and I miss you, but I probably won't be back."

The traffic was heavy and slow on the interstate heading west through the ubiquitous construction zones. For the past ten years, the interstate had been torn up at various places as Knoxville's population expanded, though I suspected it had more to do with politics and the lining of the big construction company's pockets as payback for campaign contributions. It was easy to believe, but most cynical things are. Cynicism is easy; optimism takes real effort.

The house was in a development about a half mile from the park where the geese lived and Parker Hudson died. It was easily the most impressive abode in the most impressive neighborhood in Farragut. Three stories, huge columns in front, built to resemble a European castle but on a small lot, like the houses around it, with a half-circle cobblestone driveway and a life-size statue of a naked lady holding a bowl out of which water trickled into a pool. Water lilies floated on the surface, and underneath you could see the white and orange spots of the large koi, which sold for two or three hundred dollars a pop. I rang the bell and could hear it echoing inside as I waited for a guy called Jeeves to answer the door in white tie and tails. When I was in my twenties, like a lot of guys in their twenties, I imagined myself as fabulously rich, and my chief fantasy entailed a manservant who would shave me every day, because that was the essence of true wealth in my mind: It meant never having to shave myself, because, like most men, I hated to shave. I waited, but no one named Jeeves came to the door. Maybe it would be a sweet curly-haired thing of French ancestry in one of those frilly-skirted maid numbers. I rang the bell again and after about thirty seconds I heard the lock turn. The door opened, and Kenneth Marks was standing there, wearing a business suit and holding a cup of coffee.

"Mr. Ruzak," he said.

"Mr. Marks," I replied. "I was going to say I was in the neighborhood and decided to drop by, but actually I drove straight here from my apartment. Well, I stopped by my mother's grave first."

"I see."

"I'm unarmed."

"I'm relieved."

"We need to talk."

"Urgently, I assume."

"Yeah. Pretty urgently."

He stepped back and I stepped forward and then he closed the door behind me. We were standing in a huge entryway that soared the entire three stories. The floor plan was more open than I'd expected; I'd thought the rooms would be small and I'd anticipated a lot of dark nooks and crannies, because when you think of evil, you picture a kind of spider's lair of labyrinthine complexity. That was probably a comic-book approach to evil, but I'm a product of my generation, where most movies are just comic books that move.

I followed him into the living room, or it might have been a very large formal sitting room, where one entire wall was comprised of two-story-length windows with a view of the lake and the high ridge on the opposite shore. There was a piano in one corner and a sixty-five- or seventy-inch big-screen television in the other. Above the sofa upon which I sat was a massive oil painting of the Marks family: Kenneth in the middle, with an auburn-haired woman seated beside him, and Susan and Matt standing behind their parents. Susan looked around fifteen or sixteen, so I assumed the woman I was looking at was not Lydia, but Kenneth Marks's first wife. I wondered how Lydia felt looking at the picture of the Marks family, seeing the first wife sitting by her husband and Lydia standing on the outside of the picture, as it were,

and for the first time I began to understand how terribly lonely
Lydia Marks must have been.

"Would you like anything, Mr. Ruzak?"

"No thanks."

He sat across from me in a leather recliner that faced the TV,
crossed his legs, and waited.

"Nobody knows I'm here," I said.

"Is that important?"

"I thought it might be. I'm also not wearing a wire."

"A . . . wire?"

"You know, a listening or recording device. You can frisk me if
you want."

"I have no desire to frisk you, Mr. Ruzak."

"That's good. That's terrific. You trust me. This isn't going to
work unless you trust me."

"What isn't going to work, Mr. Ruzak?"

I took a deep breath and let it out slowly, but that didn't steady
me, so I commenced to cracking my knuckles, and the sound of
the popping seemed very loud.

"Mr. Ruzak," he said. "I can think of only one reason for you
to come here, so may we proceed? I'm rather busy getting ready
for a business trip."

"That's right, you're going to Europe. Paris, right?"

He nodded. "How did you know?"

I swallowed. "I know pretty much everything by this point,
Mr. Marks."

"Really?" He crossed his legs and pulled the cloth on the upper
knee with his hands.

"Well, some things I know with certainty and some things I
know with just reasonable certainty, but others with less than certain, um, certainty. Maybe I will have something. Maybe a glass
of water?"

He got up at once, disappeared around a half wall, and came back with a glass of water with no ice. If I had Ken Marks's money, I thought, I'd have a little silver bell to ring when I wanted a glass of water. I thanked him, took a sip, and put my glass on the glass-topped coffee table in front of me. There were no coasters, and I worried irrationally about leaving a ring.

"You know who killed Lydia?"

I nodded. "You know I do."

He stared at me from across the room. I took another sip and saw it on the coffee table, the damned ring of sweated water.

"Okay," I said. "Enough beating around the bush." I was talking to myself as much as to him. "Let's strip it down to the bone. It occurred to me as I was working through this problem that the only way to go was to the top. It's like when you can't get satisfaction from the clerk, you go to the store manager. Or like my phone bill. My phone bill is always messed up. Month after month, there's something wrong with it, and month after month I call the phone company on that toll-free number where they put you on hold for twenty minutes and at the end of it you're talking to some barely literate, poorly trained customer service representative who usually has some kind of foreign accent. Like the last time I called. The rep sounded Indian—not American Indian but Indian Indian. You know, from India. Which he probably was, because of all the outsourcing. And after another twenty or thirty minutes, you're transferred to someone higher up and have to go through the whole spiel again, until you finally reach somebody invested with some decision-making capabilities. My point is, if you want any kind of satisfaction, you've got to go to the string puller."

He nodded. "The string puller."

"The guy in charge. That's why I'm here. Because this whole deal has really put me in an untenable position, Mr. Marks. I've closed my doors as requested, but I can't spend the rest of my life looking over my shoulder, waiting for the other shoe to drop. Eventually, the logic's going to overwhelm you, and my ass—if you'll excuse my language—my ass is grass."

"Forgive me, Mr. Ruzak, but I'm having some trouble following what you're saying."

"See, that's been a problem of mine for some time. I think I told you I worked as a night-shift security guard for a lot of years, and night work tends to do things to your head. You don't get the normal distractions and interactions of the waking, working world. You know, coworkers and lunch dates, things of that nature. You lose the grip on your own thoughts and you develop a tendency to ramble. You become susceptible to all sorts of verbal and physical ticks, like cracking your knuckles, for example, or mumbling to yourself. Mumbling is a particular hazard. You start to do it without realizing it, and the next thing you know, people are staring at you in elevators and enlarging their personal space. I've had a hard time adjusting."

"I can see that."

"But I just can't see this situation continuing indefinitely. Sooner or later, the hammer's going to fall, unless you and I can reach some sort of understanding."

"I would like nothing better than to understand you." He looked at his watch. "What do you want, Mr. Ruzak?"

"The, um, reword. I mean, the *reward*. I believe—um, I think I have this right—I believe the offer was two million dollars."

He laced his fingers together and studied me over them with an inscrutable expression.

"You have proof?" he finally asked softly.

"I have enough," I replied.

"You are satisfied it would be sufficient for a court of law?"

"Sufficient enough to get the task force extremely interested.

Enough for search warrants and subpoenas. Enough to make things uncomfortable for the parties involved."

He nodded. "And what is this proof?"

"I have tapes. He took the originals, but I made copies." I held my breath. If I were him, I thought I'd demand to hear the tapes. If he did, the jig was up.

"Tapes of what?"

"The witness to Lydia's abduction identifying the getaway vehicle. The patsy set up to take the fall for the goose killing."

"I see."

"These tapes are in a location known only to me and to one other person. Nothing will be done with them and no one will know about them unless something should happen to me or to someone else."

"To whom?"

"You know whom."

"The other person?"

"Exactly."

"And what if something should happen to both of you?"

"You're getting confused, Mr. Marks."

"I have been confused, practically since you walked in the door, Mr. Ruzak."

"This other person with knowledge of the tapes is not connected to the person to whom nothing must happen. Neither you nor the person who killed your wife knows who this third person is. But they have instructions from me to turn the tapes over to the authorities if something should happen to me or to the second person."

"The second person?"

"The person who was threatened by the first person."

"I thought the second person was the person with the tapes."

"No, that's the third person. I just mentioned them first."

"Would not that make them the first person?"

"Now I'm getting confused," I said.

"I thought you were the first person."

"No, the first person is the person who threatened the second person."

"If the first person is the person who threatened the second person and the third person is the person who has the instructions, who are you?"

"I guess I would be the fourth person. You'd be the fifth. It really doesn't matter how many persons there are, Mr. Marks."

"I'm relieved. You were saying you want to collect the reward—not the public reward, but the private one, the gentlemen's agreement between us?"

"There you go." Now I was relieved. "You've got it."

"I think it might be best if we backed up a bit," he said. "I'm not entirely clear on some points."

"Oh, I know you think you've got me over a barrel here, but even if I didn't have the tapes, I probably have enough. A reporter's been snooping around, and even if Gary disposes of the Ford, I've got Mike Carroll and the rental house and Gary paying him a thousand bucks to take the fall for the goslings. Plus, I know he was trying to drive home the point, but it was really a boneheaded move for Gary Paul to take me to the lake. The only way to keep a lid on this whole deal is my silence. Now, there are only two ways to ensure my silence. The ham-handed and dangerous approach of killing me—or killing the second person, or maybe she was the third person, I can't remember—or buying my silence. I figured you, being the savvy investor, would realize it's a much safer bet to give me the cash."

"Of course," he said. "The deputy. Gary Paul."

"Yeah, the deputy Gary Paul, the first person."

"You have proof he murdered my wife?"

"It's more like evidence, and it's circumstantial, like I said."

"And you won't take this proof or evidence to the task force?"

"You've got my word on that."

He studied me over those thick fingers for a long time. Then he smiled.

"Will you take a check?"

"I'd prefer cash."

"It will take a few days to arrange."

"That's fine."

"And what about, as you put it, the evil?"

"Oh, you can't get away from it," I said. "Nobody will ever go to trial for the murder, though you can never tell. Maybe the task force will break the case on their own. I've got to live with that, but at least this way there's a chance I'll be alive to live with that. That's where self-interest trumps moral character, Mr. Marks. I don't want to die and I especially don't want somebody close to me and completely innocent to die."

He nodded. "The spilling of innocent blood calls for justice. That is the ultimate moral issue, Mr. Ruzak. I am at peace with that."

He rose and offered me his hand. I took it, and his grip was very hard and he looked unblinking into my eyes. A chill went down my spine, as if I had walked over somebody's grave.

CHAPTER THIRTY-SEVEN

I DROVE BACK TO THE OFFICE AND CALLED ROGER NEW-some, my landlord.

"Ruzak!" he shouted. "How's the redecorating going?"

"That's one of the things I wanted to talk to you about," I said. "I'm closing up shop."

"What?"

"I'm going out of business. Things didn't work out and I need out of the lease."

"Oh, Teddy, that's too bad. It's dog-eat-dog out there, ain't it?"

"In a week or so, I can pay you back, as well as the balance on my lease."

"That's damn good to hear, Ted, because if you don't, I'm gonna take you to court and sue your fat ass for breach of contract."

Next, I called Felicia's number, but there was no answer. I should have gone home or, better yet, booked a flight to Bermuda, because if Marks and Gary were going to make their move, it probably would be sooner rather than later. Instead, I stayed and cleaned out my desk. I called the paper and placed an ad for a going-out-of-business sale. I figured the computer and furniture were worth at least a couple grand, even at forced-sale prices. I calculated the cost of paying out both leases, for the office and for my apartment, and wondered where I should move and how much of the two million Felicia deserved for my bulling my way into her life and nearly getting her killed. At least half. Around three o'clock, I lugged all the potted plants down the stairs and loaded them into my car, because I didn't plan to be back until the date of the sale and because, like I've said, it's all precious; life matters because there never has been and may never be proof it exists anywhere else. I drove to my apartment, where I pretty much holed up for the rest of the week, except to go out once to shop for groceries.

I had trouble sleeping at night. I figured this had something to do with my circumstances, this waiting for the other shoe to drop, because Marks was a businessman who weighed risks every day, and what was the life of some mediocre amateur detective worth against the possibility of the death chamber? Probably falling asleep or trying to fall asleep with the television on contributed to my sleeplessness, but the silence in my apartment was deafening without its sound, and when I turned it off, I could feel the nothingness represented by that silence pressing in upon me, literally squeezing my head, and my heart would pound with such force that I was afraid a couple of times it would explode. I'd crawl out of bed and stand by the window and look down at the empty street below and think if I moved to some tropical locale with a million dollars, I could live like a king, especially if I chose one of those terribly poor islands like Jamaica. Not only would I be rich but also safe, even from a terrorist attack. What terrorist in his right mind would ever think about attacking Jamaica? When I thought about Jamaica, I thought of goats, for some reason, hundreds of goats wandering dusty streets, and brightly colored stucco buildings with raggedy-assed children wandering around begging you for money. That would be my downfall: I'd give all the money away by the second week and be just as poor as everybody else there. You have to have a hard heart to make money, real money, and a harder one to hang on to it. Bill Gates gives away millions every year, but he makes that much in about ten minutes.

So I was wide-awake when my phone rang at two o'clock in the morning, six days after my meeting with Kenneth Marks. I didn't know who would be calling, but I had a pretty good idea what they were calling about.

"Mr. Ruzak?"

"Yes?"

"I am below the building, in the parking garage."

"What building?"

"Your building, Mr. Ruzak. I have a delivery for you."

"I guess it isn't FedEx."

"No, Mr. Ruzak. It is not FedEx."

"Let me throw some clothes on and I'll be right down."

I was fully dressed, didn't understand why I had lied, and was forced by my own lie to cool my heels an extra five minutes before heading down. Lying is the worst kind of buffoonery. The parking garage, like a lot of underground setups, was poorly lighted, having the lowest-wattage fluorescents you could buy, but I saw him right away, standing by a pillar about twenty feet from the elevators: a very big man wearing a jogging outfit and tennis shoes. On the ground beside him were two large paper grocery bags.

"I'm Teddy Ruzak," I told him unnecessarily.

"It would be best if you did not know my name," he said. He had a wide, flat face, a crooked nose, and large cauliflower ears like a boxer's. His huge hands were gloved and I could detect the faintest hint of wood smoke clinging to him.

"Oh, I'm all for what's best," I said. "My struggle is figuring out what exactly that is."

He picked up the paper bags and held them out. I wondered if they contained exactly a million apiece. It would fit with Marks's personality, very symmetrical, very balanced. I hesitated before taking the money. I should have been relieved. After all, ol' Crooked Nose could have put a bullet through my head just as easily as handing over two million dollars. Maybe I hesitated because another splinter had lodged itself into my brain at the phrase "confirmed your information."

I thanked him, took the bags, and we awkwardly disengaged, because this really wasn't the time or place for pleasantries—what do you say to a bagman? I walked quickly to the elevator without looking back and didn't turn until I was inside and the doors were closing. When I turned, he was nowhere in sight. Upstairs, I immediately pushed the two sacks under my bed, but there was no hope of sleep now. Lying over them, I was as restless as the princess over the pea; I was like that narrator in Poe's "The Tell-Tale Heart." So I climbed out of bed and paced the apartment as I waited for dawn. I had that same funny feeling I'd had right before they found Lydia's skull on the mountaintop. I was holding vigil. I kept telling myself I was safe now and Felicia was safe. Everybody was safe; it was over. I had started out a broke, unlicensed detective and now I was a millionaire. But the truth was, a crime had been committed, and I was about to find out I was up to my wide hips in it.

CHAPTER THIRTY-EIGHT

FELICIA CALLED A FEW HOURS LATER. SHE WAS CRYING. I'D never heard Felicia cry, and at first I didn't know who it was. Like a lot of people's, her crying voice was different from her regular voice.

"Have you seen this morning's paper, Ruzak?"

"No. Why?"

"When does it stop? When will it stop, Ruzak?"

I told her I'd call her back, then jogged down to the Walgreens and bought a newspaper. I read the front-page story as I walked back to my apartment. I read it a second time before calling her back.

"Have you had breakfast?" I asked.

An hour later, she pulled into the space next to mine at the Krispy Kreme on Kingston Pike, and her left leg seemed to take forever getting out of the car, it was so long—not the car, her leg. She was wearing white shorts, a striped long-sleeved shirt with the sleeves rolled to her elbows and the collar turned up. She had piled her blond hair on top of her head, which I'd heard women do when they have no time to fuss with their hair. Her makeup was perfect, though, and she didn't look like somebody who had been wailing on the phone just an hour before. I cry for ten minutes, and for days my face looks like somebody's used it for a football.

"This better be good, Ruzak," she said. "You better have a good explanation for this."

"Let's go inside," I said. "Look, the HOT sign is lighted."

"What's in the shopping bags?"

"I'll show you inside."

I ordered two coffees and four regular doughnuts. I followed her with the tray to a table in the far corner, away from the door and the glass facade, to which I positioned my back so I could watch the conveyor belts carrying their precious cargo.

"How's Tommy?" I asked.

"He's fine, and how have you been, Theodore? Cut the crap and tell me what's going on."

"Let me pose it as a hypothetical. . . ."

"Hypothetical? You're going to pose another hypothetical. Well, you want to know something, Ruzak? I have a hypothetical, too. Would you like to hear my hypothetical?"

She sipped her coffee, set down the cup, tore a doughnut in two, and took a bite. One of the delightful things about doughnuts is the way a fresh one will almost dissolve on your tongue. Krispy Kreme recommends microwaving the day-olds on high for eight seconds to simulate the fresh-from-the-hot-oil taste.

"There's this old man, see," Felicia said. "And one fine morning he's taking his morning constitutional and this big black truck roars past him on—"

"It wasn't a—"

"Shut up. Roars past him on the road, killing this gaggle of itty-bitty baby birdies, and he's so shocked and outraged, he hires this overweight, underqualified PI to—"

"Investigative consultant."

"Shut up. Who puts the old geezer under hypnosis so he remembers the tag number of the big black *truck* that flattened his precious ducks—"

"Goslings."

"Shut up. Then this nice lady turns up dead in the mountains, a lady who happened to have disappeared at the same time the baby birdies bought the farm in the same neighborhood they happen to have bought it, and after the old fart remembers the tag number he's fished out of a lake—"

"That's one of the things I need to—"

"Shut up! And that left four people who knew the significance of HRT seven one nine: the shrink who hypnotized him, the overweight, underqualified PI, a deputy sheriff with the Knox County sheriff's office, and . . . who else? Oh yeah, the overweight, underqualified PI's girl Friday! Only now there aren't four; there're just three, right, Ruzak? Am I counting right? Because we lost another one last night, didn't we?"

"You know," I said, "when you put it that way, the bodies do seem to be piling up faster than in a Greek tragedy, where everybody seems to die in the end, except the gods, but of course they're immortal and can't die. Felicia, I think I see where your hypothetical is leading, and—"

"You're about to tell me this is a fantastic coincidence, aren't you? You are actually about to say we can't draw any conclusions from the fact that Gary Paul was burned alive while he slept in his own bed, aren't you?"

"The only thing I can really say about that is I don't think the fire was an accident."

She stared at me for a second. *"Really?"*

"Felicia, I should have told you this a couple of weeks ago, but I know who HRT seven one nine is." I told her the full story, from the setup with Mike Carroll in the Marks rental home—which happened to be the same house Gary Paul had died in the night before—to Gary's visit to my apartment, the trip to the lake, and his threat to kill her if I ratted him out. She ate her second doughnut while she listened but let her coffee go cold.

"He threatened my life and you didn't tell me?"

"I figured I didn't have to. Not once I, um, fired you. And I was sure if I told you, you'd go straight to the cops. See, it put me in a delicate position, Felicia. If I told the cops, he'd kill you, or if I told you, you'd go to the cops and then he'd kill you, thinking I did tell. Then he'd kill me. Or he'd kill me first, then kill you out of spite. Or vice versa. Either way, we'd be dead. I couldn't see any way out of it, so I—"

"Oh my God," she whispered.

"Oh my God what?"

"Ruzak, you didn't."

"I didn't what?"

"Jesus Christ, Teddy, you *didn't.*" The color drained from her face and for a second I was afraid she was going to be sick.

"What? Oh. No, of course I didn't. I'm not . . . I could never bring myself to do something like that, Felicia. Even for you."

"Oh." She seemed strangely disappointed. "So who did?"

I watched the rows of doughnuts passing beyond the plate-glass window and their brown skin glistened with wet glaze while these two old ladies in paper hats supervised their progress.

"I think I know," I said. "And I think I know why. But I've got to be careful about jumping to conclusions. I jumped to a very big, very bad conclusion a week ago, and now Gary is dead. His blood is on my hands, Felicia; and I know, I know, he's a cold-blooded killer."

I reached under the table and put the two paper bags on the table. She gave me a quizzical look, then peeked into one of the bags. She stared inside for a long time, then looked in the other one. Then she looked up at me.

"How much?" she whispered.

"Two million. I was going to give you half. You know, for your trouble, for what I've put you through."

She was staring at the paper sacks. I slipped them back under the table, tucking them between my feet. "Ken Marks?" she asked.

I nodded. "The man who I think torched Gary brought this to me at two A.M. this morning. Probably came straight over after taking care of Gary. Now there's really only one reason I have it, just one explanation, and I think I understood even before I read this morning's paper, because he said Marks had 'confirmed my information.' See, if he was just knocking off potential witnesses, he wouldn't be paying me two million dollars for information he already had."

She looked hard at me and said, "Huh?"

"This money has meaning beyond its purchasing power, and giving it to me can mean only one thing: Ken Marks is innocent—and he is also guilty. I thought he was guilty of the one thing, but I *know* he's guilty of this thing. And now I've reached the real nub of it, Felicia, because I can walk. I've got two million dollars—well, one million, I mean—and I can go anywhere I want and do anything I want, but all I seem to want to do is sit down and cry. I thought I'd hit the wall before, but now I've hit reality with a capital *W*. Ever since I became a detective, or a nominative detective, I've been struggling with this issue of my moral character. See, I believe Ken Marks is a man of his word and a deal's a deal. If I decide it ends here, it ends here. I could even go back to being a detective, you could go back to being my secretary, and nobody would ever be the wiser. And you could even argue that justice had its day and everybody got what they deserved. Lydia got justice and so did Gary, though of the primitive variety. But still two wrongs don't make a right—or rather, one wrong doesn't make two wongs white."

" 'Two wongs white'?"

"I'm sorry, I'm very tired and talking too fast and that was like a tongue twister, like 'toy boat.' I meant 'two wrongs right.'"

"Ruzak . . ." She was searching for the right words. "Ruzak, what the hell are you talking about?"

"I'm talking about doing the right thing. What's the right thing to do? How can I be a detective now that I'm a material witness toting two million dollars in blood money in a couple of paper bags? Nothing I could have done would have settled things better than they are right now. Gary can't hurt either of us now and, anyway, nothing can bring Parker and Lydia back. On the other hand, I'm soaked to the skin with blood keeping this money and if I don't figure out what to do about it, I'm gonna end up like Lady Macbeth with the 'Out, damned spot' deal going."

"You're going to have to back up and go slow for me, Ruzak."

I sighed. "I called Susan Marks after I read the story. Her dad's been in Paris this past week, but he's coming home in two days. I've got two days to decide: Do I let it lie, which some people might reasonably argue is the right thing, or do I figure out some way to trap him, which other people might reasonably argue is the right thing? Because here's the other thing that occurred to me: What if a deal isn't a deal and Marks decides he can't trust me? Gary killed Parker to protect himself. What's to stop Kenneth Marks from doing the same thing to me?"

She sipped her cold coffee. Her nose didn't quite crinkle, but it did scooch a little—more of a half crinkle.

"I guess just one thing," she said. "Teddy Ruzak, the master of detection."

CHAPTER THIRTY-NINE

TWO DAYS LATER, I WAS WAITING FOR HIM JUST OUTSIDE the screening area at the Knoxville airport: After 9/11, unticketed people weren't allowed on the tiny concourse. I was wearing a new trench coat with the collar turned up and a floppy hat, not to disguise myself, but because it was raining and the trench coat had large pockets, in which my new semiautomatic made hardly a bulge—plus, like a lot of big men in trench coats, I looked pretty good. I came the closest I ever had to looking the part of hard-boiled private eye. I wasn't completely comfortable, though I looked good, and looking good takes you a long way toward comfort. I may have looked it, but I was a far cry from hard-boiled, and the gun might as well have been a cap pistol, given my proficiency with firearms.

This wide walkway leading up to the metal detectors and screeners was divided by a fountain constructed of boulders hauled north from the Little Pigeon River in the mountains. It was pretty to look at but very loud, a constant humming roar, so friends and family waiting to greet the arriving flights practically had to shout to be heard. The incessant sound of running water also had an effect on my bladder; I had been to the men's room twice since arriving at the airport. I stood apart from the group, near the big windows that overlooked the gates and the runway.

I watched as the plane touched down and slowly taxied to the gate. I looked at my watch. Right on time. That was good, because I had people waiting for us back at the office and I was adverse to keeping people waiting as a general principle.

He was walking by himself, pulling a little rolling carry-on. He didn't see me, or if he did, he didn't recognize me. I fell into step with him and said, "Mr. Marks," raising my voice a little to be heard over the roar of the falls.

He barely slowed down. "Mr. Ruzak." So maybe he had seen me, or was adjusting brilliantly to the surprise. Another thing that separates the very successful from the rest of us is their ability to adapt to rapid change.

"Have a good flight?"

"I had a long flight, Mr. Ruzak."

"You must be tired, and then there's the jet lag. I wouldn't bother you, Mr. Marks, but there's been a development."

He didn't ask me what the development was. He just kept walking toward the escalators that took you down to the baggage-claim area.

"Gary Paul died three nights ago when the house he was renting from you burned to the ground."

He still didn't say anything, just stepped onto the escalator, which was too narrow to stand abreast, so I rode a couple steps back from him, and for the first time, I noticed a bald spot on his crown, which might explain why he wore his hair so long: It wasn't a fashion statement; it was a comb-over. For some reason, I felt an irrational wave of pity for Kenneth Marks wash over me. It wasn't too late to call this off, and besides, who was I to think I could outwit a guy like Kenneth Marks, who made a living going toe-to-toe against the best and brightest business minds in the world? It was like a dog playing chess with Bobby Fischer. We got off the escalator and I followed him to the baggage claim, where he stood stiffly erect, his posture absolutely perfect, and again this struck me as quintessentially German, the quasi-militarist precision of the man. But speaking of precision, the Swiss are known for their watches—and army knives.

"I hardly see what that has to do with me, Mr. Ruzak."

"Really? Well, maybe not, but it's got everything to do with our little deal, and that's what we need to talk about."

"Very well."

"Not here. I don't know what your schedule is like, but if you don't mind, I'd like to take you back to my office."

"Why?"

"There's someone I want you to meet."

"Mr. Ruzak, I believe I told you my flight was quite long. I'm tired. Perhaps in a day or two . . ."

"I'm afraid it can't wait, Mr. Marks. See, a potential witness has come forward, and the three of us need to sit down and hammer this thing out before the whole shebang blows up in our faces."

He raised an eyebrow at me. "A potential witness?"

"I'm afraid so."

"A potential witness to what?"

"I'd really rather not talk about it here, Mr. Marks."

He thought about it, or at least I assumed he was thinking about it. But you shouldn't always assume just because someone falls silent that they're thinking about something.

"Very well," he said.

His luggage was one of those hard-sided numbers about the size of a large cedar chest and must have weighed about a hundred pounds. I know because I pulled it off the conveyor belt for him and walked behind him, pulling his luggage to the sidewalk outside like his coolie. A big black Lincoln was parked there, engine idling, and as we stepped out, the big crooked-nosed man with the cauliflower ears swung his bulk from the driver's seat. He gave me a quick nod, one rich man's henchman to another, and snapped open a large umbrella, holding it over the man as Ken Marks turned to me.

"I'll follow you there," he said.

"I'm parked in the garage. Why don't you have your driver pull up and I'll follow you?"

"Very well." Mr. Crooked Nose held the door for him and he disappeared behind the tinted glass.

Downtown Knoxville was a twenty-five-minute drive from the airport, which was actually not in Knoxville but in Alcoa, named for the aluminum company that was the major employer there. The rain couldn't decide whether it wanted to be fitful or torrential; I kept having to adjust my wiper speed. I'd always liked this drive on Alcoa Highway into Knoxville, with the high ridges on either side of the road, and especially in the fall, when the leaves changed, though spring wasn't bad, with all the dogwoods blooming, the white-and-pink blossoms seeming to float on pillows of bright green. The blossoms had fallen and the rain turned the leaves a deep emerald green and whispered as it fell to the carpet of rotting leaves from the year before, the compost that fed the saplings. Life was like that, indefatigable: After meteors and ice ages and cataclysmic upheavals, wars and famines and droughts and plagues, life just kept coming back for more. It's been fashionable since Hiroshima to be down on the human race and our chances for survival, but I'm an optimist, like I've said. I've never really believed we'll end our days in a single orgasmic instant of fire or go down in a long twilight struggle against forces more in love with death than with life. Even stuff like Ebola and AIDS and global warming don't concern me too much. Even though I lack the spiritual component to combat that kind of despair, I really don't think human beings have an apocalypse in their future, beyond the inevitable blowing up of the sun in about four billion years. It's easy to get down on ourselves, but if the race is really in trouble, what Kenneth Marks and Gary Paul did wouldn't be crimes and, probably most importantly, Parker Hudson wouldn't have given a flip about the deaths of six baby geese.

Crooked Nose double-parked in front of the Ely Building and waited on the sidewalk, holding the umbrella over Marks's balding crown while I searched for a parking place on Church. I saw Marks talking on his cell phone and I wondered, first, whom he was talking to; second, if Crooked Nose was the thug who'd started the fire that killed Gary; and, third, if I would ever find a place to park in this town that never seemed to have enough parking spaces. I finally found a spot on Gay Street and it took me about five minutes to maneuver my little Sentra into the spot. I'd never been good at parallel parking.

I hoofed it the three blocks back to the Ely, my floppy hat pulled low over my forehead, the gun bumping against my thigh. Marks said something sotto voce to Crooked Nose, who got back in the car. I breathed a sigh of relief. The muscle would stay outside, which indicated a measure of trust on Marks's part. He followed me up the creaky stairs, and my labored breathing sounded very loud in the close space. Marks glided silently as a ghost.

We stepped into the little secretary's area and shook the rainwater off our coats. I took off my hat and hung it on the rack by the door, then shrugged off my coat and hung that on the peg below the hat. Marks was staring into my office, at the back of the man's head sitting in one of the visitor's chairs. I nodded toward the secretary's desk as she came around to take his coat.

"Mr. Marks, this is my secretary, Felicia."

"How do you do," she said. "Can I get you anything, Mr. Marks? We have coffee, juice, Evian, soda . . ."

"The office sprang for one of those minifridges," I told him.

"Nothing, thank you." He looked at his watch.

"I guess I'll have some coffee," I told her, and waved him into my office.

I made the introductions. "Mr. Marks, this is Mike Carroll."

Marks barely glanced at him. He sat in the other chair with the same Teutonic stoicism as the first time he sat there, which seemed a very long time ago. Mike was nervous, kind of rocking in the chair, ankles crossed. He was wearing one of those woven leather ankle bracelets or anklets and a COME TO JAMAICA, MON T-shirt.

"How long is this gonna take?" Mike asked. He watched her set my coffee by my elbow and added, "Nobody offered me anything."

"We got any half-and-half in there?" I asked her.

"I'll check, Mr. Ruzak. Mr. Carroll, what would you like?"

"You got any diet Coke?"

"Just regular, I think."

"What about Dr Pepper?"

"I don't think so. I'd have to look."

"If you don't have Dr Pepper, I'll take a Mountain Dew."

She bent over the open half fridge and said, "We don't have any Mountain Dew. How about a Pepsi?"

"What about the Dr Pepper?"

"No . . ."

"Mr. Ruzak," Marks said. "Do you think it's possible we could discuss the matter you have insisted we discuss this morning?"

"All right, give me a Coke," Mike Carroll said.

She handed him his Coke and me my half-and-half.

"Will there be anything else right now, Mr. Ruzak?"

"I don't think so, Felicia."

"Do you need me to stay and take notes?"

"No," Marks said, raising his voice a little. "No notes."

"Maybe no notes are necessary, Felicia," I said.

"Okay." She flashed a smile in Marks's direction and went back to the secretary's area. From my desk, I could see her right shoulder and half her head during the rest of the meeting.

"Perhaps now you can tell me why I am here, Mr. Ruzak," Marks said.

"Yeah. I'd like to know the same thing," Mike said.

"There were just a couple of things I wanted to clear up," I said. "A few dangly little threads. See, for the past couple of months, I've been operating on this working theory, and now it's not fitting together so well, and I thought maybe you two could help smooth out the edges a little."

"I don't know what the hell you're talking about, Ruzak," Mike Carroll said. "And I don't give a shit about your theories or rough edges. Like I told you before, I don't know nothing about any murder of anybody."

"I'm glad to hear you say that, Mike. I've been going back and forth on that in the R & D phase of my theory—you know, 'What did Mike know and when did he know it?' I really didn't know how tight you were with Gary, but I figured it couldn't be too tight, since you rolled so easy on him when I waved a little cash under your nose. Spilling the beans on that gosling ruse would have been an incredibly stupid move if you were involved in Lydia's murder."

Mike stared at me and said, "Huh?"

"Mr. Ruzak," Marks said. "Who is this man?"

"This man is Mike Carroll. He's a friend of Gary Paul."

"Not a close friend, like he said," Mike said.

"You said he was a witness. A witness to what?"

"That's a good fucking question, because I haven't witnessed shit."

"Come on, Mike," I said. "There's a lady present."

He glanced over his shoulder toward Felicia's area.

"And as a friend of Gary, I thought he might tie up one of those danglies that's been bugging me." I pulled the MISSING poster from my desk drawer and held it up for Mike. "Do you recognize this woman?"

Mike's eyes cut away. "Yeah."

"Who is it?"

"I don't remember her name. I met her a couple times, maybe, but that was over a year ago."

"Who is it?" I asked again. Marks had turned his full attention on Mike.

"Gary's girlfriend," he said in a soft voice. Marks took a deep breath. I slipped the poster back in the desk, closed the drawer, and took a sip of coffee.

"How do you know she's his girlfriend?"

"A couple of reasons, Ruzak. First, he was draped all over her. And second, that's how he introduced her—'Mike, this is my girlfriend.'"

I turned to Marks. "Lydia managed your properties for you while you were overseas?" He nodded. "That's it, then," I said. "That's the piece I didn't have. I couldn't figure what Gary's connection to Lydia was if it wasn't Mr. Marks here. Thanks, Mike. I think I've got it all now, Mr. Marks, and if you don't mind, I'd like to run my working theory by you and see what you think."

He gave another brief nod. He was the picture of studied calm. It played counterpoint to Mike's obvious discomfort.

"Can I go now?" Mike asked.

"I don't see why not," I said. "Mr. Marks probably wouldn't want you here for the next part."

He set his Coke on my desk—I hadn't seen him take the first sip—fairly sprang from the chair, spun around, and headed for the door. I picked up the can so it wouldn't leave a ring and put it back in the minifridge. I grabbed a bottle of Evian because coffee dehydrates you and my mouth was very dry. I sat behind the desk and called out for Felicia to hold my calls.

I took a sip of water and said to Marks, "Did you know Americans spend more on bottled water than on gasoline?"

"Do they?" He had laced his fingers together, his elbows on the armrests of the visitor's chair, staring at me over his diamond rings the same way as the first time he'd sat in this chair.

"That's what I heard," I said. "But it's one of those statistics you sort of take at face value. We live in an age of specialization, Mr. Marks, and I bet eighty or ninety percent of everything we believe is based on something we haven't experienced firsthand. People say it's also the age of cynicism, but we trust a helluva lot, when you think about it. Like during the Cold War: It was pretty much accepted fact that the Soviets were ahead of us or at least equal to us in nukes, when they never actually were. We were always kicking their butts in the bomb department, but it suited somebody's purpose to convince us we weren't. Or those nutritional labels on foods. How do I really know there're X number of carbs in a Twinkie?"

"What," he asked, "is a Twinkie?"

"A snack cake that's supposedly very bad for you. Twinkies seem smaller now than when I was a kid, but the world seems smaller, too, even mailboxes, so it's hard to tell."

"I have had difficulty, Mr. Ruzak," Kenneth Marks said, "since meeting you, in deciding whether these digressions are designed to make their objects uncomfortable or to put them off their guard, or whether there is any design to them at all—in other words, are they a means of avoiding the matter at hand or merely the meanderings of an undisciplined mind?"

"Probably more the latter," I said. "My brain's like that stereotypical guy in his underwear sprawled all over the sofa on a Sunday afternoon." I reached under the desk and pulled out the paper sacks and set them on the desktop between us.

"What is this?" he asked.

"The money," I said. "All of it. You can count it if you want; I don't mind."

"You are returning it?"

"I'm afraid I don't have a choice, Mr. Marks. No matter how I spin it in my meandering mind, this money really came to me under false pretenses, and to keep it kind of elevates, or de-elevates, me into a league I'd really rather not belong to."

"What league? What are you talking about, Mr. Ruzak?"

"The league of bad moral character, Mr. Marks. See, I lied to you to get this money—well, the money wasn't the point of the lie, really—that's one strike. And keeping the money when I know why you gave it to me is the second strike. Two strikes implies a third, which, I guess, is that keeping the money and keeping my mouth shut will probably land me in prison."

"What do you mean, you lied to me?"

"About the tapes. I don't have any tapes or any other kind of proof linking Gary to Lydia's murder. But I figured I needed you to believe that so you'd get Gary to back off Felicia."

"Who is Felicia?"

"My secretary. You just met her. She's sitting right over there. See, I figured Gary was working for you. That was my big mistake, my big boner."

"Your . . . big boner?"

"You bet. And it just goes to prove what sorts of heartache and mayhem can come from erroneous beliefs. I thought you hired Gary to kill Lydia, so when Gary threatened Felicia, I thought the only way to protect her was to go to you and pretend I didn't know that piece of the puzzle and take you up on your offer. Only that wasn't a piece of the puzzle, because the puzzle was something entirely different; I knew it was Gary but thought it was you, and it wasn't you at all."

He was staring at me dead-on when he said, "I didn't kill my wife, Mr. Ruzak."

"I know that now. And my point is, if I'd known that then, I wouldn't have lied and I wouldn't have taken your money, but I did and now Gary Paul is dead, which could lead somebody to believe I just used you for two reasons: to get rich and to get rid of Gary Paul."

He nodded. "It is a very compelling argument, Mr. Ruzak."

"You bet it is, and that makes me nervous as hell, Mr. Marks. Somebody could look at these facts and come to the conclusion that my goal all along was to put Gary six feet under."

"And was that your goal?"

"I'm not that sneaky or that clever."

He nodded. He didn't elaborate, so I didn't know if he agreed with the first part, the second, or both.

"I didn't kill my wife," he repeated softly. "I loved her." And then Kenneth Marks did an extraordinary thing, the last thing I would have expected him to do: He began to cry. He buried his face inside his bejeweled hands and sobbed like a baby. His big shoulders shook and his knees pressed together as he leaned forward, and there was really nothing to do until he could get a grip on himself. I looked over his shoulder toward the secretary's desk. She had turned around and was staring at his bowed back as he cried. I held up my hand, signaling her to stay put.

"Have you ever loved someone so much that the thought of losing her is simply unbearable, Mr. Ruzak?"

I thought about it. "No."

"After she disappeared, and particularly after they found her, the only thing that gave me any peace was the thought of ripping her killer's head from his shoulders. I would fall to sleep every night with the fantasy of dismembering him slowly, of disemboweling him and scattering his steaming entrails as carrion, of ripping his heart still beating from his chest. . . ."

"Okay," I said. "I get it. Let me ask you something, Mr. Marks, because these danglies have been driving me crazy. . . . You didn't know Gary and Lydia were lovers, did you?"

He shook his head. Reminding him of Mike's revelation helped him get a grip on himself, I think.

"I knew him, of course," he said, removing a white monogrammed handkerchief from his pocket and wiping his face. "Or rather, I knew of him. I rented that house to him."

"And Lydia would manage your rentals when you were out of town."

He nodded.

So did I. "See, that dovetails pretty neatly into my current working theory. I wondered how the two of them hooked up, given the fact that Lydia was so shy and a virtual shut-in. However it happened, Gary and Lydia became lovers, and I bet there was some kind of falling-out. Maybe she tried to break up with him, or maybe he was trying to extort some of your money from her, or maybe there was a big fight and he hit her—maybe didn't even mean to kill her—but anyway, that morning he was on his way to the mountains to dump the body when he hit those geese. That got Parker Hudson involved, which got me involved, which ultimately got both Parker and Gary dead. And that leaves just one question, Mr. Marks, beyond the normal, unanswerable ones about the human heart: If you had known they were lovers, would you still have killed him?"

He hesitated only half a breath. "Of course I still would have killed him."

"But without any proof. You never asked to listen to the tapes. You just took me at my word and killed him."

"No, I did not, Mr. Ruzak. Gary Paul confessed."

"He did?"

"I made sure one was forthcoming before I exacted justice."

"Well, that's very thorough. You're a . . . very thorough man, Mr. Marks."

He stood up. "Are we finished, Mr. Ruzak?"

"I think that's the difference between you and me, Mr. Marks," I said as she got up from her desk and came into the room to stand behind him. "If I had known the truth, I wouldn't have asked for your two million dollars. I wouldn't have pretended to know things I didn't know and to have things I didn't have. That's what really gets you into deep water in the moral character department."

"You are going to the authorities, then?" His arms hung loosely at his sides while he clenched and unclenched his fists.

"Well, that brings me to my last lie," I said. "I mean, in regard to this case. I guess to represent it as my last lie ever would be another lie, since the odds of that are pretty slim and it's one of those promises most people are doomed to break. The money is tempting, Mr. Marks, plus the fact that you've shown you're not the kind of man who lets moral issues stand in the way of your desires. Like one day you might decide it's too dangerous to allow me to walk around knowing what I know and do a Gary Paul on me. So the truth is, I've already gone to the authorities."

He glanced over his shoulder at her, then looked back at me.

"Mr. Marks," I said. "This isn't my secretary. This is Detective Leslie Garrison with the Tennessee Bureau of Investigation." Then I added, I'm not sure why, "I'm sorry."

He remained stock-still as she stepped up behind him and pulled his hands behind his back and told him he was under arrest for the murder of Gary Paul. We stared at each other as she read him his rights, and his expression didn't change. After she asked him if he understood his rights, he said to me, "You are a . . . very complicated man, Mr. Ruzak."

"It'd be easy to think the worst of me at this moment," I admitted. "Like Hamlet—was he insane or just acting insane? I just want to do the right thing, Mr. Marks. Sometimes that brings more grief to people than doing the wrong thing, but it's like that old saying, It's better to be lucky than smart."

CHAPTER FORTY

Two days after the arrest of Kenneth Marks, the police picked up the man he hired to torch Gary Paul, the wood smoke–smelling crooked-nosed man, whose name turned out to be Kaczmarczyk. That had to be Polish, and I felt a little like an honest Italian burdened with the stereotype of the Cosa Nostra.

Two months later, the case was still getting a lot of press. Strangers were recognizing me on the street and some even crossed it to shake my hand. The phone was ringing off the hook, mail was pouring in, and people were showing up at the door. Even a couple of those network news-magazine shows had called me, interested in doing a story. Felicia told me she could put in her full forty hours if she could bring Tommy to work on the days when the baby-sitter fell through, and I said sure, the more the merrier, and the kid turned out to be a terror, crawling all over the furniture, tearing stuff out of my filing cabinets, and jumping into my chair every time I got up, spinning in it like he was at the teacup ride at Disney. Felicia and I took a meeting about the Tommy issue and she said he'd be much calmer if there was a TV somewhere in the office where he could watch his shows, so the firm sprang for a television and cable service so he could loll in his pajamas in Felicia's area and watch *Blues Clues* and *Little Bear*, and whenever an episode came on with Little Bear's big seafaring father in it, he'd point at the screen and yell, "Roo-ZACK! Roo-ZACK." And Felicia would laugh one of her nose-crinkling laughs.

One morning when Felicia had brought Tommy with her, I went outside just to get a breather from the bedlam, and there was Susan Marks sitting on my stoop, hugging her knees and looking at nothing in particular, just like the day she came to ask for my help. I sat beside her on the steps and looked at nothing with her.

"I can't even begin to imagine what it must be like," I said.

"Matt's the one I'm really worried about," she said. "He's had a total meltdown. He lies in his room all day with the door closed, listening to Led Zeppelin."

"Well, everybody has to find their own way."

"You're so . . . philosophical."

"I don't blame you for being sore," I said. "But you gotta understand I wasn't trying to trick him—well, I did trick him when I brought him here that day. I was talking about the other trick, the one that got Gary killed. But it really wasn't a trick on my part, since I thought your dad was involved in Lydia's death. I've learned a big lesson about going off half-cocked, but like most big lessons, it came with a pretty hefty price tag. Some people might say I'm too trusting. For example, I trusted myself that I knew the truth, and that got Gary Paul killed. You know, that thing about unintended consequences. Are you talking about this with anyone? I know this great lady doctor who might be able to help."

She didn't answer. Instead, she pulled a long white envelope from the pocket of her khaki shorts and held it out without looking at me. Inside was a check for $500,000.

"What is this?" I asked.

"A check for five hundred thousand dollars."

"The reward?"

She nodded.

"But that was for the arrest and conviction. Nobody was arrested or convicted. They were offed in a house fire."

She didn't say anything.

"It's like blood money," I told her. "And rewards are offered for doing something honorable."

"You won't take it?"

"Okay," I said. "I'll take it." I didn't want to add insult to injury by arguing with her about it—plus, it was half a million dollars—so I stuck the envelope in my coat pocket.

"What did you decide?" she asked.

"About what?"

"The dog."

"I haven't yet. I've been, um, kind of wrapped up in my work."

"It should definitely be a Great Pyrenees," she said. "The personalities would mesh perfectly."

"What, they're dim-witted?"

"They're guardians," she said. "They're bred to watch over things, like sheep or goats. Very gentle and loyal and big and . . . and kind." She still hadn't looked at me. A tear rolled down her cheek and she brushed it angrily away with the back of her small hand. I should have taken that hand, seized it, pressed it to my breast, and promised her the hurt would go away and everything would be fine and she would never feel pain again, but I was through with the empty promises.

"You're never going to go out with me, are you?" I asked. "That's why you brought up the dog."

"I can't even tell you what I'll be doing next week," she said. She finally looked at me. The sun peeks through the clouds and says, I'm still here.

"Well," she said, sighing. "I'm late for work."

She stood up and I stood up and there was really nothing to say.

I had a couple of suggestions, like usual, but I held my tongue. She started away, her arms folded over her chest. Suddenly, she turned, came back to me, and, rising on her toes, kissed my cheek and called me "Mr. Ruzak."

I went back upstairs. We were hip-deep into summer; it was eighty degrees by ten o'clock, and despite the two fans, one in my office and one in Felicia's area, the dry-cleaning fumes lingered like the smell of a dead animal rotting beneath someone's porch. I figured maybe with this five hundred grand, I could move into better space, but I had already signed the contract to remodel and still had seven months to go on my lease.

Just before lunchtime, Felicia ushered in a little guy with a cheap suit and an even cheaper haircut. She left him in one of the visitor's chairs to run back and answer the phone and to tell Tommy for the six hundredth time to be quiet.

"Mr. Ruzak," he said. "My name is Walter Hinton and I'm with the Tennessee Private Investigation and Polygraph Commission."

"Oh," I said. "You bet. Good to see you. You want anything? Coffee? Coke? Evian? We just sprang for a refrigerator and it's fully stocked. We even have lemonade, if you don't mind the kind in those little pouches with the plastic straw."

"I'm actually more interested in seeing your license."

"My license?"

"Your license to privately investigate criminal and civil matters in the state of Tennessee. You see, Mr. Ruzak, we've reviewed our records and can't locate either your application or a copy of your exam."

"That's probably because I haven't applied or taken the exam. I was meaning to take the exam, but a murder case came up and I missed the test date."

"So you are aware you must be licensed in the state of Tennessee?"

"Oh sure, but see, the thing is, I wasn't what you might call actually practicing anything. I was consulting."

"Consulting?"

"Yeah. The name on the door's a little misleading, mostly because people have trouble adjusting to new ideas. It says 'The Highly Effective Detection & Investigation Company,' but really I'm an investigative consultant."

"I'm sorry, Mr. Ruzak, but I fail to see the difference."

"It's more a distinction than a difference. Are you here to shut me down?"

"I'm here to determine if you're in violation of Tennessee statutes."

"Would it make any difference if I told you I'm already on the list for the next test?"

"Only if you shut your doors until you pass and receive your license from the state."

"Things are really hopping, Mr. Hilton. . . . Hilton. Any relation to the hotel people?"

"No, no relation, because my name isn't Hilton; it's Hinton."

"Oh, sure. I should have written it down. Do you get that a lot?"

"Get what a lot?"

"People who think you're related to the hotel Hiltons."

"No, because my name isn't Hilton; it's Hinton. Mr. Ruzak, are you trying to provoke me?"

"I wouldn't dream of provoking you, Mr. Hinton. I know what that's like, someone getting your name wrong. People get mine wrong all the time. When I first opened up shop, I couldn't even get the right name on the letterhead, but I straightened all that out."

"It just seems to me you're trying to muddy the waters, confuse the issue."

"I've certainly been guilty of that. I was saying that with things so busy around here, the issue with the license puts me in a diffi-cult position."

"In all honesty, Mr. Ruzak, the state could care less about your position. The law—"

"Oh, I'm a firm believer in the law. One of the reasons, maybe even the chief reason, I went into this business in the first place."

"Then you'll understand if the state fines you and secures a court order to shut down your operation here."

"I was thinking about taking a vacation."

He smiled a humorless, bureaucratic smile.

"At the end of which, you can take the test, we can review your application, and, if so warranted, we'll issue you a license."

"I can't think of a more satisfactory resolution," I said. We shook hands and I walked him to the door.

Felicia said, "Busted."

"Maybe I need a vacation," I said. "One of the biggest mistakes people make is rushing through traumatic experiences looking for closure. Nobody takes the time to absorb anything anymore."

Like he always did when he caught me standing still, Tommy came over and sat on my foot and held up his fat little hands.

"Ride! Ride!" he shouted, lifting his wide face up at me.

"So now I cancel all your appointments and take the phone off the hook?" Felicia asked.

I grabbed Tommy's hands and lifted my leg straight out, whooshing him about two feet off the floor. He screeched with delight. "Roo-ZACK! Roo-ZACK!"

"I don't know, what do you think?" I asked.

"By the time he gets that court order, you'll have taken the test."

"You're assuming I'm going to pass."

"You don't have a choice, Ruzak."

"Well, we could probably afford the fine," I said. I lowered Tommy to the floor, pulled the envelope from my pocket, and showed her the check. She grabbed it out of my hand and stuffed it into her Louis Vuitton knockoff purse. At least I *hoped* it was a Louis Vuitton knockoff purse.

"I need a raise, Ruzak," she said.

"Done," I said. Meanwhile, Tommy was back on my shoe, shaking his fists at me. I gave him a couple more rides, then swung him by the wrists onto the love seat, where he curled up and hooted with joy.

I looked at Felicia, and she was actually smiling at me. She pulled the hair back from her face and asked, "Did I ever thank you for saving my life?"

"I'm sure you did," I said.

"Well, in case I didn't, thanks."

"You're welcome."

I sat down at my desk and looked out the window. The sun was directly overhead and bright summer light filled the space between the buildings. Felicia left with Tommy; they were going to the Subway at Market Square and she asked if I wanted anything. I told her I'd brought my lunch. The phone kept ringing, but I let the machine pick up while I stared out the window at the brick wall. I heard the outer door open and close again, and I said, "Hello, Eunice."

"Goodness, how did you know it was me?"

I swung around in my chair to face her. She was wearing a yellow summery-type frock and a bonnet over a poofy blond wig. She looked like what Dolly Parton might look like in another thirty years, depending on the extent of plastic surgery she might get. She was wearing the same orthopedic shoes, though. She sat in a visitor's chair and plopped the ubiquitous purple purse in her wide lap. Purple purse, yellow dress. Mrs. Eunice Shriver clearly did not know how to accessorize.

"I saw your reflection in the window," I explained. I made a show of pulling out my yellow legal pad and clicking out fresh lead in my mechanical pencil.

"I see you're quite the celebrity now, Theodore," she said.

"I'm thinking of writing a book about my exploits," I said. "The working title is *The Gosling Affair*. What do you think?"

"It's not the sort of book I would read," she sniffed.

"What's your taste? I'm thinking *Gone with the Wind* or maybe those Harlequin romances. Or those true-crime paperbacks."

She let the question slide past her. Maybe it was too intimate a detail. "It's a poor title, Theodore. People will think it's about a love triangle among birds."

"You know," I said, "you might have a point there. I can't stand those books with the anthropomorphic animals, like *Watership Down* or that one they made us read as seniors, *Animal Farm*. It's kind of a creepy literary device and it disturbs my sense of the cosmic order. I have a couple other working titles. *Murder Most Fowl. The Wild-Goose Case. Fowl Play.* But there was a movie a few years back with that name; I think it starred Mel Gibson and Goldie Hawn. It was spelled differently, maybe, but I think there was a scene that involved birds—not geese, but chickens. I don't remember much more about it, except that Mel Gibson showed his ass in that movie. I was also leaning toward *Theodore Ruzak: The (Unlicensed) Master of Detection,* which sounds a little self-serving, which is why I put the *unlicensed* part in."

"Theodore," she said. "I really didn't come all the way downtown to discuss literature with you."

"I didn't think so."

"It smells like a child's been in here."

I gave the air a sniff, but all I could smell were dry-cleaning fumes (they were worse the hotter it got) and her perfume or body powder, or whatever it was.

"That would be my secretary's," I said. "She brings her son in occasionally."

"Oh. I thought perhaps you were diversifying into day care."

"I hadn't thought of that. It's generally a good idea not to throw all your eggs in one basket."

"Theodore," she said, "I am a busy woman and a paying client, and I would appreciate it if you would stop changing the subject and going off on wild tangents like talking animals and books and movies in which Mel Gibson exposes himself."

"You're right," I said. My stomach growled. My pimento cheese sandwich was no more than five feet from her in the minifridge by the bathroom door.

"Have you any leads in my case?"

"Not many, but I've ruled out the mayor."

"I'm not sure that's altogether prudent."

"I can't find a motive," I said. "Do you even know the mayor?"

"Goodness, what a question!"

"In fact," I said, "I can't really find a motive for anybody to kill you. Why would anyone want to kill you, Eunice?"

"Do you doubt, Theodore, after all I've done, after the kind of life I've led, that I would come to the twilight of my life with no enemies at all?"

"I don't guess many people do, even the Pope. Maybe certain people do, like hermits or mentally disabled people. I'd guess it'd be hard to hold a grudge against the retarded. Although there's always stuff in the paper about some state wanting to execute a retarded guy, and that's like all of society being your enemy."

She puffed out a hard jet of breath and said, "I have the perfect title: *Theodore Ruzak: The Long-Winded Detective.*"

"I am profligate," I admitted. "Particularly with breath. And thought. I waste a lot of thought. If my life had taken a different path, I'd be sitting in some ivory tower right now, working on a paper about the economy of thought. But that would make me like that televangelist who preached against the evils of prostitution while he cruised truck stops."

"That is a horrible indulgence, Theodore, though quite understandable. A man such as you must get quite lonely at times."

"Oh, no. I said I would be *like* that. I've never done anything like that—never even thought about it."

"Then why did you bring it up?"

"I'm not sure now, but it probably was related to something we were talking about."

"I am an old woman and my memory is certainly not what it used to be, but I'm fairly confident, Theodore, that our conversation had nothing to do with prostitutes."

"Well," I said. "There you have it."

We smiled at each other for a moment. We were on the same wavelength, which was comforting and disturbing at the same time.

"But I was going to say," Eunice Shriver said, "there are certain people whom I have named in the list I gave you who would be more than happy to see me six feet under. Another reason I came today is to give you an additional name."

She reached into her purse and handed over a single sheet of typing paper. I wondered why she'd bothered. She could have just told me the name, but maybe she wanted everything in writing.

I looked at the name and said, "Oh, come on, Eunice."

"Would you not say that revenge is a very strong motive for murder?"

"Eunice, you had nothing to do with the death of Parker Hudson and you know it."

I had raised my voice a little, and it was probably that more than what I said that made her stiffen and pull back in the chair.

"Also," I said, "how would his poor widow know that you did?"

"Because," and now her voice dropped to a whisper, "because Parker and I . . ."

"Eunice."

"We were . . ."

"Just stop, Eunice."

"Lovers!" She pulled the white hankie from her purse and dabbed her eyes. I was about to light into her, but that was something her kids did all the time and it sure hadn't fixed anything.

"This is pretty serious," I said. "And Mrs. Hudson knew about it?"

"Not during the time of our torrid affair, no. Later."

"Eunice, you didn't call Mrs. Hudson, did you?"

She didn't say anything. She wasn't looking at me, but over my shoulder toward the blank brick wall on the other side of the alley.

"Jeez, Eunice, talk about salt in the wound. Why would you do something like that?"

"Because the truth will out, Theodore. The truth will always out. We were taking our usual morning stroll around the lake, Parker and I, when we saw that awful man Gary Paul hit those goslings. Parker saw inside the car and shouted, 'There goes Lydia!' "

" 'There goes Lydia'?"

" 'There goes Lydia!' And I asked him who this Lydia was and he told me."

"He told you? He told you what? Oh. He was seeing her, too?"

All she could do was nod. I said, "So you killed Lydia because you were jealous?"

Another nod.

"And you told all this to Mrs. Hudson?"

"I couldn't keep it in any longer," she whispered.

"Yeah, you seem to have a problem with that. Okay, look, this is what we're going to do." I wrote a name and phone number on the top sheet of my pad, tore it off, and handed it to her. "This lady is tops in her field, Eunice. She specializes in the treatment of serial criminals and adulteresses."

" 'Dr. Stephanie Fredericks,' " she read, frowning.

"Call her and set up an appointment. Today, Eunice. I'm one hundred percent certain she'd love to meet you. You're worth at least one, maybe two articles in *The American Psychiatric Journal.*"

"Do you really think so, Theodore?"

"I'd bet half a million dollars on it."

She went limp with relief. That's all she was really after: a plan of action, a road map to the way out. She even gave me a hug at the door.

Felicia and Tommy came back about fifteen minutes later, while I was eating my pimento cheese sandwich at my desk. Tommy ran straight to me, crawled into my lap, and grabbed the Clausen pickle spear from the paper plate. Pickle juice ran down his forearm and dripped off his elbow onto my $75 pair of dress slacks. Then he wiped his sticky face on my $150 dress shirt, closed his eyes, and fell asleep.

Felicia came over to move him to the love seat, but I told her it was okay because with his head right under my nose, I could smell his lavender-smelling hair instead of the dry-cleaning fumes. She returned to her desk and I sat there with her kid in my lap, and I was thinking this was it. This was what I had been waiting for all those years on the night shift with the aching somewhere in the vicinity of my heart, not Tommy Kincaid snoozing in my lap, per se, though that was part of it, but the whole thing. For the first time in a long time, I didn't feel like Mr. Sad Sack Teddy Ruzak schlepping through the second half of his life like he'd schlepped through the first. For the first time in a long time, I didn't feel so crummy. For the first time in a long time, I actually felt pretty damn good.